SECRETS OF
THE BONES

BOOKS BY TERI A. JACOBS

THE VOID

SECRETS OF THE BONES

TERI A. JACOBS

WILDSIDE PRESS

Wildside Press
www.wildsidepress.com

CHAPTER ONE

"That the sons of God saw the daughters
of men *were* fair; and they took them wives of
all which they chose."

Genesis 6.2

"There were giants in the earth in those
days; and also after that, when the sons of God
came in unto the daughters of men,
and they bare *children* to them, the same
became mighty men which *were* of old, men of renown."

Genesis 6.4

"These are the Grigori, who with their prince
Satanail rejected the Lord of light ... "

Book of Enoch, XVIII

I.

The smell of suffering summoned them from the darkness.

From the dark of their prisons beneath the heavens, beneath the worlds,
beneath the hells . . .

Quivering, stinking flesh of the wretched awoke their hungers,
hungers deeper than the abyss, and drew them out of their silence and
their pity. After centuries of chained unrest and torment, they escaped.

The Fallen crept through torturous chasms and entered into the world.

Ravenous.

II.

Midnight in winter was her hour of sorrow, the time of black reflections and cold silence, the only time she allowed the tears. Tears for her child taken from this world during some other winter, some other midnight.

Aimless, Rani walked the near-empty streets and wept. The wind carried awful tones through the alleys, reminding her too much of her son's murderer when he pressed his mouth against her ear. His blood-hot words had awaken her from sleep, only to bring her into a nightmare.

"Little Boy Blue asleep in the hay, blue-black bruises around his throat, never to wake another day."

And then his murderer had disappeared, literally, as if he'd walked through a door made of the air. But this fact didn't shock her, not after all the strange she'd witnessed and experienced. What had rattled her was that he was invisible, unknowable, invincible, and left no evidence behind, except a corpse in the crib.

Her son, her little Stephan.

Her little boy blue.

She shrieked into the wind.

The homeless, lost in their own despair, ignored her, looking beyond her as if she were an apparition. She passed them like a bad memory.

Turning off Broadway, Rani left their haunted faces behind. If only it could be so easy, she thought, simply turning a corner to change her fate, but her life went from one bad direction to another. At the end of her road, only monsters ever waited.

26th Street seemed a different world, darker, colder, the realm of the dead perhaps, with its cemetery quiet and vapors. Steam hissed from the vents, rising from the subterranean tunnels like souls escaping from Hell, enveloping her as she crossed over a vent.

The damned have warm hands, Rani thought and shivered. *Warm hands, cold hearts. The hearts of thieves, liars, and killers of young boys.*

6

Beneath her boots, the sidewalk squares became gravestone plaques, and every one bore her son's name, Stephan, in baby blue blood.

The *clack, clack* of her heels reminded her too much of his small bones breaking, crushed by the monster that still stalked the winter nights, and she stopped.

A black church loomed beside her.

Bells rung by the wind called her in for a blacker mass.

The red-lit stares in the courtyard belonged to the rats, but other things waited on the slate roof and watched with red-hot eyes, a hideous audience silently cheering for her to enter the church.

III.

They saw her without skin.

Beautiful, her raw meat of muscle, sinew, and fat, the tempting organs and bone hidden as if within wraps of scarlet and white silk.

Sweet, earthy, the odor of her aching womb drifted up toward them. Winds ripe with her scent wrapped around their heads, in memories of the daughters of men and their lithe legs parted and clasping. On their split tongues, the virginal taste of the daughters of men lingered still.

The smells of fornication dragged them into the unhallowed church, and, in the shadowy vaults of the ceiling, they prayed for the sacrifice of her body and her blood.

IV.

Rani opened the iron gate. The rusty hinges greeted her with a screech, and the rats scurried noisily across the pavement and into the storm drain. An eerie welcome.

The brown-black silhouette of the Gothic church was foreboding with its spires and tower. Over time, the stones had breathed Manhattan's polluted air and absorbed this necrotic hue, and, even though she restored historic architecture for a living, she decided she liked the untouched character of the church. An ominous, brooding relic of disrepair, a symbol of disintegrating faith.

Rounding the transept, she noted the nave's grisaille windows were intact. She reached and touched the glass, her fingertips gliding on cold darkness until faint buttery light flickered within like fire beneath her fingers.

Come to light, come to death murmured the voice within the stones. The voice of midnight and winter and murder.

Rani withdrew her trembling hand.

The stones snarled.

Behind her, the click of claws and feral growls of dogs.

She turned and gaped. These dogs were larger than wolves, with red-matted fur and red-glowing eyes. In their massive jaws, the beasts held skulls.

Misshapen, infantile skulls dripping blood and wailing as if with the voice of her dead son.

She screamed, and her screams silenced the phantom cries but not the laughter coming from the stones, from the shadows behind her.

Hands clasped the sides of her head and held her skull.

Smoky breath enveloped her, and her attacker whispered into her ear, "Where is your Little Boy Blue?"

Thumbnails pressed into her nape.

"His soul waits in darkness, in agony. He cries for you—don't you hear him crying for you?"

Yowling winds rushed between the buildings, and her son's cries echoed in the eaves, the terrified cry of his birth and his death. The wracked cry of her nightmares. The grim herald of the season of death, which had her wandering the streets at midnight.

Tears for Stephan fell.

"Come to light, come to death, and we will release his soul."

The vise of his hands vanished, and Rani was left standing alone, shaking, straining to follow the sound of his footfalls. But there was none, only his cold laughter in the dark stones.

As if listening to the calls of their master, the dogs turned ears to the winds and whined. They retreated into the streets with the skulls wailing between their jaws, sirens fading into the distance.

His soul waits in darkness, in agony.

The church groaned with the tones of anguished prayers as heavy walls settled on old foundation, and Rani felt drawn toward it. Toward the somber sighs of a dying heart.

Come to light, come to death.

Her heels hit hollow on the steps like hammers against empty skulls, like the sound of her dreams, where men built buildings from bone. The sepulchral sounds ushered her inside.

Inside, where a sanctuary of bodily incense, dim golden glows, and the sharp hymn of whips against flesh welcomed her.

Crimson drugget led from the vestibule to the black-velvet screen before the tribune. She walked up the aisle, feeling anxious as the thud-crack of whips intensified, feeling dread as the sensation of being watched descended upon her.

The central nave and radiating chapels were devoid of pews and people. Still, she felt prying eyes and searched the triforium, arcades, and ceiling, somehow believing something lurked in the arches, pillars, and vaults.

Only shadows cast from candlelight wavered along the intricate marble ceiling.

Shadows of dogs quarreling over bones.

Rani inhaled the strange odors of wax and wounds and burning myrrh.

Behind the screen, she spied their strange sources.

A black-vinyl-clad beauty tipped flaming candles over the naked woman kneeling on the steps in front of her, the red-hot wax streaming down and hardening like clotted blood on the ropes binding her wrists, her ankles, and her breasts. The tortured girl hissed for more.

Another woman, in stiletto boots and PVC gown, had her worshiper on his hands and knees, his bare ass rosy like communal wine. Others waited in breathless circles for their taste of her flogger.

At the altar, one man punished another servant of pain, while others masturbated to the rhythms of her cries.

Rani flinched with the *swoosh* and *swap* of the cane as it struck the woman's red-welted bottom.

Sweat, tears, and delirious bliss glistened on the woman's face, and her eyes were soft and unfocused, her sight seemingly turned inward on the enthralling ecstacy of pain. Anticipating the cane, she held her breath and swirled her hips slightly. Waiting and wanting . . .

The cane stung her flesh. Again and again, and her flesh sighed apart in red weeping lines.

And her rhythmic cries touched Rani, touched deep like groping fingers into her open sex.

Enthralled herself, Rani was unaware of the growing stench of burning myrrh and of the nearing presence of those who wore that stench as their perfume.

Unaware until blackish smoke lashed down onto the men.

Unaware until the men howled and crawled away from the altar like beaten dogs, their backs slathered with cuts spitting bloody froth and pus.

Unaware until the smoke became grotesque pillars of men and came onto her with talons and ripping teeth.

CHAPTER TWO

... angel as you are, that insect lives in you too,
and will stir a tempest in your blood.
Tempests, because sensual lust is tempest —
worse than a tempest!

Dostoevski, The Brothers Karamazov

A pleasure so exquisite as almost to amount to pain.

Hunt, Letter to Alexander Ireland

Talons and ripping teeth.

Her skin, their canvas for splattering art.

Her body was hurled upon the altar and surrounded by things in the vestments of otherworldly flesh.

Hands, inhuman, maleficent, and scorching, burned upon Rani, and her clothes fell in ashes beneath her. Her skin reddened in deep degrees until blisters pearled and popped in rankled ooze. The unearthly men licked them with languid sighs.

Their tongues, stroking velvet and shredding thorns against her broken skin, orchestrated her pain. Her voice split her throat in volumes, an organ piping high and piercing.

Cutting along her abdomen, tracing the slats of her ribs, the curves of her breasts, the circles of her nipples, their tongues made ducts from which they lapped with sanguine greed.

"*Milk,*" the myriad of unearthly mouths hummed.

"The milk of Asherah, the Mother of God and of the sons of God."

"The rich milk of her sweet, lurid womb and the waste she birthed."

Sickened by the sucking sounds of their blood-milking, Rani swooned into delirium, into ruddy darkness filled with wolves and the howling bones of the dead, where soft fetal bones harangued her for marrow and milk.

Unsavory, the taste of uterine water in her mouth. Salty and pissy.

Upon the ceiling, shadows moved like spiders on webs wove of tierceron ribs and rose tracery and dangled above their prey.

Waiting, wanting . . .

Her body ached, an ache bordering on brutal euphoria, as their mouths softly kissed her labia, as their tongues razed her clit. Caressed as if by a whole bouquet of blood red roses.

Does it hurt? She had asked, and the Singapore whore who masturbated with a razorblade answered with a teasing grin, not anymore.

Not anymore.

Opiated with endorphins, her blood flowed through shrieking veins, numbing the shrieks as if pounding them into senselessness. She had gone over the threshold of pain into the wasteland of pleasure. Their pricks of tongues drew her to the edge of an excruciating orgasm.

MADNESS, this is MADNESS, her mind screamed as their withered faces withdrew from her lap and regarded her with flaming eyes.

Star-bright eyes, peril eyes.

"Madness," she mumbled breathy, desperately wanting the madness to bring her to that fatal climax.

Rani arched her back and pushed her swollen, open sore of a clit against the mouth of a nimbus-faced man, who flicked his razor-kiss against her.

The orgasm cut through her, its blades of keen pleasure whirling inside her.

Unbearable pleasure, more intense than the vehement agony of childbirth, gripped every cell in her body, and she couldn't even scream because of her constricted, convulsing throat. It lasted mere minutes. When it ended, she collapsed, her body rubbery and slick with fervid sweat, her mind reeling between heaven and hell.

The creatures from either heaven or hell stood around her, with white wings fanned and tattered, with skin blushed with the light of dawn, with melancholy faces bowed.

"We are the Grigori," she heard in the dreary song of their telepathic, celestial voices.

Unknown winds stirred from the sacristy, bringing the stale dust of the Eucharist and the mournful cries of infants.

"We come for our sons born and slaughtered."

Rani trembled in fear, for their faces suddenly stormed into turmoil, ashen ovals wet with tears made from lightning. The Grigori fashioned swords from their falling tears and brandished the bright blazing steel before her, pointing them at her eyes, mouth, and pubic mound.

"We come for our sons waiting and unmade."

Then she succumbed to another onslaught of vicious rapture.

Azure-burning hands spread her arms and legs, opening her body to them. Between her legs, her own heat warmed the air with wanton perfume. Star-bright eyes glowed brighter with hellish fires as the Grigori savored the scent of her arousal.And theirs, like jasmine, intoxicated her, giving her drunken hallucinations of Sodom, of lush bodies making ardent, adulterous love in the flowers and flames.

Swords gored into her sides and thighs.

Spears of their sublime cocks thrust into the blood-wet slit of her wounds.

Glorious pain, her body afire as if in the embrace of the sun. Burning in lust beyond human feeling. This must be Elysium, her mind and body sighed as the fallen angels ravaged her.

In her ear, one of the Grigori whispered his name, *Shemyaza*, and her raging heartbeat quivered into a murmur. Her breath silenced. Her womb though yearned for more than his voice inside her.

And this he knew and complied, ripping into her in one fell thrust, splitting her man-made cunt with his god-almighty cock.

Her eyes rolled back. Cold sweat mixed with the dew of the warm blood on her skin, making her body super slick on the altar. Rani slid into his thrusts. Crying out, she felt gutted as his huge cock rammed deeper than humanly possible, striking into the core of her body. Into the core of pleasure itself.

Hyperventilating now with his fast and furious rhythm, she rode the fire-cracking fuck and swore she'd pass out from this awesome feeling building and building within her. It threatened. Rani wondered if her body would literally explode, all her juicy sex coming strewn apart and wet-spotting every inch of the walls. Moments of blackness took her. And then she came. Soul-shuddering hard.

Shemyaza withdrew from her, with his cock still twitching and spilling clouds of white upon her. Sweet warmth dribbled onto her mouth, and Rani tasted not only honey in his seed but Paradise.

But, in the aftertaste, came the bitterness of his exile from God's Kingdom, his punishment for fathering ogrish sons who devoured the men and beasts of earth.

As she lay shivering in shock and ambrosial satiety, the fallen angels licked her wounds, healing the flesh again, sealing them without the trace of even the faintest silvery scar.

Rising on the altar, she sat as if on a throne, her imperial guards at her sides, her subjects fawning.

Shemyaza placed his flaming fingers against her forehead. His perilous eyes bore into her.

"We are the Watchers."

"We are the Keepers."

Candlelight faded flame by flame. The Grigori disappeared into the darkness, the hint of burning myrrh left behind, but Rani felt them from afar, watching, waiting, wanting.

And she knew they were watching for signs of sons growing within her.

CHAPTER THREE

The boundaries which divide Life from Death are
at best shadowy and vague. Who shall say where the
one ends, and where the other begins?

Poe, The Premature Burial

I.

Her son's corpse hung from the branches of the ash.

"I charge thee, I conjure thee, I command thee, on pain of the torments and wandering of thrice seven years, which I, by force of magic rites, have power to inflict upon thee, by the sights and groans I conjure thee to utter thy voice."

Creak of tree bough shuddering; the wind soughing through snow; the strangled mewling of an infant.

"I conjure thee utter thy most sonorous, woeful voice! Thy mother cannot hear thee yet . . . "

The man made small cuts in the corpse, a star upon death-dappled flesh, and Stephan's dead gray body, awakened by the knife and the spell, stretched wide its worm-riddled mouth. Loud, horrible, haunting, its cry resounded through the woods and carried far upon the icy winds.

Its sunken, milky eyes wept black tears.

Louder, more pained, it cried for the comfort only its mother could bring.

II.

Midnight ended with his cries.

The wind pushed his cries against her, into her breath, into her blood, where the anguish wrenched her apart from the inside. Her heart felt crushed and twisted. Every beat, every breath was a struggle, and Rani didn't feel like fighting.

She wanted to lie down and die.

But she kept hearing the loathsome voice say, *Come to light, come to death, and we will release him.*

His soul waits in darkness, in agony.

The Grigori waited in darkness as well, waiting for their dead sons to come back to life. Would that happen to Stephan? Would he come back to her?

"Why not?" she asked the weeping winds, pulling the borrowed coat tighter around her nakedness. It made bizarre sense—someone had him to release him.

Standing on the street corner, she raised her arms and opened them to embrace the wind, to embrace his cries.

"Come to Mama . . . "

Her voice broke into sobs. God, this awful emptiness she held instead of her son.

Ice on the storefront awning shattered with his terrible, needful cry.

Right now, more than anything, she needed the voice of her son's murderer to tell her what to do. She would do anything to put an end to the nightmare of midnights.

III.

He removed the corpse from the branches and dropped it unceremoniously to the ground, where it landed on hard-packed snow with a gross thud of bones and rot and a wretched squeak.

Climbing down from the tree, he pulled a large black cloth from his bag and laid it on the ground next to the corpse. He lifted the dead, flailing baby and placed it on the rectangle of funeral fabric.

Waxy, unblinking eyes stared at him. Years ago, the blue of the irises had faded throughout the whites of the eyes, and now it was like staring into balls of bluish ice. But the eyes were not cold like ice; they were very much heated with feeling.

Especially with fear.

"Thee, Stephan Izhar, whom I have formed from chaos are mine to do as I will. By the power of the Prince of darkness, I, master of Magic, confine thee, Stephan Izhar, by this shroud."

He folded the cloth over the head.

"As my magic will confine thy life in death . . . "

He folded the cloth over the legs.

"Thus will thee, Stephan Izhar, return to the blackness . . . "

He folded the cloth over the right side of the body.

"From whence thy came . . . "

He folded the remaining segment of cloth over the left side of the body. No shred of the dead's gray, only the black of the cloth, the black of death.

"By my power I hold thee, bound by my will."

He put the swaddled infant into a box, which stank of river and decay, snapped the padlock, and lowered the box back into its shallow grave.

"By my power I hold thee in darkness, bound by the will of the Brotherhood."

Shoveling the dirt upon the box, he smiled.

The Brotherhood.

His Brotherhood.

His brothers who would die without question, without delay for the Order; his brothers who would kill without hesitation.

His brothers, who waited for her to help build them a Higher Order.

"Come to light," he said and in the dying fire spied her image and stuck his knife through the heart of the red-orange flame. "Come to death."

Her eyes went to ashes and her lips went to deep red flame.

The face of a painted harlot, of Jezebel who calls herself a prophet and is teaching and beguiling God's servants to practice fornication.

Worse than Jezebel, she calls the angels down to fornicate.

17

He stomped out the fire, snuffing the image of her face, and laughed, for the prophets of God are called to destroy all the Jezebels.

And then they will cut open her body and steal the thirty Keys of power from her vile organs and call the angels down themselves for rightful purposes.

The Brotherhood will not suffer a woman to have sluttish control over the Divine.

But she will suffer.

Yes, indeed, he thought as he walked through the darkened woods, in the unseen company of darker things.

CHAPTER FOUR

In revenge and in love woman is more barbarous than man.
> Nietzsche, Beyond Good and Evil

Sweet is revenge—especially to women.
> Byron, Don Juan

There will be a time to murder and create.
> Eliot, The Love Song

I.

Dawn broke bleak upon Greenwich Village. Gray cumulus clouds shrouded the sallow light of the winter sun, and, though the sky brightened, it still had the wan look such that of a cadaver in the morgue under the fluorescent lights.

A grim day promised, with the threat of snow. Not the snow of Christmas, not the fat flakes flittering to the ground like wondrous white butterflies, but of the unrelenting sheet of dull, furious snow.

Stiff and nauseous, Rani stumbled away from the window, her vigil of the last few hours done, and threw herself on the bed. Michael rolled over and draped an arm over her abdomen. His hand rested on her breast; his finger and thumb kneaded her nipple.

Her eyelids fluttered in the heavy temptation of sleep.

The radiator rattled, and, in the mind-haze between awake and asleep, she heard the hiss of angels.

"We come for our sons."

"We come for slaughter."

Hands clasped over her eyes, she dared not witness the Grigori coming on the morning sun. Nightmares were meant for the night. But she saw their star-shining faces in the dark of her mind. Watching, waiting, wanting.

Her cunt quivered and warmed. Her heart pumped hot blood, heated by the lust fraught by fucking demon-angels.

Rani groaned as the radiator hissed only dry air.

"What's wrong?" Michael yawned, cupping her breast in his hand, his touch smooth and soft as the finest suede.

"Nothing." She rolled into his arms and slid her tongue between his supple lips. Pausing in her kiss, their lips still pressed, she murmured, "Hurt me."

Nodding solemnly, he stroked the wild coils of her sable hair and kissed her tenderly. He understood her need, for one pain to replace another, and shifted fluidly across the satin sheets, as if his nude body slid through a shallow pool of blood. She half expected his backside to be smeared red when he leaned over to reach into the night stand.

Scars tattooed his back. Years of cutting had made his back a living scroll work of archaic, alchemic symbols, and the ritualized rigor of his black arts had made the sight of his blood on his back almost ordinary.

Michael withdrew a roll of bondage tape from the drawer. The tape was nonadhesive, made from PVC film with self-clinging agents, something akin to Saran Wrap, only it came in black, pink, and red patent latex. This he wound around her head, over her mouth.

Her lips tingled from the pressure of the tape. She tongued the gag, and it was like licking a balloon that had lost its rubber zing. She tasted her own spit with a honeyed trace of the demon-angel's sperm.

Spreading her arms and legs, he buckled her wrists and ankles into restraints and strapped the cuffs to the posters of the wrought iron bed.

He teased her nipples with a white feather, like one torn from an angel's wing. It was soft as the downy velvet of angelic lips, sharp as the pointed shaft of angelic tongue.

Her areola tightened and her nipple hardened beneath the light touch of the feather. Michael bent down and took her nipple in his mouth, at first sucking gently, then biting it. All the while, he brushed the feather against her goose bumped skin, stimulating her nerves.

Rani muffled against the gag and writhed. Ruined. The Grigori had ruined her, and her body trembled for Michael to slash the feather across her side over and over and over, until it made a new hole for him to fuck.

The feather tickled her vulva instead.

The radiator hissed, and she closed her eyes, pretending the feathery wisp was the Grigoris' breath upon her.

With a final sweep, Michael tossed the feather aside and opened an exquisite box crafted from obsidian rock and mother-of-pearl. An array of clips awaited use—plastic, wooden, and metal clothespins, binder clips, butterfly clips, all varying in size and color and degrees of tension, the higher the tension, the greater the pain. He gathered a handful of metal clothespins. High tension.

Usually, the threat of the clips sent her body into a cold sweat, but this time her clit twitched, excited. It hardened for the coming of the burning bite, the throbbing numbness, and ultimately for the scathing return of blood when the clips were removed.

She sucked in her breath as he clipped on the first. It felt as if the Grigori with their terrible teeth like tiny daggers chewed her cunt apart with each one thereafter. By the seventh clip, tears ran down her cheeks.

But she loved it. The paradox of pain.

He breathed on her seething labia. Her body clenched, holding in screams.

His tongue seized upon her clit, then moved up and down between the clipped, inflamed lips of her sex, and Rani wept as he brought her closer to the state of being with angels. He stuck his tongue into her but pulled away suddenly as if her cunt had grown teeth.

As he removed the clips and gag, as she lay shaking and in tears, he rubbed the pain-pinched flesh of her labia and stared at her with pain-perplexed blue eyes. Like Stephan's eyes.

He wiped his lips slowly. His saddened eyes shifted downward, and, like someone who had been bitten on the mouth, he looked at his hand as if checking for blood.

"Sulphur and incense . . . "

Dawn filtered further into the room, bringing frail light and vigorous shadows, and Michael sat between her thighs, his Grecian-sculpted face half lit. He bowed his head. His dark tousled hair fell over his eyes, veiling his emotions.

"You stink of sulphur and incense. You taste saccharine, like dandelion wine or honeysuckle flowers. Like the whore of an incubus."

The sheet crumpled in his fist, his knuckles pearly against the ruby fabric.

"Did you steal a page from my handwritten text and perform a Goetic evocation? Did you give your soul as well as your body?"

"No, Michael . . . " she began, feeling as if she was part of the Spanish Inquisition with her wrists and ankles still in restraints.

"No?!" He pounded his fist onto the bed. "You can't pretend it didn't happen. I recognize the smell, Rani. It stinks of demons and angels, all the things you have dismissed from your life. Or so you have told me. *In flagrante delicto.*"

Pushing off the bed, Michael paced the wooden floor, slinking through the stream of dusty dawn. His abdominal muscles were taut and rippling as he moved. He glared at her. Incredibly, she felt aroused by the intensity of his eyes, like she was trapped prey and he would pounce at any moment. She squirmed against her bonds. Her juices trickled along her perineum, wetting a tiny spot beneath her.

Invisible fingers parted her labia; tips of claws dug into the pink flesh and clamped onto her as if with a hundred clips.

Rani's gasp whistled through her tight throat.

Stabs of immaterial tongues sent her reeling into a world of black, but, within the pitch, the faces of the Grigori shone with devious light . . .

II.

Her scream ringing in his ears, Michael stood and watched her body buck then slump upon the bed. Blood stained her inner thighs, and he would've assumed it menstrual if not for the ravaged appearance and the wet slur of things unseen.

He smelled their presence. An overpowering odor of sweet smoke, which became heavier with each passing second, a good indication that the spirits were gathering the salts of the earth and the dust in the air to manifest bodies.

His heart pumping hard, he felt lightheaded as the dim ether hanging above Rani consolidated.

No esoteric illustration of old could compare to the sight of these angels of agony.

Michael dropped to his knees in awe. Their wondrous and gigantic forms blinded him as if he had stared at the sun for too long, left only with the impression of dark brilliance imprinted on his retina.

Tremors wracked his muscles. Their awful glory rendered his limbs useless and stupefied him, paralyzing all but his most primitive senses. Deep down, he was aware of his raging erection. It was as if their wafting power stroked him hard and kept him cruelly tottering on the verge of a mind-altering orgasm.

Pain welled in his balls as though sulphuric acid instead of semen filled his sacs.

Incantations spewed from his mouth, spittle strings of gibberish and futility. The angels glanced his way, annoyed with his pittance of power.

Doubled over, he vomited and the liquid fire in his balls spread into his gut. His scars burned and chafed. It seemed the theurgies written in his flesh whispered in the voice of many.

In the voice of angry angels.

He shuddered, even in their silence.

They returned their attentions to Rani, licking the bright rosy stains from her thighs, tearing the lesions wider and wider to keep the blood flowing.

"Drink the milk of her womb," the vampiric angels commanded in deep tones, and he crawled toward the bed, unable to deny them.

Michael placed his mouth on a driblet of blood hanging from the hood of her clitoris like a marquis-cut garnet. Her life essence was meaty on his tongue.

"Asherah, the Mother of God and of the sons of God created Man from a bloody clot of her womb."

He nodded as if he understood the significance of their words, and the angels' shimmery eyes bore into him, daring him to truly understand. Their eyes seared a vision into his mind, of another Michael with wings of the color of emerald and his flesh covered with saffron hairs, each of them containing a million faces and mouths and as many tongues. Of the archangel Michael, who trussed these great angels up and forced them to watch their progeny die.

"We are the Watchers."

Their profound sadness weighed upon him, their chains of misery crushing him, and he thought he would die under the immense strain of their watchful eyes.

The scars on his back itched with the creepy-crawling of insects, of their iridescent beetle-brow eyes burrowing into him.

Another vision gripped him. Vibrant-dark, the angels knelt in crimson foam, their white wings drenched with the bloody spray, their hands clasped on rosaries of intestines, their tallow-dripping eyes wasted by the ongoing sight of their colossal infants making oceans of blood from their gluttony.

"We watch for the first rains of blood."

III.

She dreamed. Feverish dreams of midnight wraiths coiling from the mouths of angels, in billows of ashes, soot, and smoke, in swan songs, melodies of susurrous gas chambers and incinerators and the last sweet gasps of many.

She dreamed. Horrible dreams of long, inhuman fingers, more bone than flesh, raking away her belly and revealing her womb. Within the bloated amnion, faces with a million eyes blinked at her, their million mouths blowing bubbles. Her womb was a stretch of pink outer space, little eyes twinkling like stars, little bubbles swirling like clear, empty satellites.

She dreamed. Painful dreams of embryos erupting from her bulbous womb and crawling on cold slime-slick trails toward her breasts. Millions of mouths shrilled for marrow and milk. Millions of mouths with millions more teeth fastened to her breasts. Skin shredded. Mammary flesh and fat mangled. Blood flowed in hot sticky trails . . .

Then the dream was nothing more than darkness and the sounds of sucking . . .

#

Choking on guttural screams, Rani woke and twisted hard against the restraints, hard enough to pop her shoulder joint.

Michael pressed on top of her. His voice, his kisses, his hair-stroking hands soothed her, and she settled against the sheets, panting like an overheated pet.

"The angels have gone," he said, undoing the buckles of the leather cuffs.

"Gone?"

He nodded, gaze downcast, his hand idling between her legs. "Even the marks they made on you."

Groggily pulling herself into a sitting position, her back pressed uncomfortably against iron bars, she took a deep breath. Myrrh and copper permeated the air.

"What did the Grigori do to me?"

"Grigori? Grigori, Watchers, hmmm . . . " Michael chewed on his lush, lower lip as he slipped out of bed and out of the room. His back was livid and seeping, and Rani wondered what the Grigori had done to him.

The padding thud of feet, the click of locks, the shuffling of papers, the loud toppling of books and curses resounded through the hall.

Returning with a book hefted high in his hand, Michael grinned. "Here, the Grigori in *The Book of Enoch*. A superior order of angels of the 2nd or 5th Heavens, depending on if they are holy or unholy. God had sent these angels to watch and subtlety assist mankind."

We are the Watchers clicked in her mind.

He flipped through the pages until he came to the passage he wanted, reading aloud:

"And those men took me and let me up to the second heaven, and showed me darkness, greater than earthly darkness, and there I saw prisoners guarded, waiting the great and boundless judgment, and these angels were dark-looking, more than earthly darkness, and incessantly weeping . . . "

Thumbing through a few more pages, he read more:

"And the men carried me up to the fifth heaven, and I saw there many troops, Grigori, and their appearance was human and their size greater than that of great giants and their faces withered, and the silence of their mouths perpetual . . . "

Michael held up one finger, grinning broader, and then he sat upon the bed and looked to the index. Nodding his head emphatically and giggling, he practically shouted as he read yet other paragraphs from the book:

"And now giants, offspring of spirit and flesh, will be called spirits on the earth, and earth shall be their dwelling. Their bodies emitted evil spirits because they were born from human women and the Holy Watchers. The giants afflict, oppress, destroy, attack over the earth. Although they hunger and thirst, they do not eat. They offend. These spirits will rise up against men and women because they proceed from them.

"The giants will slaughter, unpunished, until the day of the great judgment. Then the age, the Watchers, and the godless will be wholly consummated. As for the Watcher who sent you to intercede for them, tell them: 'You were in Heaven but the mysteries were not revealed to you. You knew worthless ones, and in the hardness of your hearts you revealed these to women, and through these secrets women and men work much evil earth.'"

He placed the book onto her crossed thighs. Its leather binding was coarse, nearly crumbly, and it weighed heavy upon her lap, even though the volume was not thick.

"Wow, incredible," he breathed, leaning against her, kissing her shoulder.

"Incredible, how?" Rani rubbed her temples, irked by Michael and his prophetic books, disturbed by the wicked memory of the Watchers, of their swords, of their gruesome pleasure. She thought about the giants, the offspring of the heavenly spirits and earthly flesh. History repeated in her flesh, she feared and kneaded the space between her eyes.

"Incredible because the Grigori appeared to you twice without evocation." Michael rolled once again out of bed and fumbled with a pile of clothes tossed on the floor. "Working magic requires a union with the divine, and I say . . . " He shucked on his pair of wrinkled wool pants. "You now have the ability to work magic."

His indigo eyes brewed with excitement, brightening like a twilight sky in the midst of an electrical storm.

"What magic, Michael? What do I need with magic?"

"Alchemy, divination, communication with the Watchers. Transforming through destruction and chaos. Gaining transcendental wisdom. Traversing the darkness for the light of mysteries. Succeeding in the human goal, to have the godhead on your shoulders . . . "

"Not my thing," she said, interrupting his rattle, setting the book aside. But the gold embossed lettering kept her attention as it changed from gold to glossy rose, then flickered back again to glitter. Trick of light or madness of mind, she couldn't decide.

"Not your thing?" He grabbed her hands and pulled her standing in front of him, his bare chest rising and falling with rapid breath, his skin's warmth touching hers intermittently. "Not even if these angels are said to carry swords of punishment?"

Michael yanked her hair, pulled her head back, and pressed his mouth against her ear, whispering, "You can call the angels to punish the man who killed Stephan."

Shivers tingled from her ear and down her spine.

Punish the man who killed Stephan. Her vengeance dream . . . her nails pierced in his throat, mincing his breath and murderous voice . . . her hands wrenched on his head, pummeling his skull against a rock.

Fingers buzzing, she wondered if it mattered whose hands delivered the murderous sentence. Surely not, as long as his life emptied red from his body.

"All you have to do is call them by name and command them by your will."

She groaned as he pulled down harder in her hair and bit the pulsing carotid path of her neck. "My will . . . "

As if her will held power enough to bring her son back.

But then, by the angels' will, in the dark of her womb, the seeds for destruction were implanted. They will give her different sons, ones who would cry for marrow and milk.

"Why have they chosen me?"

His lips were a feathery touch against hers.

"They have their purpose."

His hands sliding down her shoulders, her sides, resting on her backside curves, he pulled her closer. She sank into his sultry embrace, her cheek resting against his hot silken skin, her ear filled with the erratic deep-drum sound of his heart. His breath seemed to hitch and shudder inward.

"Something wrong?" she whispered, her lips upon his chest, feeling as if she spoke directly to his troubled heart.

"Anxious. Concerned." His lips soothed her brow. "I have always sought the mystic, but the mystic has always found you. And I'm afraid I'll lose you to it this time."

Rani kept silent, afraid as well, because his words felt right.

With a finger beneath her chin, Michael raised her face and grimly searched her features, as if reading some secret tarot inscribed onto her flesh. "Please don't do anything until I return from my morning lectures."

"But I have the restoration proposal on the Trinity Church to prepare."

"You know what I mean . . . "

With her tongue, she toyed with his silver nipple ring. "Mmmhmmm."

She massaged his flaccid penis through his pants. Smiling as he stirred and swelled beneath her fingers.

Michael pushed away from her. "We don't have time for this, Rani. Perhaps the Grigori have chosen you for this reason—you, the perfect whore."

Said without malice, possibly even with a hint of admiration, desire.

He crushed his lips against hers before walking away.

Mouth smarting, as if slapped instead of kissed, Rani fell onto the bed. She watched, through tear-puffy eyes, Michael pull on his favorite sweater, the thick yarn dyed as if with blood and bruises. Another layer of abuse on his back.

"You'll be okay?" he asked, the *Book of Enoch* tucked under his arm like an accessory. He hesitated at the doorframe, his eyes sullen, his mouth terse.

She nodded, and he hurried away to make the eight o'clock class at the University.

With only the quiet ticking of the clock as her companion, Rani turned on her side and stared at the walls. So much like a cell, a cage, with the bars of sickly sunlight surrounding her. Dust motes were suspended in the streams. She thought of Stephan, suspended in the unabated dark, of hands squeezing his tiny throat. His sweet-milk breath souring foul in suffocation.

Freedom craved. From this life, that death.

Call them by name and command them by your will.

Rani sat up, crossed her arms over her eyes and rocked against the headrest rails. The bars clanged like bells breaking.

"Stephan," she whimpered.

Clang.

"Stephan . . ."

Clang.

"Stephan . . ."

Clang, the sound echoed for an hour, the minutes marked upon her shoulders and back as if by time's violet-staining hands.

Time was the absolute executioner, and life was only a question of time running after you.

Every night, in that moment before she drifted into sleep, panic settled in her. She feared slipping into the darkness within her mind. If all the world's a stage, and all the men and women merely players, then sleep's but a rehearsal for death.

Rani feared death, not the act of dying. The prospect of being stripped of her self-awareness terrified her, and she struggled to reconcile the idea of eternity compared to her fraction of existence in the ultimate scheme of things. No doubts she would be dead longer than she had ever lived.

Why give her a taste of life in the first place? she always wondered at night, in bed, on the brink of practicing her eternal sleep.

But now . . . she could think of nothing worse than that sleep being disturbed.

His soul waits in darkness, in agony.

"Stephan . . . "

Clang.

His agony, his agonizing cries. Vile hands continued to wring his tiny throat. The anger coiled tight in her gut unraveled.

Her will, her will, her will . . .

"Shemyaza . . . " she wailed, tossing her head side to side.

Walls rumbled; windows rattled. The dust and shadows collapsed together like a dark star imploding, and, with a clangorous cacophony, the Grigori leader hailed into the room.

With rage-rimmed eyes, Shemyaza approached her.

"Avenge my dead son," she growled, half in fear, half in defiance. "Tear out the murderer's heart as he has torn out mine."

The demon-angel knelt beside her and placed his head upon her belly.

"Mother of the sons of the sons of God will have her vengeance."

CHAPTER FIVE

And the angel of peace who was with me said to me:
"These two monsters, prepared conformably
to the greatest of God, shall feed . . . "

Book of Enoch

I.

They scoured the sky, hidden within the swatches of dirty clouds.

In the sprawl of asphalt, concrete, and steel, humans bustled along the sidewalks in a mass flow like ants but without direction, pushing onward in desperate stride, seeking nourishment where no nourishment could be found. Manhattan reeked of exhaust, both the combustible and the human.

Buildings towered into the sky like walls of mazes. In the days of Moses, only the hill towns of the Anakites, the giant descendants of the Nephilim, matched these heights. And they watched these inhabitants devour each other as well.

A whiff of murder drew them down.

Nestled in the black labyrinthe of the fire escape rails, they watched the alley brighten with the flash of knives. The victim lay in a slushy puddle of urine and steaming blood, his body jerking still with the squelching thrust of blades. He had no screams. A garotte jeweled his throat in a slim necklace of rubies.

His eyes stared up at the Fallen, unseeing yet full of the dreadful sight of death.

Wiping their knives against the victim's jeans, the gang of four exited the alley and slipped back into the hurried flow, unsuspected of any crime.

But, although they had left the body behind, they had absorbed the smell of the spirit murdered. Such pungent trails always attracted dogs, demons, and angels and made for such easy tracking.

Slinking down, the Fallen enveloped the dead body like a grisly shroud. The blare of horns and the squeal of brakes concealed the thundering snarls and the wet ravage of meat, and the dark, littered alley floor kept secret the snaky flows of blood.

Only a greasy smear remained when the feast ended.

The angels had delivered him from this world.

His soul would wait by a gorge filled with venomous reptiles until the day his murderers perished from this earth, then he would watch these small dragons stalk the murderers with terrible hisses and snapping jaws. The bite of these black reptiles burned. His soul would be soothed as his murderers writhed in this torture, as raptorial worms oppressed them in dark slithering clouds.

#

Before his fall, Shemyaza would visit the gloomy places of the damned and watch the punishments, half in fascination, half in confusion. His vast heavenly knowledge never helped him understand the wrath of God, how He could destroy that which He had helped his wife create. It was akin to a child molding clay and throwing a tantrum that the clay refused to fit neatly into the shape within his mind. The child would flatten the sculpted figure with fist or foot, then begin the process again in frustration. Doomed to ever perfect it.

The Grigori leader would descend from his mount on Hermon and sneak into the bowels of the earth through volcanic vents. Winding through convoluted passages of glowing rock and rivers of magma and fire, he encountered numerous rooms, rooms used loosely, for

Hell was boundless and without boundaries, only infinite in tortures. It was as if pockets of dark space opened up, as if with curtains pulled apart, revealing all the punitive acts within.

Hell was like some grand, subterranean theater, garishly papered in gold flames and screaming mirrors. An echelon of stages existed throughout the multitude of floors, linked by inverted stairwells and hidden halls, and merciless angels directed these hideous flesh-propped and wailing stages. Chains and hooks dangled from scabious ceilings which swelled with fetid breath.

All-in-all, Shemyaza had enjoyed the shows.

Those who had blasphemed hung by their tongues. Bodies pirouetted, forever twisting tongues, wearing tulles of incarnadine bits of tissue and spittle.

Those who waggled their tongues in deceit spent an eternity with their lips cut off, their tongues stuck with sharp prongs, and their intestines pulled up through their throats and mouths. Repeatedly.

Those who turned away from righteousness drowned in a great lake full of molten mire. Scorched skins dripped from skulls in blackened wax and ochery fluids of pus and blood. Eyes boiled over, and mouths bubbled with red-viscose shrieks.

Women who ensnared men to destruction with their beauty hung from their hair and necks; and the men who had lain in their traps hung by chains, by red-hot hooks pierced through their thighs and genitals.

Children murdered by their parents skipped in circles around their damned parents, cursing them in sing-song voices and giggling as Temlakos, the angel of all fire, tormented the mothers and fathers. Milk spilled from severed nipples, curdling, congealing into foul smelling beasts which devoured ever-slowly the flesh of their doomed parents.

Opposite that place, the discharge and excrement of the tortured ran down into another gorge and became a lake. Those who produced children outside marriage or procured abortions sat in the lake, with discharge coming out of their throats. Many premature children sat on the brim, weeping, smoldering these women with the fire-rays of their eyes.

There were men who defiled their bodies by behaving like women, and women who behaved with one another as men with a woman, and they were cast from precipices. Then the angels would drag them up the high slopes and throw them down again without rest from the battering plunge.

In pits, in heavy chains, sinners of all manners of cruelty and with no compassion stood knee-deep in blood and fire, unable to cry from mercy. Four legions of evil angels struck them with stones and wounded their faces like storms.

And many, many more torturous chambers of the iniquitous . . .

Shemyaza cherished those stolen moments. The cacophony of tormented voices and explosive, crackling angel-laughter was forever locked in his spirit, sweeter than any melodious harp or lute played for the Majestic ear, inciting in him an obsession, an intense passion filled with the passions of thousands upon thousands of forbidden affairs.

His sons had inherited his love for the wicked.

Such pleasure, such savory flesh, and he anticipated the moment he would taste her child's murderer.

#

The air tasted and smelled already of him, the bitter of Turkish smoke, the sharp dust of corpses, the subtle spice of vanilla, a child's distinct flavor. Her earthen-mother scent mingled as well in the effluvium.

Assassin winds, they blew into pores of the bricks, through the fibers of plaster and insulation, around pipes, wires and support beams, and out of the ducts. The Fallen came into the murderer's den.

In his hands, he held a skull, turning it over and inspecting it with a perplexed gaze. His thoughts peppered the air.

Exceptional cranial bulging, as if the brain ballooned in utero . . . encephalitis? But the eye sockets . . . too big, too round for human eyes . . .

They circled the man and crouched like crocodiles lurking on the river's bottom for unsuspecting prey, jaws agape.

What, draft?

He glanced up from the skull as the Keepers of Secrets revealed themselves.

God Almighty . . .

II.

Seven entities beyond his imagination surrounded him. His eyebrows singed beneath their fiery gaze, their eyes like glowing coals, and his spit dried in the heat of their breath against his face. His skin burned, tightened, blistered, and crusted.

By impulse, he reached up and scratched his cheek, his fingers drawn away, his nails embedded with tiny strips of his flesh. He dropped the skull with a clatter.

Winds beneath their wings stole his screams.

Winds beneath their wings knocked him into the window.

The needling of glass stung his ear, his cheek, his brow, his eye. Falling onto the ground, he dumbly stared at the window, at the shattered web of cracks, at the stained glass. The sun glimmered crimson.

Swords sliced apart his gut; talons emptied it, uncoiling visceral ropes.

No pain, only disgust and detachment. No pain. No pain until those talons scourged through liver, pancreas and stomach, until those talons ripped into the beating pulp of his heart.

His world went red with the sight of his heart in the grip of a beast, then it went oblivion-black.

But, God Almighty, he still felt them feed . . .

III.

Rani doubled over, clutched her belly as if punched, and sank to her knees. Ribs in vise, she couldn't breathe. The very air around her was crushing her and rambling in the tongues of the ancients.

Feast, the binding winds sighed.

And black-green vines sprouted from between the seams of the hardwood planks, twining her wrists, raveling up her slender arms, twisting around her neck and pulling her head down until her mouth touched the ground. The vine bloomed. Nothing as sweet as roses.

But a human heart, thrashing on thorns and pumping grumous nectar.

The vines wound faster, constricting her, pinning her mouth against the heart, and the slick muscle pulsed against her lips.

"Feast," Grigori voices demanded from the growing shadows.

Slammed with angelic fist ... *breathless, aching* ... and stabbed with angelic cock ... *groaning, aching* ... , Rani hungrily bit into the heart, and, as the tough meat released blood into her mouth, she came.

Softly in the air the sound of an infant mewling in gratitude for the symbiotic taste of blood she gave him . . .

CHAPTER SIX

If there is anything worse than the
wrongs wrought by wicked men,
it is the evil done by good men.

Newton, Religion of Masonry

I.

"In the presence of Almighty God, I vow to keep the secrets of our Lodge under no less penalty than that of having my throat cut across, my tongue torn out by its roots, and my body buried in the rough sands of the sea."

The initiate opened his mouth, and the Grand Master poured hot wax on his tongue, sealing his pledge.

"You have stepped from the darkness and into the light. Into the truth and wisdom of the Masonic Brotherhood, with faith in the Universe as friendly, faith in man as a spiritual being, and faith in the power of spiritual ideas," the Grand Master began, leading the rites.

"Our lives are the living stones, building an ideal, temples of the brotherhood, truth, morality, relief, and love."

The Grand Master laid the candle's flame against the initiate's chest.

"We are generations of builders, adding an arch, pillar, or spire. Our faith is the cornerstone; our sweat, tears, and blood, the mortar. Temples rise, built by love of many and the loyalty of many."

Hairs curled away into ash and flesh smoldered.

"Come build Solomon's Temple with your brothers. Through the body of change and death, you will have the perfect body, which shall not be subject to death. From the material of the physical body, we will build this deathless body and you will be eternal in the heavens."

Into a ring of bubbling red, his flesh burned, and another member of the order knelt beside the initiate, with knife and silver dish in hand. He cut off the blistered patch of flesh. With deft hand, he edged the knife in the skinless wound and carved the sun over the initiate's heart, as badge of light, illumination, and God.

The initiate garbled in pain, his tongue blistered and swollen from the wax.

"Julian Starks, we enlist you as a fellow worker with the Eternal. Life will reveal its eternal quality and promise to you as you have made an eternal promise to the good of the Freemasons."

Arms linked tight around his arms pulled him to stand in the center of their circle, and Julian watched as the dish was passed from brother to brother, as the Freemasons had a communion with his seared skin.

#

Yesterday it seemed he had taken his Masonic oath.

Not this faded decade, with only its vivid memory marked upon his mind and body.

Julian paused before the mirror, modeling shirtless for the silver-backed glass, tracing the sun scar with eye and finger. It had gone lunar-pale with time, an improvement over the gaudy pink of healing tissue. On dull, wintry days like today, he had the impulse to saunter over to Last Rites Tattoo Studio on 214th and have it emblazoned gold, with black tendrils of death spoked around it, with white-phantom screaming faces etched within the spokes like some haunting mandala.

The dead might as well scream upon his flesh. Their screams already had imprinted within his body, not only in memory but in vague spasms of his heart. An aftereffect of his necromancy, his pulse disrupted by their electromagnetism. Freud might've called it guilt.

"The bastard, he believed animism and sorcery were neuroses." In an affected German accent, Julian told his reverse image, "'Every neurosis results from premature sexual activity, especially that of molestation in childhood.'"

Twilight cascading in dreamy blue along the walls; breeze sifting lazily through the curtain sheers, bringing the damask of magnolia blooms and the beauty of a ghost.

A ghost of hyacinth mists and lovely smile of dew.

Prepubescent night of wonder, of her ivory-lilac hands and his budding manhood.

In the mirror, he focused on the shadows behind him and charged the amorphous shade to coalesce into his *neurosis.*

"Flesh she will eat; blood she will drink."

Julian cut across his thumb with an x-acto blade and anointed his forehead with his blood.

"Dark is she, but brilliant. Black on black, she leadeth forth the hordes of the abyss and leadeth men to ruin. Look on her in lust and despair."

The shadows shimmered, as if the oily darkness captured the fiery arch of a rainbow. Darkness pressed outward with an emerging beast, and she broke from the shadows, no longer cloaked in the illusion of a midsummer fairy but a thing borrowed from myth. Her black head crawled with serpent hair and her eyes dripped poisonous blood. Standing with brass-studded whip and wrapped in gray gauze, she grinned, her hideous-wide mouth stretching wider as if she meant to swallow him whole.

Her breath warmed his nape. She had drunk the wine of sacrifice recently, and Julian swooned in its piquancy of narcissus, honey, and blood.

"Lilith," he sighed as her deadly hand reached around his shoulder and covered his scar. He flinched. Her touch was cold, colder than deep-cavern stone, and as substantial as his own, even though her hand was only finely crafted air.

"Yesssss," her hairs hissed.

"Show me . . . "

Her other hand pushed through his back, an icy gurgling spear of gas lancing through his insides, and exited the other side through his navel. With index finger pointed, she touched the mirror. The glass rippled as if made of crystal water. Rings spread outward, warping their reflections into some Picasso rendering of fragmented faces, then spiraled, blending their reflections as if mixing various pigments on a palette into a swirl of brownish-black.

Within the vortex was another dimension. A landscape of black liquid sands sucking in and spitting out scorched corpses and screeching demons.

Dead and demon alike reached for the mirror.

The mirror split through the center as monstrous claws pried apart the translucent satin of the undulating glass. Adorned with the grue of broiled flesh, a demon with seven serpent heads, fourteen faces of man, and twelve dark wings pushed through and entered the room. The demon held a dismembered head.

The Grand Master's head. Two hollows of eyes stared at Julian in madness and spite, his sockets like the insides of conoidal shells, dark pink ridges winding into depths and hypnotizing Julian in horror; his mouth, an awful gape of soundless fury.

Lilith pressed against him. Her cold reptilian flesh gave him little comfort as she wrapped limbs around him and turned him to face her. The serpents on her head lunged at his forehead, their forked-tongues striking flesh and savoring the anointment of blood.

"Hisssss sssoul isss ssssacrificcced," the asps said.

Then the room emptied of all demons and visions.

Julian turned before the mirror, once again admiring his sun scar which twinkled for a brief minute, smiling because his scheme had worked. Sometimes it paid to sacrifice a little of your blood to demons instead of the whole lot . . . *razor sliding into his skin, making scarlet-black cuts . . . brass chalice filled with his body's wine . . . Lilith greedily draining the chalice and licking clean his wound.*

Lilith had predicted mortal danger. Through cunning and dark-enchanted perfumes, he and Lilith had transferred the danger to the Grand Master, and the wrath of the Jezebel had been taken out on the wrong man.

CHAPTER SEVEN

What, silent still? And silent all?
Ah! no;—the voices of the dead
Sound like a distant torrent's fall.

Byron, Beppo

Thrilling to think, poor child of sin,
It was the dead who groaned within.

Poe, The Sleeper

I.

Michael cringed. His skin itched, vibrating as his scars shifted and murmured. Given voice by spirits he had raised from graves and harbored in his flesh, by spirits roiled by the omen of the Watchers.

Like leaves in the wind, the voices rustled throughout the classroom. Several students lifted their heads from their texts.

Michael cleared his throat, directed the students to turn the pages, and read a passage from T.S. Eliot's *The Waste Land*.

"A woman drew her long black hair tight/And fiddled whisper music on those strings/And bats with baby faces in the violet light/Whistled, and beat their wings/And crawled head downward down a blackened wall/And upside down in air were towers/Tolling reminiscent bells, that kept the hours/And voices singing out of empty cisterns and exhausted wells."

Voices within his scars echoed from the empty of his soul.

"In this decayed hole among the mountains/In the faint moonlight, the grass is singing/Over the tumbled graves, about the chapel/There is the empty chapel, only the wind's home./It has no windows, and the door swings,/Dry bones can harm no one./Only a cock stood on the rooftree/Coco rico co co rico/In a flash of lightning. Then a damp gust/Bringing rain . . . "

Affected by the sounds of his scars much like winds in an empty chapel, the students drew their arms against their bodies. Some shivered; some giggled. But all felt the mysterious airs drift about them and whisper of gloom and despair.

"Co co rico co co rico is an allusion to *Hamlet* when the cock crows and the King's ghost fades. It signals the departure of ghosts and evils spirits. Co co rico co co rico . . . "

"Co co rico co co rico," the students repeated, then repeated again with conviction.

His scars burned and breathed, hitching deeply like a body expiring. Sweat swelled at his temples, and he steadied himself against the podium until the vertigo and rigor spells subsided. A shudder twisted through his back, then stillness.

Wiping his brow with his sleeve, Michael shrugged off the ominous brooding of the spirits and carried on with his lecture as if nothing happened, and his students gratefully ignored the out-of-the-ordinary and concentrated on literary theory.

"*The Waste Land* exemplifies an archetypal work, that the structure of myth and ritual are linked with the structures of literature. Eliot admitted he based a great deal of the poem's symbolism on Grail legend, the questing knight, the grail and lance as fertility metaphors for female and male, the conquest which would restore life to the land. Which brings us to another archetype."

Michael stepped aside of the podium and faced the window. "*The Waste Land* was in effect about spiritual dryness. About man living in a waste land of winter, loneliness, ruin and death, hoping for the barren earth..the dying god . . . to be renewed with spring . . . to be resurrected . . . "

Spring . . . life . . . a colorful, fleeting illusion. In spring, when the cherry trees of the Brooklyn Botanic Gardens exploded with delicate, pink flowers, the sight reminded him too much of souls exploding from dead bodies in blood-sprinkled clouds. An unsettling sight and an ugly sign of new life.

But it was not life becoming anew as the cycle suggested but life always returning to its fruition of darkness and indefinite dormancy. To the primordial state of genesis.

"Though Eliot ended the poem on the note of hope . . . "

Bleak beyond the window, layer upon layer of corpulent gray clouds settled over the cuspated heights of Manhattan. It looked as if the snow would come biting down.

The class waited for him to continue. They stared at his back, their eyes reaching out with ennui and impatience, and his scars stirred beneath their psychic touch.

"Gods never rise once fallen. They become the demons of other religions and the old faiths become waste lands."

Wind buffeted the windows. Tinkling of bells drifted throughout the room, the tone unusual and subtly alarming, and chairs screeched as a few students pushed away from their desks and hurried from the room. Michael dismissed the rest of the class with a theatrical twist of his wrist and wave of his arm toward the door, pantomiming to the laughter of his scars.

Special effects, he would explain later if asked.

After the last student exited the room, he fell into his chair and bit into his lower lip. His scars stung as if the spirits were ripping exit wounds through his flesh.

Blood seeped into his mouth. Light, salty, lacking that meaty quality of Rani's blood. *The Mother of God and of the sons of God created Man from a bloody clot of her womb.* Perhaps his sip of Rani's blood created the voices of his theurgy-scars.

The spirits had been silent before, silent as the graves he had raised them from.

Ringing winds sounded again. Leaning his head back, closing his eyes, he thought of sea-shell chimes and pearl-strung shades and the murmuration of his nanny's voice as she rocked him in her ample arms and read him "The Lady and the Merman." A modern fairytale by Jane Yolen, his nanny's favorite author.

#

He would nestle against Diane's soft pillow of a body and feel as if he were adrift at sea, the walls of the beach house awash in blue moonlight, calm waves of ocean. Sea breezes would flirt with the chimes, bringing marine and salt perfumes as gifts, and dance gaily among the pinkish shells. He pictured ladies twirling, their glass slippers clinking across the ballroom floor. A mind for fancy, his nanny would say, but then she filled his head with fanciful tales nightly.

As she read, he would forget he existed and become part of the story, flowing right into the illustrations it seemed and coming through the other side into another world where the imagined was real.

The Lady began as everyone had, as a child born of a mother and father. On her very first day in the world, her father, a sea captain, looked upon his daughter and turned away, angry and disappointed by the infant's plain face. He set sail without another glance at his newborn girl, a burden in his mind.

Michael would curl his hand into a fist, angry himself at the father, because he knew the story. He knew what would happen next, having heard it repeated often, having lived it.

The mother would die. The child would grow, feeling unloved and hurt, always searching for her father's sail, waiting for his return, waiting for his love.

Sometimes, sheltered in his nanny's arms and in the blanket of twilight shadows, Michael would shed a tear for the Lady, never admitting he meant the tear for himself. He was an ugly child too, ungainly in sports, and unmanly gifted in poetry and language. A sad specimen of son to his burly father, who, though no sea captain able to sail to faraway ports, kept his distance nonetheless.

Once, the Lady asked her father how to heal the wounds between them. His nanny would choke on her voice every time and stroke his cheek as she relayed the father's answer: *Salt for such wounds.*

Salt of tears, sweat and sea.

Salt of suffering.

Like the cry of gulls, suffering had echoed in the walls of the beach house when Diane had passed away and left him alone. A tortured retreat, returning to his place of comfort with her ashes in an urn. "The Lady and the Merman" had beckoned, and he had read it aloud, his voice lacking her soothing lilt.

Salt for such wounds.

Michael had taken the fish gutting knife and splayed open the vein of his forearm's underside. He was mesmerized by the blood spilling over his pale flesh, mystical scarlet springs on white sands.

Coming through the door, his father had stopped in the threshold. He had looked with disdain upon Michael, who sat cross-legged, knife poised in one hand, blood cascading down the other, his palm upturned as if begging. Then he had turned and walked away, shutting the door as he did. Leaving Michael alone.

Alone with the sea-shell chimes singing and pearl-strung shades clapping and the blue-wash walls shimmering in shadow-frolic. Alone like the Lady standing on the rocks, watching the figure of the Merman surge above the foam, yearning for love. Alone, still a boy, sitting on the floor, grinding the salt of corpses into his cut, watching his nanny's ashes soak in the blood.

Healing the deepest wounds.

"Can you love me?" The Lady had asked the Merman.

But the Merman gave no voiced answer, only pointed to the sea before he dove down in the deep. The Lady, after one glance at her father's house, followed him . . .

Michael had picked up the story book and read, tainting the pages with his ash-clotted blood: "The sea put bubble jewels in her hair and spread her skirts about her like a scallop shell. Tiny colored fish swam in between her fingers. The water cast her face in silver, and all the sea was reflected in her eyes.

"She was beautiful for the first time. And for the last."

"Can you love me?" he had asked the wind, and not even the distant slur of the ocean had answered him . . .

#

The cockled scar along the underside of his arm murmured in warning.

Shaking off the reverie of shell song, Michael stood, gathered his belongings, and rushed from the building. All his scars seemed to rumble with her name: *Rani*.

Something was happening. Something bad.

His heart raced faster than his feet as he bounded down the outside stairs and sprinted down the sidewalk, bumping tourists milling on the corner of Washington Square, crossing the street with no heed to the horns. He slowed his pace to a brisk walk when he reached Bleecker Street, his bronchial passages clenching with cold breath, his diaphragm in stitches.

Heading west on Bleecker, he caught a whiff of sweet smoke in the air. He imagined Rani carousing with the angels, her lips split and bleeding from Seraphical fellatio, her mouth full of their shining cum. He imagined their swords splicing her in half, their tongues lancing through her guts, their mouths full of her flesh.

We watch for the first rains of blood.

His calf muscles cramped; his stomach cramped. The thought of losing Rani sickened him, and he ran again, despite the protests in his body and the winds pushing against him. In his peripheral vision, the brick buildings of old turned into a bloody blur. The street trees were like stick-men magi in procession, bowing slightly in the swirling winds, bowing toward the stars which had fallen upon Rani.

At the corner of Minetta Lane, he stopped and clutched a light post to catch his burning breath. The air had grown thinner in oxygen, thicker in sweet smoke.

A gay couple walked by him, eyeing him, then glanced conspiratorially at each other, tiny grins teasing their lips. Their auras shimmered in pale violets and specks of spirits flitted around them like glittery butterflies.

The site of the old Minetta Court was a refuge for restless spirits, drawn to this place because of its slum-starveling past, where the dangerous and desperate once dwelled. Michael sensed malevolency in the air, as if hoodlum spirits stalked him from alleys, intent on mugging his body and possessing him. His skullcap tingling, he released his hold on the lamp post and lumbered away.

He braced himself for an onslaught of spirit, but he walked without hindrance, without any sense at all except the graying sight as the world went irreal.

Ghosts loitered on the steps, in the windows of the buildings, on the rooftops. Every coal-dusted eye swivelled toward him. Peckish grins spread upon the raven-gloomy faces.

Ghosts rose like bluish smoke from the cracks in the sidewalks and the sewer grates, hissing foul of stagnant breath and fouler curses.

Ghosts in rags of rot crowded the entire area. Hollow voices begged for him to barter his soul and sacrifice the blood. *"Raise the dark beast."*

The hairs along his crown stood pin straight as a spirit worked its ways through his skull. It traveled down into him, lifting hairs at his nape, chest, navel, groin, thigh, shin, and even the hairs upon his toes. Every nerve and follicle in Michael's body tingled with the settling of the static-charged body-thief.

"Raise the dark beast," it demanded.

The beast, a demon-deity of towering mass and blood-red skin, a hungry horror of black-shining claws and blood frenzy.

The beast which lorded over the flies and the dead.

The beast which wished to walk again from his nightmares, but which he kept trapped within the shadows of his soul by the power within his scars.

Each year, he needed another theurgy cut into his flesh, another conjuring of a sorcery-strong spirit to aid him in the Keep. His scars were the locks to gates, always under pressure and weakening.

Of late, he dreamed about a plague of flies swarming a body with squirming skin. The maggots would feed through the skin into the body, and the mask of worms would slip away, revealing Rani's face, beautiful even pocked with burrows. Then the dark beast would burst from her body in showers of blood.

"Raise the dark beast."

And the howl of the beast escaped his throat. His lips were forced to form her name and call spirits upon her . . .

CHAPTER EIGHT

To keep from the evil woman,
From the smoothness of the alien tongue,
Lust not after her beauty in thy heart;
Neither let her captivate thee with her eyelids.

Proverbs 6.24-26

Who felt the touch of her swift hands, —
What lord of sunstruck Eastern lands?
Who felt the soft white bosom swell
Of Jezebel, of Jezebel?

Barlow, Jezebel.

I.

The sickness struck suddenly, and blood she had consumed sprayed from her mouth and splattered all over the floor. So much blood, Rani couldn't breathe. Her sides and throat ached from the force of her retching, and, on wobbly hands and knees, she crawled toward the bathroom and left a copious trail behind her.

Pulling herself up against the sink, she filled the porcelain basin. The Grigori held her head as she vomited. The Grigori kissed her lips, chin, and neck, mouthing the waste upon her skin.

Rani trembled with the touch of their lips. Deep in her belly twinges of pleasure replaced the sickness.

Shemyaza whispered in her ear, his lips ever still and silent, but his voice seeping inside and soothing her nonetheless.

"Mary dreamed of an angel."

"And the angel of the Lord came onto Mary and conceived a child with her . . . "

Shemyaza positioned himself behind her, talons gripped around her breasts, his cock maneuvering into her cunt and tearing her open again. Rani opened her mouth, but her gasps and groans were breathless and therefor soundless.

"Mary birthed the hybrid Messiah, half Man, half Son of God, and taught him the art of illusion. The Nazarene hid his Nephilic nature well, except in those moments witnessed as miracles, except during those forty days in the desert where he fulfilled his hunger for the flesh of man and beast."

His thrusts sounded wetly.

"The first born of the dead appeared to his disciples without illusions, and the prophets saw for the first time his heavenly disguise. Thus they saw the Lord's face, ineffable, marvelous, very awful, and very, very terrible.

"Stand before his face into eternity . . . "

Rammed against the edge of the counter, her face bowed within an inch of the mirror. Her reflection was obliterated in the core of Seraphical light which embraced her, the image of the Fallen, darker than the earthly dark.

Dark as eternity.

His talons pierced her breasts.

Blood dripped from punctures, *plink-plink* of red rain running down the drain.

Laughter spilled from her lips, crazy kind of laughter, like that of Old George who would push his mower in the streets and cut grass which only he saw, who bray-laughed at the moon and the hearse. How his laughter had frighted her. Especially when she was five, with his mouth pressed against her ear and his laughter tingling her lobe, as his rough hands fished down her shorts, as his thick finger hooked into her tiny, unyielding vagina.

Doubled over, she spewed blood-browned bile into the sink.

His laughter, like thousands of flies buzzing around the dead and the weeping, whirred from the pipes. It was Old George laughing and unzipping all over again.

Rani fell against Shemyaza as if some force knocked her back, and the Fallen Seraph wrapped his arms and wings tightly around her.

"Jesus never wept upon the cross but laughed until tears streamed down his face and the day turned black with his mood. And he died with a hard-on."

Again, that crazy laughter.

Shemyaza drew his talons down her back as he slunk to his knees. She arched her back, hissing and gasping. Nearly fainting as his talons pierced into the meat of her ass and spread her. His tongue explored her, like a skewer being thrust into her anus. Into her cunt. Into the other holes he was making.

Buckling under the pricks, Rani gripped the counter and steadied her balance, edging from his tongue but not shifting away completely. Sort of maneuvering herself in a position to deny him nothing of her sex yet control his depth of penetration. Like she does with a guy with a long cock. Holding and pushing on his hips, keeping his thrusts shallow enough not to hurt her.

But after awhile she wanted the hurt.

She rocked her pelvis against him, harder, faster, reckless, making him pierce through her skin and be deep inside her. The tiles reverberated with her cries.

When he abruptly withdrew his tongue and stood, she whimpered, "No, no."

But she panted, "Yes, yes," as he eased his swollen purpling cock into her.

Shemyaza toyed with her pussy, pushing only an inch into her, then slipping out and rubbing his moistened head against her clit. All of it warm and wet and highly arousing. Rani thought she would burst if he didn't fuck her hard and break her apart right then and there.

But he stopped. Even the blood-twitch in his cock stilled.

She waited.

She wanted.

Then he clasped his teeth into flesh between shoulder and neck, and she flinched under his bite, automatically pushing her body down, away from his teeth but onto his cock. Pain stabbed her cervix as it was torn open. Blood streamed down her thighs and breast.

The bathroom filled with nightshades.

Fleshed with this substance of darkness, seven female spirits appeared and knelt in front of her. Their black-wisp of hands caressed her. Their black-wisps of tongues probed the contours of her cunt and licked at his glistening cock as it slid in and out of her. The women of darkness also attended the other Grigori and cocks straining for attention.

Rani shivered, feeling these sensations like chilly winds whispering along her skin.

Star-shining eyes closed, Shemyaza appeared more human, his face beautiful and almost feminine like the spirits adoring him. Delicate and dewy with light. No wonder he had his pick of the earthly women. She felt her love swell for this awesome creature, touched that he had chosen her of above all others. Her orgasm slipped in quietly, a deep throbbing coil which took her breath away.

"Oh god," she sighed, and the fallen angel smiled.

On his knees again, Shemyaza buried his head between her legs and attended to her lesions, humming as he healed her, and the lower half of her body reverberated with the bass of his voice. Her lower belly undulated as if his echoes were moon-melody and made waves in her amniotic fluid.

Already her organs felt like they were changing, almost as if his spit was surgically rearranging her insides to accommodate the growth of the monstrous fetus.

Her blood whined through her veins, melodic of discordant violins and swarms of flies, and she listened with disbelief to the unnatural symphony within her. Even felt the kick of unnatural life within her as the fetus danced in utero.

She automatically cupped the budding swell of her belly, her hands waiting to catch the next movement. Strange awe, feeling the knot of a tiny heel bump against the supple wall of her flesh, feeling the testament of life, though it made her squeamish as if some alien had infested itself within her, her belly moving of another's accord. Maternal instinct conflicted with her fears that she was a host to horror.

Against her belly, against her hand, the fetus played his devil's tattoo, rapping gently, timidly, coming off more as nervous ticks than ambitious life. She pressed upon her belly. Indistinguishable limbs, thin as pencils and sharp as their lead points, jabbed at her hand.

Millions of mouths shrilling for marrow and milk.

Millions of mouths with millions more teeth fastening to her breasts.

Rani dry-heaved. Her belly bobbled with the riling unborn.

Looking down at her stomach, she watched the flesh push outward and stretch into a topographical map of a blue-veined mount. She didn't doubt this *child* would erupt from her in a thunderous, scarlet gush.

Sounds of evil children giggling in the quaggy drain issued forth.

"Little Boy Blue, come blow your horn. The sheep's in the meadow and the cow's in the corn. Little Boy Blue asleep in the hay, blue-black bruises around his throat, never to wake another day . . . "

Louder their giggles gurgled up from the drain. Colder the air turned.

"Sacrifice the children to the dark beast . . . "

Flame colored Shemyaza's irises and smoke poured forth from his anger-twisted mouth.

"Sacrifice . . . "

The Grigori surrounded Rani, guarding her from the winged wraiths which flowed upward from the drain with the speed of God's breath, from the frost bite of their snapping, death-cold mouths.

"Sacrifice . . . "

Savage winds buffeted against her, blowing into her mouth, ears, vagina, and anus like arctic fists knocking her out cold . . .

#

. . . imprisoned, the blankets her shackles, the mattress her bed of nails, the bleeding her punishment.

Eggshell walls closing in. Dreary patter of rain upon the roof, the windows, the walls, tears of the dead children deserted to heaven falling down upon her.

Plip-plop of water dripping from the ceiling into the plastic pail,

52

counting the seconds while she waited. Waited for the rain and the blood to stop.

Immobile, afraid to flinch a single muscle, afraid to jostle the tenuous embryo from her already hostile womb. Six weeks pregnant. Twelve weeks beyond the last miscarriage. Six weeks pregnant and bleeding again.

Staring through her tears at the ceiling, at the spreading water stain as if it was some sign heralding disaster for her, some premonition of the crimson-child stain which would spread upon the crotch of her panties. Her hand between her thighs, her middle finger plugging the dam in desperate hope.

Haunting, the filmy image *of the ultrasound, of the larval human and its transparent heart beating in hummingbird-flutter. Haunting, the image of life struggling hard since inception to survive. Haunting, knowing the life was doomed . . .*

II.

Winds with Cherubim faces, with six pairs of eyes peeking from front, side, and back, hailed upon Rani, and Shemyaza and the other Grigori fought flaming sword with flaming sword. The clashes of their azure-shining weapons resounded in stormy volumes and lit the small bathroom in blaze-blinding bolts.

Old memories in his mind, *Gabriel charging their offspring to turn upon each other and strip flesh from bone,* Shemyaza set his sights on defending his unborn son with every ounce of force, vehemently unwilling to repeat history. His hands blackened in his rage. His sword smoldered the very air into ash and the lesser Cherubim into silvery pieces like glittery discards of fish scales swirling in the deep after the marlin's feeding frenzy.

Spurred on by his ferocity, Shemyaza'a brethren slashed the winds embodied of chariot angels, and the walls were streaked with steaming mercury, with Cherub blood. More winds came. Came as fuel for the Grigori fire.

The Warriors fell away one by one, unmatched against the Watchers' might.

But, in their retreat, promised to return. *"With Gabriel."*

#

Gabriel.

His nemesis.

The second highest ranking angel. The angel of annunciation, resurrection, mercy, vengeance, death, and revelation. The angel with one hundred and forty wings who dealt destruction to Sodom and Gommorah, who dealt destruction to the giant angel-children.

Gabriel had incited the sons of the Watchers with the bait of a trussed angel. But, when the Nephilim had reached the angel bleeding from the stump of his wings, the angel of death had pulled the bait away, leaving the Nephilim to fight amongst themselves.

Hunger blood-piqued had set them into deadly feast. Teeth sharpened on human bone, they clamped onto the nearest body of flesh and, just as crocodiles fed, ferocious-twisted themselves upon the ground, tearing off limbs and pulling apart large bodies. Slaughter-mass of shredding skins, splattering organs, and cracking bones had ensued. They had devoured each other with red-grumy grins until only one remained. One who had gorged on his brothers' meat and could not move, who had lain in bloated agony as Gabriel gutted him.

Bound by Raphael and helpless, Shemyaza had suffered the sights of his sons reduced to corpus mangles of blood and bone, to wailing puddles of digested ichor. His screams had been carried away by the torrential winds and rains.

Rains which were sent by God to wash away the rivers of blood made by his sons.

Eternal darkness kept, the Watchers had endured their punishments with quiet weeping, their minds tormented by the last lights, the last day when their sons died in an unfair war. God had given and God had taken away. Without warning. Without justice, for the Archangels had kept their freedom, even after embracing sins which had imprisoned the Grigori.

Uriel had disclosed the heavenly mysteries to Ezra and gave the cabalas to man.

Raphael had handed Noah the *Sefer Raziel*, the book in which all celestial and earthly knowledge had been set down.

Gabriel . . .

Silver pearling from his pores, Shemyaza sweated the heat of his anger.

Gabriel who had come in unto Mary and found favor in her womb, whose son was worshiped as a God-child and ascended to the right side of God himself. Whose son escaped the scourge.

Centuries of silent wrath found voice.

"Gabriel, confront me again and I promise you will hang on the big black Tree. Let Adam's sons pull out the feathers of your one hundred and forty wings as grim souvenirs. Such is their nature to collect and dissect . . . "

III.

Dust flies from the wheels of the chariot as the slayer races across the sands. His eyes glow as if the desert sun burns in his pupils, and his mouth twists down, feral and maddening like an Ahazu-demon's smile. With an appetite greater than the Ahazu-demon, he comes for her and raises his sword high, the sword slick with her son's blood.

Prophets gather in the shadows of the room, praying, dancing in circles, cutting themselves, their blood singing to the ground.

"Oh god, help us . . . "

She paints her eyes with kohl and dresses her braided hair with ornaments.

She waits at her window, looking down at the man who orders her thrown from the balcony . . .

##

Falling, falling down into a black well . . . spinning, spinning in black waters . . . drowning, drowning in black omens and the blacker cries of the child inside her . . .

Her eyes flipped open, and vertigo slammed Rani, drilling her it seemed into the bathroom floor. Shadows shifted, spiraled, and whorled upon the ceiling. Shadows of the empty room.

The Grigori, the dead brides, and the threatening winds had gone. Only one thing remained, the tinsel-ooze glimmering upon the orchid tiles. Pockets formed as the stuff slid down the walls. Pockets of pink mouths laughing.

Little Boy Blue . . .

The laughing silver faded into the grout, into the walls, into the spaces between voids where all the unseen horrible waited.

Wrapping her arms around her head, squeezing elbows over her ears, she stood. Pain shot through her jawbone, from teeth to temple, and it felt as if some sadistic dentist had cracked enamel off the pulp and capped her teeth with ice.

Rani shuddered as she tongued the teeth which had filled the gaps, deep gaps she remembered tasting of metal.

When she was eleven years old, the dentist had decided her mouth was too small, her teeth too numerable and large for her gum lines. He had decided to remove four permanent teeth. So, sentenced to the chair, with her mouth puffy and stretched wide with clamps, she had braced herself for the dental pliers he held in his hand.

And thereafter she had learned too late that Novocain was ineffective for her.

She had screamed and screamed while the dentist twisted and twisted upon her bicuspid. Twisting forever it seemed until the root tore excruciatingly away from the jawbone with awful crunching noises. Like chunks of meat and bone through a hand-cranked grinder.

With an efficient yank, he had pulled her tooth and displayed it before her, proudly stating she had three more to go. Her siren-loud wails had caused the octogenarian's heart in the adjacent room to arrest.

The things she suffered for her perfect smile, courtesy of braces which cut into the soft of her cheeks and the inside of her lips and the denti-extraction.

But her reflection in the mirror was anything but perfect.

Once again her stomach pushed blood into her throat, but she swallowed it, swallowed her fear, and backed away from the mirror.

Away from the face of another woman, from the magnetic allure of her death-shadowed eyes and her death-promising lips.

CHAPTER NINE

I had a dream which was not all a dream.

Byron, Darkness

Her lips were red, her looks were free,
Her locks were yellow as gold:
Her skin was white as leprosy,
The nightmare Life-in-Death was she,
Who thicks man's blood with cold.

Coleridge, The Rime of the Ancient Mariner

I.

Bedfellow of the battered sky, the snow fluttered down with melancholic airs, flirted about Michael in vapid white frolics and landed little frigid kisses on his lips. The wind wrapped about him as if with the arms of hysteric lovers, holding him against his will and wailing for him to stay. As he ran, the cold brought tears to his eyes.

His scars settled into snowy silence.

His maligner settled into the pit of his heart.

Very little time remained before his blood carried the cold daemon throughout his body and turned every cell into ice. His insides would expand and crack. Then the fiend would feed upon him, licking and sucking and chewing on him as if he were a cherry snow-cone.

Cursing his haste this morning, he sprinted around the street vendor and his tables of books and skirted between parked cars into the street. A dreaded exorcism, the draining of the cryo-tainted blood, awaited to rid him of this possession. But if he had grabbed the scarab from the night stand, he would've been protected. He should've known, by the grim-heavy atmosphere, that the spirits would come out to play. *Red Rover, Red Rover, we dare Michael over.* Over to their darkside forever and ever.

Beetle-black limousines pulled beside him, slowing, keeping their speeds to his pedestrian crawl. The rear, tinted window of the second car lowered, and blue smoke spilled forth.

"Michael, come," rasped the voice of an ancient, of Jichun Xu, his *Mao Shan* mentor of long ago. Jichun beckoned him with the wiggling crook of a finger and the point of his six-inch, indigo-painted finger-nail. A threat Michael could not ignore.

Automatic door locks clicked, and Michael opened the door, ducked into the backseat and the blue smoke, and slid across the leather seat. The air was thick and sweet as sorghum. Light-headed within seconds, he succumbed to the familiar fear of being this close to Jichun again.

His heart contrasted with his slow, shallow breath, coming in double rapid pangs and troubling missteps of rhythm.

"Long time, Michael, since you visit me." Jichun placed his hand upon Michael's thigh and his nails of dangerous twilight rested within inches of his crotch.

Nails with a penchant for deep flesh.

Hands seen too often gloved in red.

"We parted," Michael paused, biting his lip for the right word. "Unkindly."

"Yes, regretful. But I can make you forget all trouble."

"Offering jade dreams again?"

Jichun laughed, geisha mirth tinkling in the sound. "Something far better. Higher than mountain, stronger than water."

"What then?"

By removing his hand and waving his nails in front of Michael's face, Jichun dissipated the blue smoke. He sat, dressed smartly in a black ankle-length coat and wool cap snug on his bald dome, with a gold toothed-grin stretched wide on his opal-fine face. Small round sunglasses hid his eyes, ghastly eyes without iris, without pupil, without capillary. Twin globes of cadaverous hued, scleral blanks.

Quicken cold in his heart sent Michael's teeth chattering.

"I don't have time for guessing, Jichun. The cold daemon awakens."

"You have bad luck with daimons," he giggled.

Michael reached for the door handle.

"Wait." Jichun stayed Michael's hand with his own, those nails persuading him further. "I have come into possession of the *Pao_p'u_tzu.*"

"Which means nothing to me."

"The *Pao_p'u_tzu* means everything to you."

Brushing the hair from his forehead, frowning, Michael glanced from what whirred beyond the window in sleeting grays and faced the smug master of *Mao Shan.*

"4th Century work by Ko Hung documenting alchemical formulas. Ring bell?" Jichun asked.

Michael's mouth dropped in soundless answer.

"I have detailed method of creating *Chin-tan.*"

"*Chin-tan?*" Michael repeated in disbelief.

The fabled gold elixir, the consumption of which led to immortality.

Jichun nodded. Slipping a curled claw under his sunglass rim, pulling the shades low on the flat bridge of his nose, he stared at him with cyanic eyes. It was always as if Michael looked into the shielded eyes of a serpent.

"Why are you telling me?" Michael asked, alarms of his fear taking a toll on his heart. "You must need something because you loathe sharing."

His nails toyed with his ear.

"Yes, regretful."

Already the maligner set upon chilling his blood. His fingers, toes, ears, and nose burned and ached as if on the verge of frost bite. Turning his hands palm-up, he noticed the tips of his fingers and parts of his palm had indeed blackened. On his left hand, the life line looked like a thin white worm which had burrowed from the dirt and died.

"Take the mercury from your woman." He inserted a syringe into Michael's pocket.

"The mercury?"

"Yes, from her womb, the fluid of its vinegar and silver child. Fail and your daimon feel like jade paradise."

And then Jichun, without moving, pushed him from the speeding car.

II.

Misty veils smoked from the mirror as the reflection of the other woman, *of Jezebel*, seeped through the glass and touched upon the ground.

Unable to tear her eyes from the advancing phantom, Rani backpedaled from the bathroom. She tripped over the threshold strip and braced her fall with her left hand. Impact stress pinched her wrist and snapped her elbow. Still, she crab-crawled backwards down the hallway on the pads of her palms and heels.

The spirit of Jezebel rose to the ceiling, a rippling mass of silver darkness, and hovered above Rani. She reached for her.

"Please stop," Rani whimpered, collapsing in the corner of the hall. She tucked her knees to her chest, hugged her legs, and hid her face.

As lily-bouquet drifted over her, she rocked herself, mumbling in childish tones, "Only a nightmare. Asleep but tired, tired, so tired . . . "

Weep into your pillow, Rani. Quiet, don't disturb your sister.

She rocked to the hushed cadence of a child's cry.

Airs, fragrant, cool, pastoral, inviting, enslaving, collected upon her and blew the breath of the incorporeal into her mouth. Opium smoke, she mused as harlequin chimera paraded in her mind.

Faces with variegated flesh and colorless grins pressed upon her. Motionless mouths laughed buzzing flies.

Do not disturb your sister. She finally fell asleep. After all those hours of kicking and scratching and fighting the sleep she feared. Because if she didn't wake, her soul was for the Lord to take.

Rani rocked harder.

In her arms and nestled against her bosom, Stephan had been rocked. Powder, baby soap and sweat had enveloped her then, not perfumes of the casket and grave. She had kissed his tender cheek. So warm, so soft. Then had laid him gently in his crib and swaddled him in his terry-cloth blanket of moon and stars.

For his soul to be taken.

Weep into your pillow, Rani.

And she wept now in the crook of her arm, muffling any sound.

The brush of lilies was upon her arm.

Rani dropped her arm and looked up, but the dark-veiled reflection vanished into the hall mirror, laughing and crying at once. The image stayed briefly in the glass. Tears ran black from her eyes. Words spilled red from her lips.

"Take him out and stone him to death."

"Who?" Rani breathed, standing, seeing her own image betray her in the mirror, the laughter, the tears.

The other woman had vanished. But, in the mirror, the glimmer of blood remained.

She slapped her hands over her eyes. Her palms were shades of crimson-veined dark. Again the sober cry of a child, like a child lost and searching for his mother, echoed. Its tone dissolved into burbling like that of a child drowning in his tears, in his snot, in the pool of blood his murderer left him in.

Shaking in sickness, Rani steadied herself against the wall and, with her back pressed, shuffled her way down the hallway into the bedroom. Aria of dying child and snakes rippling through sand followed her.

She wept . . . *quiet as tears falling on clouds, quiet as clouds falling to the ground* . . . as she threw open the closet door and shoved the clothes and hangers aside . . . *screech of her sister disturbed.* Reverting to childhood escapes, she stepped into the closet. She wished she had her Mr. Honey Bear as she shut the door behind her and found herself boxed in familiar darkness.

Rani crawled behind her long dresses which hung like mortuary curtains and sat amongst her pile of shoes, the edge of the soles like chunks of bone.

The closet, her sanctuary from the madhouse beyond.

"No candy kisses from sugar lips," she whispered in the voice of a frightened little girl. "No pretty prince for the princess of Pandora."

Spoken like a threat, a promise, a mantra.

In her box, her locked tower, her kingdom of umbra, she had dreamed of other worlds, worlds whimsical only to the witches and ogres, dense with black forests and blacker enchantments. She had pretended her body was wrapped in a cocoon of midnight silk . . .

. . . there, on the branch of a dead tree, her cocoon would sway in the wind. She would hear the sway of other things, of creaking ropes and hanged fairy-queens, of unicorn horn wind-rattles, of flapping strips of flesh which leaved the trees.

. . . there, the dog-star spiders would chew through the stygian cocoon, and she would slip through the rend and land upon the ground covered in golem-jelly and moon splash. Then the spiders would drop on tether webs and feed upon the viscosity.

. . . there, in the dark of the wood, she would rise in butterfly-triumph. Metamorphic, nightmarish, body torsional as her mind, arms many and defensively radial off her body. She had no mouth. She had no screams. But she wished for this change because, in the world beyond the closet, she wouldn't make any sounds to wake the monster of her sister . . .

Hands clasped tight on her lips, she had no mouth. She had no screams. At least screams which could be heard by the monster of midnight and murder.

III.

Michael rolled and hit the curb.

Breathing in exhaust, he staggered to his feet, his legs and mind unsteady. He patted his pocket. The syringe had not broken its needle into him by some miracle.

Miracle, he scoffed. Wicked miracles of angels, spirits, and demon-gods. And another miracle bided on his delivery of *mercury*.

"How convenient," he said sourly.

On the other side of the street stood their quaint brownstone. Tidy-packed next to other identical three-story homes, their place had one outstanding feature—the twists of English ivy and climbing roses trailing the golden-orange brick from ground level to roof. The roses were bare of leaf or bud in winter, but the thorns gave a plentiful show as if with Liliputian swords.

A creepy facade with those thorns, with those shadows. Shadows which skipped the other Grove Street addresses.

Cold lethargy deadened his limbs. He loathed to walk, wondering if his cells had turned to ice yet, if his blood and bones and organs would crack apart if he moved.

The sign of angels and spirits was present in the air, in drifts of sweet rot. Concern for Rani spurred him on.

Or did the mercury, silver, gold?

He patted the syringe again.

From her womb, the fluid with all its vinegar and silver child.

"Silver child?" he mumbled through lips numb and puffy as if with novocaine. A trophy was all he could think of, with its metallic flesh and hollow insides. But he couldn't connect it to her womb.

Unless she was with child.

Fathered by those who were made of the stars and smelled of sweet smoke and beget evil giants.

Michael chewed his lip as if the chapped pieces of skin would give him an answer. Such cold skin too.

He was afraid. Afraid of the snow, the way it flurried down like scattered fleece torn from all of heaven's angels. Afraid of the cold that was death's embrace which was taking hold of him. Afraid of following through with temptation and obtaining the *mercury and silver* for the alchemy of immortality.

Bones chattering in his body, he moved from the curb.

The rose vines seemed to have multiplied, nearly shielding all the brick with their twining sticks and thorns. He thought of razor-wire snares guarding the treasure within as he stepped up the porch.

Once in the house, Michael backed against the door and suppressed a yelp. A red carpet of blood welcomed him home. A path smeared the floor from this room, down the hall and into the bathroom, which he followed with carefully avoiding steps.

Blood had splattered the bathroom walls in explosive pattern, as if some holocaustal execution had taken place, and filled the catch-basin of the sink like a trough. His throat burned with bile and suppressed screams.

"Rani?" he shouted, terrified she had been butchered and her answering voice would be the gurgle of the drain.

Only the wall boards creaked and the icy wind tapped on the windows though.

"Rani?" An urgent, emotional bark.

His joints stiffened with the spreading cold of his daemon, and, lumbering off, he continued his search. He clutched his chest because his heart thumped a deadly rhythm and his breath hitched from his mouth in frosty puffs. Before long, his daemon would freeze his body and finally have its victim taken down and immobile. A hunter like the Komodo dragon with its toxic bite. The ambling predator relied on the lethal bacteria in its mouth and disregarded the chase but followed at leisure the scent trail left by its dying prey. Then fed in peace.

Like his daemon will.

Panic gripped him further. Adrenaline flushed enough heat through his veins to push him along. He found a trail of little crimson tear-drops leading into the bedroom, into the closet.

"Rani?"

No response.

Upon opening the closet, he found Rani huddled in the back, her mouth, chin, throat, and chest painted in blood, her eyes wild, her hands grappling a hanger which she had twisted into a hook. Michael couldn't help but think of metal hangers and hooks, of blood, of silver child and silver needles.

His mouth watered for the drink of *Chin-tan*, for the liquid gold, and, before his mind could react, he withdrew the syringe.

To turn mercury and lead into gold.

CHAPTER TEN

Lo! as that youth's eyes burned at thine, so went
Thy spell through him, and left his straight neck bent,
And round his heart one strangling golden hair.

Dante Gabriel Rossetti, Lilith (For a Picture)

Or like the tears of mist and fire, Wept by the moon, that wizards use To secret runes when they require Some silver philter, sweet and dire.

Clark Ashton Smith, The Tears of Lilith

I.

Lilith straddled him, sliding back and forth against him, upon him.

Her slate wings were spread as wide as her legs and fanned outward like a peacock's tail in pride. Scales within the leathery fibers scintillated like specks of obsidian glass catching starlight. Even her nipples were black and shiny, and leaking bright red milk.

Leaning forward, Lilith pressed her breast against his mouth. Back and forth went her hips. Back and forth went her breast, smearing her blood on his lips and tongue.

Bringing divinations on the taste of her blood, dry and chthonic as the wastelands she created beyond Eden where the very air sucked the moisture from bones . . .

. . . desert winds whispered in his ear, whispering of secrets.

"The Angels who fell from Heaven saw the daughters of Cain perambulating and displaying their private parts, their eyes painted with antimony in the manner of harlots, and, being seduced, took wives from among them."

"The Angels who fell from Heaven produced monsters and ravaging beasts."

"The Angels have fallen through *hubris*, which means pride, and lechery, after taking seductive flesh, and God in Heaven especially punishes *hubris*. He destroyed the sons of the Angels."

"You shall act as God's instrument and destroy the son the new harlot carries."

Another voice rose above the others. *Hers*, the whore with a face as sharp and distinctive as her character, who lacked the soft, subdued qualities of the ideal woman.

"If you are Elijah, so I am Jezebel . . . "

Elijah who killed her prophets of Ba'al. Jezebel who killed God's prophets in return.

"If you are Elijah, so I am Jezebel . . . "

Unnerving, a woman who wouldn't back down.

Downright frightening, a woman who not only stood her ground but rushed forward in attack. And this woman had seduced a legion of force for her battle.

Angry winds spat, "And in her was found the blood of prophets, and of saints, and of all that was slain upon the earth."

Salt-rot was upon his tongue and voice.

"For true and righteous are his judgements, for he hath judged the great whore, which did corrupt the earth with her fornication, and hath avenged the blood of his servants at her hand."

"You shall serve as that judgement, none of her powers shall strike you down . . . "

And the voices faded until all he heard was the wet slap and slide of Lilith astride him. Her hips still rocked hypnotically back and forth.

"Sssssssweet Julian," she sighed, staring deep into his eyes, into his brain, triggering his orgasm with merely her wanton look.

Julian gripped the sheets and tensed beneath her while her cunt squeezed and squeezed his cock, milking him hard for semen and blood.

Head and back arched, he cried out.

Then screamed as she forced him to come again.

Rolling off of him, Lilith stretched onto her back and wrapped herself in the blue velvet duvet. She glanced at him. Brimstone smoldered in her eyes, and Julian turned away, dropping his eyes as the Christ on the Cross glowered at him as well.

He was ashamed at his coupling with Lilith, but, without her, he would fail God. Fight fire with fire, tooth for tooth, eye for eye, whore with whore. Adam's first wife, who refused missionary position, and the mother of demons, who devoured human children, would understand the Jezebel and the angels fallen from *hubris*. She had the light of heaven still within her.

Which brought him closer to God.

"I must destroy the son she carries," Julian said, breaking the silence. "But she will be protected by the Watchers. Tell me how I should proceed against them and their whore."

Lilith shifted on the bed, and he felt her weight against him, her breath hot in his ear.

"Proceed against the whore only. Because I have already taken measures against the Watchers."

"What have you done?"

"Nothing that concerns you, sssssssweet Julian." And she twisted his head toward her and kissed him.

Her tongue darted between his lips and inside his mouth. It was pronged and piercing. Salty copper ran along his tongue, down his throat, and into his windpipe, choking him, reminding him of his first encounter with her, the mother demon of snakes.

Blood had flowed down his throat then too, but not his own blood.

#

In the midst of some Ohio Valley woods, with locust trees in honey-scented bloom, a field of alfalfa, clover and blue grass opened up, and seven-year old Julian sat in the center of this secret circle.

The sun was hazy and dreamy-warm in the palest blue of sky. The wind carried puffs of dandelion seeds, and it seemed magical as if fairies danced in the air, their white-petal skirts twirling and billowing. They danced to the songs of cardinals and finches, the whistles of river reeds, and the thrumming wind through the trees. They also danced to the hiss of snakes slithering along the ground.

Unafraid, Julian stayed put, giggling even as the feathery tips of long grass tickled his arms like flickering tongues of serpents. He made binoculars with his fingers and searched for the snakes—-startled blades of grass swaying to and fro, the fleeting flick of shadow. Nothing seen, only heard, the *shush* of scales through the grass.

"My daddy would find you," he whispered to the snakes, slapping the ground with his hand in order to rouse one from hiding.

His daddy, *the snake wrangler.*

Countless times, Julian had watched his daddy rustle a copperhead from beneath firewood piles and porches, within crawl-spaces, under rock hangs, and even from engines of cars rusting in lawns. His daddy would always smile at him, tap his nose to indicate his sense of snake, and prod it into the clear.

Then, like dark lightning, the snake would ripple across the ground.

Countless times, Julian had felt his skin jump off his bones as the snake zipped toward him. But his daddy would always grab its tail and pull it away. Then Julian would watch in heart-stopping awe while his daddy wrestled with the whipping coils, dancing it seemed with the snake as he avoided the strike of poisonous fangs.

Hands working magic moved faster than the eye, capturing the copperhead behind the jaw.

Hands working miracles soothed the snake to sleep.

After depositing it into a wooden coffin-box filled with other listless vipers, he would drive hours through the sidewinder-curvy mountain roads, and they would deliver the box to the spry reverend of the Pentecostal Church of Appalachia.

Sometimes Julian and his daddy would stay for the service, and

Julian would feel the power of the reverend's voice booming during the sermons.

"Luke 10:18, He said to them, 'I watched Satan fall from heaven like a flash of lightning. See, I have given you authority to tread on snakes and scorpions, and over all the power of the enemy; and nothing will hurt you."

The reverend reached into the box . . .

"Mark 16:17, And these signs will accompany those who believe: by using my name they will cast out demons; they will speak in new tongues; they will pick up snakes in their hands, and if they drink any deadly thing, it will not hurt them; they will lay their hands on the sick, and they will recover."

. . . and pulled out a four foot copperhead, its crisscross pattern of pink and orange scales deceptively pretty like a Chanel scarf, which he wrapped around his neck . . .

"Numbers 21:6, Then the Lord sent poisonous serpents among the people, and they bit the people, so that many Israelites died. The people came to Moses and said, 'We have sinned by speaking against the Lord and against you; pray to the Lord to take away the serpents from us.' So Moses prayed for the people. And the Lord said to Moses, 'Make a poisonous serpent, and set it on a pole; and everyone who is bitten shall look upon it and live.' So Moses made a serpent of bronze, and put it upon a pole; and whenever a serpent bit someone, that person would look at the serpent of bronze and live."

. . . continuing the sermon even with fangs in his throat.

"Your Lord asks you to take up the serpent. Will you join His faithful by taking up the serpent?"

. . . his voice booming straight into the soul, stirring the zeal of the Holy Spirit.

The discoloration from the bite would disappear as soon as he passed the snake along, and Julian would doubt the snake had ever even struck the reverend, who like his daddy, had hands working magic and miracles.

But no doubts as Julian had taken up the serpent and fell into a fibrillating trance. Faded into the white. As if into clouds, into heaven, into the whites of God's angry eyes.

Fangs pierced into his wrist. Like crucifixion nails into the Nazarene. And he too threw back his head and howled for God.

God came in venom and wrath, boiling in this blood, and he wished now he had been forsaken as well.

Sinking to his knees, Julian had wet his pants as the snake bite commandments rushed through his veins. He had heard the reverend's voice, like thunder breaking in storm clouds, compelling him to look upon the serpent and believe.

Believe in God, in His power over the enemies of Devil and Death.

Believe, abandon your body as God's vessel, abandon your heart and let the Holy Spirit in.

Believe, the power of God is within you, preparing you to serve His will.

And Julian looked upon the serpent, into its coal-black eyes, and believed . . .

Serve His will, the wind, grass and snakes seemed to say.

"I will find you," he grunted. "Then tread upon you."

Crawling upon his belly as snake hunting snake, Julian sought their whereabouts. Thistle weeds pricked his skin and wild roses thorned him. Chiggers made buffets of his shins and ankles, and pollen dusted his eyes, making them itch and water. After a short way, abrasions formed on his elbows and knees, but the snake-cut trails in the long grass led him on despite the irritations.

Birdsong erupted into sharp cries. To his left, three whippoorwills scattered in flight, the startled flap of their wings sounding like belts against flesh.

Goose bumps flew up his arms. Even the air smelled of alarm, sort of metallic, like tornado-brewing sky.

He was afraid to raise himself off the ground, feeling much safer hidden in the sprouts of prickly weeds and thorns. His breath seemed amplified. The ground thumped hard with his heartbeat.

All other sounds were stifled in the pretense of danger.

He waited and waited while the air thickened with the static of the sly hunter closing the distance. Whimpers edged into his throat, but he choked all sound back. And waited.

His nose itched something fierce. Staying as still as the world around him, he wrinkled his nose and twisted his lips to one side. But failing as he sneezed and blew up a cloud of dirt in his face, causing him to sneeze again.

Silence ticked away. *Tick, tick, tick, tick* of the sound bomb ready to explode.

Breath held, he waited.

Not long.

The winds came, roaring like semi-trucks barreling down high-ways. Something else came too in terrifying noise, like brakes locking in an unending squeal, like tires screaming on asphalt. He couldn't help but lift his head.

But it wasn't an eighteen wheeler crashing over guard rails and careening over a bridge; it wasn't the familiar neck-straining, morbid-curious sighting of wrecks.

It was of wreck's carnage though.

Carnage smiling and standing before him in the red colored grass.

As his eyes worked up the slough of crispy black and crimson-cracked flesh, he held his screams. His mouth dried, his spit seemingly sweating through his face instead. The ground turned wet and warm beneath him even before he reached its face.

Face, an unlikely description for the split of skull, the skins peeled off the crown, frayed and hanging like rotted fronds of ferns, the eyes misplaced and misshapen, the mouth yawning terror. Hisses expelled from her mouth as if snakes coiled within her. Her tongue slithered from between shorn lips, forked and bloodied and vibrating like a rattler's tail.

Julian screamed then.

Deep bow and contortion-bend, the nightmare was on the ground in front of him, its head near his head, its mouth near his mouth, its screams eating his screams.

She put her slick fingers in his mouth, stanching his screams with the grue of her damaged digits.

"Sssssshhhh, child."

Her voice oozed into his ear, molasses sweet and slow, catching his breath and his heart, and his anxious-ridden muscles softened. He felt as if his body would melt into the earth. Closing his eyes, he shunned *her* present state of gun-blasted face and pictured her as her voice suggested, golden-haired, luminescent-skinned, pretty as Cinderella at the Ball.

Other stuff oozed into him.

Pus, amber and thick as tree sap, and sloughy skin trickled along his tongue, flowed down his throat and clog-pooled in his pharynx. He breathed her infectious fluids. And in his lungs discarded memories instead of oxygen were exchanged in his blood and played within nightmarishly his mind.

. . . sandstorm and screams . . . winds stinging flesh as if the sand had turned to glass . . . the people running with hands over bleeding eyes and trampling a woman giving birth to a giant . . .

. . . the infant's head pushing through, audibly popping femurs from hip joints and crushing coccyx, stretching and tearing her flesh from her bones . . . the huge infant coming into the world glazed red . . .

. . . its mother's body becoming the mess of the afterbirth . . .

. . . the black skinned creature kneeling between those unhinged, shattered thighs and snatching the gross-mass of newborn . . . licking off its blood grease . . . eating its mouth before it sucked in its first breath . . .

Julian didn't understand what it was he saw in his mind, but he understood the fear that rattled his teeth. Fear of the monster, the ghoul, the horror creeping from the dark, of being eaten and digested in those bellies. His daddy once explained the law of natural order, that man was at the top of the food chain, not destined for the menu, but Julian believed with unnatural things that a different order existed and man was the only meat.

And the unnatural thing was prying apart his lips and spitting the old blood she had drunk into his mouth . . .

#

Wet-snap of lips unlocking, Lilith released him from the kiss as well as his felt-like-he-was-there memory. Thirty years later, and he was still sucking down the blood of her kiss. But the blood brought voices. Voices of God telling how he should *serve His will.*

"The Nephilim were on the earth in those days—and also afterward—when the sons of God went into the daughters of humans, who bore children to them. These were the heroes that were of old, warriors of renown."

Old warriors of renown. The Mighty Ones of Eternity, the People of Shem. The Giants of Canaan, monsters begotten of monsters.

"I have determined to make an end of all flesh, for the earth is filled with violence because of them; now I am going to destroy them along with the earth."

Disturbing remnants of the Flood lined his bookshelves, skulls of the People of Shem, of the unnatural which surely fed upon humankind.

"Only, you shall not eat flesh with its life, that is, its blood. For your own lifeblood I will surely require a reckoning: from every animal I will require it and from human beings, each one for the blood of another, I will require a reckoning for human life."

Dead, empty stares upon him, Julian gathered a hammer and sickle, which he wrapped in black cloth, and the skulls complained in terrible noise, the echo of the slaughtered dying, as he steeled himself for the blood reckoning.

CHAPTER ELEVEN

No kind of sensation is keener and more active
than that of pain;
it's impressions are unmistakable.

Marquis de Sade, The 120 Days of Sodom

It has, moreover, been proven that horror, nastiness, and the frightful are what give pleasure when one fornicates.
Beauty is a simple thing; ugliness is the exceptional thing.
And firey imaginations, no doubt,
always prefer the extraordinary thing to the simple thing.

Marquis de Sade, The 120 Days of Sodom

I.

A silhouette with malice-bright eyes lunged into the closet.

Rani raised the hook-twisted hanger. She was loathe to strike though, having witnessed her sister wield a shiv of bone over and over into herself. That impression, of flesh submitting with wet grunts as if rutting with that bone shaft and exposing its secret raw places, repulsed her. She feared her sick potential. Like her sister, she might enjoy how it felt for flesh to fatally submit to her hand.

"Help me," Michael said, collapsing at her feet.

Helpless he looked, curled and shivering on the floor. How easy it looked, she thought, shirking the rest of the thought, as she lowered the hanger by her side. She felt a buzz in her fingertips. Almost as if her fingers would betray her and enact his sacrifice.

Light angled across his face, cutting it diagonally, etching a mask of a split personality on his face. One half light, the other dark. He sobbed, and his tears cascaded across the bridge of his nose and dropped across the dark half, losing the glitter of crystal along the way.

It reminded her of the well, how its obscure depths swallowed the shiny silver and copper of tossed coins. *Our offerings*, her sister had urged. *Or else the well will swallow us.*

Offerings. Sacrifices.

Rani brushed her tingly fingers across Michael's cheek, cringing inward for the touch, like the midnight touch of Stephan, because his skin was toughening and cool. She looked to the empty syringe clutched in his hand and wondered if he'd injected heroine or something far worse into his veins.

The gnarly network of his vessels strained beneath his cold skin, looking as if pumped full of motor oil instead of blood.

"What has happened?"

"Flood of blood . . . " Michael laughed, giggled almost, as he loitered on the edge. "Tides and tyrants of red . . . god dead, dead, dead . . . "

Blood. The vision of his face streaked with smiling cuts and incarnadine teeth of serrated tissue.

Her hand on the hanger, Rani vacillated between the psychotic and the placid. *Take him out and stone him to death.* The recent, other plague of voice. She fought the urge, shoved the flexed hook away and tucked it beneath a box.

"Bleed me," he said, gripping her hand and pulling her near. His breath was ripe, carnivorous, like that of a dog's after it had gnawed upon hour-old bones.

"Bleed you?" she echoed.

"Retrieve my notebook from the den. Orange section, the bloodletting exorcism. Do exactly as inscribed. I cannot . . . I cannot . . . " Cackling laughter, then hideous howls which aspired to curdle all the blood of the world.

Behind Michael, wan light, like pale blood of the sun, flowed across the walls. Shadows of faces, with many eyes and many mouths, disappeared into the streaming light, and each face seemed the mask of her sister, the final impression of her theatrical grimacing grin fading away into the light which was almost dark.

Fading with that crazy laughter.

But it was her own, not a figment of her imagination nor of the dead. Even if, with the shift of light from a passing cloud, the wall took on the facade of her dreams, where the walls were built of stacked skulls, where omen laughter echoed from the hollows.

Michael guggled in pain, drawing her back into focus. Black ichor stained his lips; his flesh blued from either cold or lack of oxygen.

Scrambling from the closet, Rani narrowed her eyes. Sun-lit sheets of snow beyond the window cast blinding whiteness into the room and into the aching slits of her eyes. Cold bombarded her, and she shivered. She felt like Lucy stepped from the wardrobe, thrust into the land of ever-evil winter and dread, thrust onto a strange quest.

She hurried down the hall, the back of her mind registering the inexplicable amounts of blood splatter, and barged into Michael's den. A path between knee-high book stacks led toward his desk, an antique partner's desk with tiger-oak inlay. Instead of brass handles or knobs, the drawers boasted the half faces of the Winds, and it had always unnerved her, with her fingers gripping and pulling the upper jaw of Boreas or Zephyr. It didn't help that the drawers, through humid time had swelled and stuck, grinded and groaned upon opening.

No scrap of paper was tucked within though. The drawers held knives and nails and other various sharp objects, tools of his black trade she supposed. Until she met Michael, she thought of magic in terms of candles and crystals, spices and spells, but she learned soon enough how much magic centered on blood and bone. *Life beget life*, and so it was the same with sorcery.

As Rani shuffled through the notebooks on the desktop, she grazed her hand on the glass-shard pentacle mosaic glued onto the wood. She hissed and curled her hand into a fist, fingers holding the gash on the meat of her palm. Blood dripped through, crimson-tinting one point of the star.

Sharp and bloodied like the canines of a predator.

The other glassy teeth glistened as if with salivation, and the window rattled with the wind, like teeth snapping and clattering. Beside the desk, on the low bookshelf, rows of animal skulls grinned, exposed canines larger than in life, dead-lethal. The dog-skull, with its permanent snarl, frightened her. In the other room, Michael groaned, but somehow it sounded nearer as if it were growls coming from the skull.

Sucking on her palm, Rani continued searching for the notebook and ignored the empty stares of the morbid hungry. She found it at last, tucked inside a black binder, its orange tab glaring like a warning sign.

She had avoided Michael's magic throughout their relationship. But, here she was, her heart thumping shaman-drum, her foot tapping nervous need, her fingers rifling through pages of hand-written ceremonies.

Too many exorcisms, she thought, turning page after page of demon scourging rituals. Michael had been meticulous in his notes, detailing the rites with step-by-step illustrations. After awhile, Rani looked upon his notebook as an obscure anatomy text or mad laboratory experiments.

She rouged the pages as she read. Apt, bleeding on the bloodletting passage. Her hand ached, not from the cut but from the pending weight of the knife, and Rani inhaled deeply, trying to calm her anxiety. But her hand only trembled more, excitedly she feared.

She pulled open the desk drawers again. Grate and groan of the horrors waiting within and of the terrible waiting to happen in the other room.

Eyes roaming the clutter, Rani picked out the iron knife. Its handle was wrought of wood and reinforced with bone and horn, though the bone had blackened over time and mites pitted the wood. No taint touched the blade however. Its edges recently sharpened and glinting, the blade looked keen enough to flay the skin off, layer by layer.

She pulled the knife out with some reverence. She treated it like a god who at any moment would determine her unworthiness and strike her down. Dangerous images were scarlet and seeping in her mind. Her sister, with her bloodied hands, offering her the bone. And that awful moment Rani had reached for it.

Fingers tingling again, she tested its resilience. Unbendable too, this knife was intended for piercing sternums and cutting out hearts and offering the gods who wore garlands of severed heads and hands, those throbbing rosy bouquets.

With the knife, she pushed around the other sharp instruments, the shifting like metallic clawing, and looked for the fleam. A common phlebotomy tool. Three blades coming out at right angles from the brass handle, described his notes. All the blades of varying size, for varying degrees of bloodletting.

Her mouth went dry upon sighting it, like a crude, torturous switchblade. As primitive and raw as violence itself. She picked up the fleam and squinted at the rust upon the blades, at the antiquated blood, at the iron stain of hysteria and diseased humors.

Knife and fleam in hand, Rani looked around the hermetic mess for an onyx skull and a puce vase with embossed Edwardian script. Books clogged the majority of the shelves. She huffed as she walked along the bookshelves, perusing every shelf and nook. Between Agrippa's *Occulta Philosophia* and Boethius' *De Consolatione Philosophiae*, the onyx skull perched vulturous, black-pearl eyes watching, waiting, wanting.

She removed it from between the brittle-bound books, and the quartz cranium wobbled and clanked, threatening to slide off and crash to the floor. She pushed it against her chin, holding the lid on. Then she set everything back on the desk, atop the notebook, and lifted the cranial lid. Inside the hollow, it stank of decomposing flesh.

Her stomach turned. She had the discerning idea of a chalice filled with abortive potions, of that grume sludging down her throat and implanting into the walls of her stomach, growing and growing until it and the other unborn squeezed all her organs together into livid mush.

Leaving the objects on the desk, she once more went around the room. She spied the puce vase on a pedestal tucked in the cobwebbed corner. Maneuvering before it, she gripped the gold-porcelain scrolls of the handles and pulled it against her.

Something sloshed within.

Rani read the Edwardian letters. *Leeches.*

The fine-art vase nearly slipped from her hands. Of all the gross things in this world, she hated worms most. Almost to the point of phobia. Brought on by a childhood incident when she had shown her nanny the *pretty white worm,* and the nanny had become hysterical and screamed the fear into her, making her immediately shake the *filthy thing* off onto the carpet. Which had made the nanny scream more. Maggots however only fed upon dead flesh, but leeches liked their food fresh and hot.

As the contents of the vase sloshed with her steps, disgust wiggled in her belly.

Leeches, knives, and fleams. *Oh my.*

Mad-moon laughter tickled her throat. Old George had touched her deeper than her tiny twat, deeper than his fingers could ever go, had left more than shame inside her. If lunacy were a seed, then he had filled her hole with more than a handful.

Quiet, make no sound, do not disturb the disturbed.

Gathering all the ritual things, Rani chortled, whole-body shaking, and walked the coagulum-path. Shadows whispered their dirty secrets as she came upon Michael.

He lay naked and fetal-curled, his knees drawn in tight, his arms drawn around, except his skin pallor, like clay, put him at the opposite spectrum. His body was not fetal-curled but laid down in the burial position favored by the ancients.

He stared blankly, without blinking, certainly with the look of the dead.

" . . . as an offering to Aliyan Ba'al . . . "

Rani jumped back a step.

His slack lips leaked black ichorous words.

" . . . as an offering to Aliyan Ba'al . . . "

Unexpected, this chant coming from that still mouth.

Cold emanated from his body, but the chills crawling along her flesh were brought on by his listless chant, that insect-tone of his voice coming from elsewhere than his mouth. She shivered as she set everything down and sat beside him, ignoring the caressing cold on her bare crossed legs. The notebook acted as a blanket. At least until she read what the ritual entailed.

Then the cold burrowed into her bones.

An offering indeed, she thought as she heated the iron knife over a candle flame and read the first line of magical commands, words nearly unpronounceable, words which thrashed off her tongue.

The blade turn meteoric.

"Experience scattering by the sword," she intoned, turning his body onto his back.

Blade-blazing knife in hand, swung crisscross like a scythe, Rani cut Michael's chest. Skin split apart like mud into a garden plot of wounds.

Michael threw his head back shrieking.

Her hand planted the knife in his flesh, over and across and over again, but she was digging her own pain. She was her sister and her child's murderer, relishing the hurt she inflicted and crying laughter.

Blood harvest splattered her face and streamed down her cheeks. Upon her lips, she tasted the chilly mineral rains of spring and the fertile dream of green.

Rani traded the knife for the fleam. On his arms and upper thighs, she applied PVC tourniquets, and the veins in the crook of his arms and knees bulged sacrificial blue.

"Experience winnowing by the pitchfork."

Grimace-mouth holding grim breath, she lanced the veins of his arms with all three blades, like seraphical teeth and talons sowing deeply into flesh. She cut behind his knees, along his inner thighs, and upward on the thick carnal vein of his cock.

Angels breathed in her ears, on her nape, between her thighs, breath of ambrosial vapors, murmuring for her to sip the wine of her lover. Eyes half-lidded, Rani pressed her mouth against his phallic wound. Her tongue slipped between the parted lips of inflamed flesh, deeply teasing him, tasting him raw. Like salt and iron.

Salt of tears, sweat, and sea, of suffering, the angels whispered. *Salt for such wounds.*

His body came in blood.

In salt.

From all his gaping wounds, crimson watery salts drained, and she stared at his body, at the red-riddled, ripped quilt of his skin, then down at her hands, wetly colored with him. Her hands, like her sister's hands.

But unlike her sister, the wounds she'd inflicted were not fatal, Rani reminded herself and continued the ritual.

"Experience gathering," she said, spitting bloody words. "As an offering to Aliyan Ba'al . . . "

Rani positioned the skull beneath his left arm, where the onyx bowl caught his blood, which oozed downward, stringy and grumous like clotted menstrual flows. After the count of twelve, she moved it beneath his right arm, then returned to his left and repeated the pattern again until his blood topped the skull. The black pearls in the sockets shimmered darkly. Michael's blood within the skull was as black and shiny as those eyes.

Next she lifted the vase onto her lap, removed the top, and breathed foul airs of stagnant aquarium water. Soft bodied things unfurled, setting off a domino of little awakening splashes. Without looking inside, Rani turned the vase upside down onto Michael.

Dozens and dozens of leeches poured onto him. Wriggled onto him like a second layer of murky skin and took feeding-holds with their large sucker mouths and fine conical teeth.

She crossed her arms over her eyes, sickened by the sight of his body pasted with slick bloodsuckers, and chanted over and over, "As an offering to Aliyan Ba'al . . . "

Chanted louder and louder, because the fetal-angel within her womb was making sucking sounds.

II.

Her chants drew the cold daemon from his soul.

It entered his veins, like menthol in his serums, and his body felt afire and cold all at once.

Called on by the piper ritual, the icy fiend seeped through all the stringy and globulus layers between skin and bone.

And from his scars, it was vomited in wintry gales and susurrous spews.

Still, Michael heard other chants than hers.

Raise the dark beast.

He felt another thing rise from hidden depths within his body, colder than the coldest daemon, darker than the darkest evil.

His scars were no longer soft and rustling but raucous in terror. His flesh weakened even further, and more than blood and daemon would flow from him soon.

III.

Once again, the chittering came. As if the very essence of air had been affected by the harrowing cold which emanated from Michael and shivered.

Her own teeth chattered. Her heart even felt like it was chattering arrhythmic and slushy from this frigid mass which enveloped her. But then it ended, and warmth returned in the downy press of angels.

Rani lowered her arms and watched in dread as the leeches turned frosty-silver and slid off his body, leaving skids of blood behind. Michael's skin had shaded frosty-silver well. Except where vibrant rings of the leeches' mouths puckered the skin unmarred by wounds.

Salt for such wounds, the scars along Michael's body murmured with the voice of the angels.

Salt for such wounds, she mulled, her mind full of images, of lepers soaking in the Dead Sea, the supersaturated salt water soaking into their shred of sores and dissolving the disease, and of angels licking her wounds and sealing them. *Salt for such wounds.*

Her salt.

And she picked up the knife again.

In his mirror image, Rani dragged the blade into her skin, exacting mark by welt-splitting mark. She cried out in volumes worthy of Sheol and its burning damned. Her flesh seared as well with fiery red wounds and the smoke of angels.

She cut an agonizing copy of the scarlet canvas.

Angelic swords cleaving her flesh; angelic cocks clasping her clefts.

The cuts scathed her skin, her veins, the very pit of her belly, downward and inward, through and through. This torture aroused her entirely. Other fluids besides blood wetted her.

Rani straddled Michael and laid down upon him, placing cut against cut, cunt against cock. As if he sensed her heat and painful desires, even though unconscious, he became erect and moved autonomic beneath her. He tilted his pelvis, maneuvering into her. Lubricated with blood, their bodies and their sexes slid together.

The knife penetrated her as well, as she thrust it into her side, angel-style.

Grunts of cries. She twisted the knife deeper and tormented herself further by envisioning her sister beside her, bloody hands trembling like her own and reaching, offering her the knife. Telling her to dig it all the way to the bone.

Angels touched her, abused her and rocked her body against Michael's. The pressure built deep within.

Release it, the angels sighed.

And she withdrew the knife. It exited with a sloppy smack and, when she threw it, the knife landed with the sound of a broken bell. *Clang, clang.*

Her body convulsed with orgasm. Fitful and shameful, like the time Old George coerced her to *relax, release it . . .*

Rolling off of him, Rani wept from every inch of her flesh, in tears, sweat and blood. In salts of suffering.

The unseen Watchers shrank her lacerations with their celestial salts of spit, as well as Michael's.

Michael gasped as their tongues whorled upon his scars. "No, the gates . . . unsealed . . . the dark beast."

With an audible snap, like fish being slapped against decks, his scars opened, and the wells of his flesh brimmed with midnight-oil blood.

Rani sat, then stood, then rushed away.

Not because of what was happening to Michael, but because the wind cried again with the heart-breaking voice of her son.

CHAPTER TWELVE

Ceremonial magic to which reference
is made here depends from formal RITUALS,
being processes of evocation, compulsion,
entreaty, and other devices whereby the
spirits of height and depth, spirits of our
four quarters, spirits of the elements, with
other hosts and hierarchies, were rendered
subservient, ex hypothesi,
  to the will of man.

                Arthur Waite, Secret Tradition of Freemasonry

I.

In an unquiet cemetery, the wind sang through the shrouds of snow and graves, and the buried dead hissed in settling dusts of decay.

Julian sat within a crypt vault, his back against the coffin, listening to the somber symphony, biding his time until the night resurrected all things dark.

In the four corners of the crypt, candles burned. Light flickered across the solemn faces of the Brothers which stood beside each of the four candle pillars. They looked more like guards instead of priests, their hard eyes shining predatorily, their hands clasped on *devil sabers*, knives with sinuous blades and handles made of twisted horns.

Dangling on scarlet ribbons, the medallions of the Royal Arch lay against their chests and seemed like gold burning hearts with the reflective candlelight. That jewel, the heart of their sublime degree with the Divine. Double triangles intersected within a circle, and in the center was a sun with diverging rays, within a triangle, and underneath, and suspended to this, the triple tau.

The Royal Arch symbol contained written pledges. On the obverse circle, the engravings read: *Si talia jungere possis sit tibi scire satis*—If you are able to unite these things your knowledge is sufficient. On the triangles—*Eyphkamen, invenimus,* we have found it; *Cultor Dei,* Worship of God; *Civis Mundi,* Citizen of the world. The reverse circle had *Deo, Civati, Fratribus, Honor, Fidelitas, Benevolentia*—For God, for the State, for the Brethren, Honor, Fidelity, benevolence—inscribed, and on those triangles were wisdom, peace, strength, concord, truth, beauty. On the ribbon under the circle, *nil nisi clavis deest,* Nothing is wanted except the key.

The keys within the Jezebel, Julian thought. And they had ways to get what they wanted.

A fifth candle waited unlit from atop the coffin, the center of the vault, the center of the ceremonial square. Beneath the candle lay the heart of the corpse, and, when Julian put flame to the wick, its heart would beat again.

He struck the sickle against the granite floor. Sparks sprayed, amber of his anger.

The smell of wax and ashes piqued his sense of failure, all the times he held ceremony and the hierarchy of spirits refused him. But she . . .

Twang of the sickle.

Spark of cold stone.

Breath of his curse, and the candlelight wavered, dancing down, dimming, and the wind slammed the heavy door, stranding them in the near dark.

On the sickle's silver, the battle of light and dark teased him. He turned it, catching a flash. *God's wink.*

God had winked at him many times in the blade of a knife.

And, once upon a mobile in a dark nursery.

#

Julian had shared a special moment with the child, both in awe of the scintillating stars and moons which circled above the crib in plinky song. But then the infant had yawned. A tiny sweet sound from his tiny sweet throat. Which had sent tiny pinprick shivers down Julian's spine. Gripping the crib rail, he had watched the child's eyelids flutter with heavy sleep and finally draw down over those blue-black irises.

Little Boy Blue fast asleep in the hay . . .

Not tending the sheep.

Like all false prophets, all false shepherds must die.

With a fingertips upon his lips, Julian felt the kiss of his pulse, mnemonic of that time when he first touched the child's soft skin and soft pulse. A pulse that had faded softer and softer with the grapple and throttle of his hand.

The smell of milk, powder and the baby's surprisingly sweet wastes had filled the nursery. Another scent had lingered beneath these. Burnt linen, he had realized. The odors of an inhuman man named Gabriel who had come weeks before during an Enochian ceremony, who had worn clothes of burnt linen and a hot cindery grin.

Gabriel, the angel of death who had commanded them to kill the child, had come as witness.

And catalyst.

Pinprick shocks had shivered through every nerve. Julian's hand had involuntarily clenched, thumb and fingers pressing harder and deeper and deadly into that small neck. Blood and bone had popped beneath the soft skin.

Little Boy Blue fast asleep in the hay, blue-black bruises around his throat, never to wake another day.

This he had enjoyed whispering in the mother-harlot's ear.

So many sounds he enjoyed throwing her way since, like a juicy bone to the dog.

II.

She ran from the choir of cries, her son in woeful strains, Michael in tenor-terror, her shadow in mirror-shatter warble. In wild-stride, she hit her hands against the wall as if pushing them away, as if the walls were crashing down upon her. But it was only her mind crumbling.

Hear it, eunuch-song piped from her womb.

And hear it, she did.

The snarl and growl of pack-feeding dogs.

Such intensity, the sound bit into her and shook her nerves. *Dogs tearing away her flesh.* She slowed at the end of the hall, scouting the living room and all its darkened places, expecting the glow of hunters' eyes all fixed upon her. But only the glare of winter flurried through the open door, with fangs of cold bared upon her.

Rani walked and stood in the doorway, unashamed for her nakedness, unafraid of the snow and its lash and sting against her exposed and frost-vulnerable skin. No icy assault could numb her raw grief.

Especially not with Stephan out in the darkness, waiting.

In the distance, the rabid winds attacked, and her son's cries crescendoed into shrills. *Dogs ripping into him, quartering him.* She ran down the steps and into the street, screaming for Stephan, screaming as if he was dying all over again.

Horns blared, and cars swerved to avoid her, narrowly missing her and the parked cars.

"Crazy bitch!" the driver yelled, and his fraternity passengers whooped and whistled as they passed. Even crazy snatch had an allure because then these frat-brats could do with her as they pleased.

No one to listen to her screams now; no one to believe her later.

Rani shuffled across the slick asphalt, feeling helpless, hopeless, completely lost even with her front door fifteen feet from her. Her dead son was out there, somewhere, needing her as much as she needed him.

He waits in darkness, in agony.

He waits as if in an underground torture chamber, waits as if he could be released from the chains and nails. Has been waiting for seven years without release. All this time, she thought she endured only his haunting, a phantasm of her irreparable grief, but his cries were not figments, fragments, of her torn heart. His cries were as real as his death. Perhaps she had instinctually known because of her wanderings, subconsciously seeking him out in the alleys and subways and all the dark lairs. A mother always knows . . .

And she knew she had to unearth the secrets of his grave.

III.

Beneath the odors of wax and ashes, a hint of burnt linen wafted in his breath, and his body responded as if infatuated. His glands pumped giddy hormones into his blood, and his heart thumped it all madly into his groin. Julian shifted to his knees and sat upon his feet, then prostrated himself to the power of the air before standing tall and commanding. His erection bobbed between hands in prayer.

"O Ye swords of the South which have forty-two eyes to stir up the wrath of sin: making men drunken which are empty."

The four Freemasons turned their heads and faced the center of the crypt. Confusion, anticipation, expectation and fear, ran the gamut of emotions through their eyes as Julian called out the 13th Key.

He had no sweet-wood table, no Enochian letters bordering the laurel top, no white linen cloth spread downward to the floor, no wax of Sigillum Aemith nor the seven tins, ensigns of creation. But he had the most elemental value—loving dominance.

"Behold the Promise of God, and His Power, which is called amongst ye a bitter sting!"

Winds generated from the ceiling and shot down, stinging indeed into their eyes like arrows. Arrows unlike Cupid's darts which flew from gilded strings but from Cherubim's bows, from strings fashioned from the ligaments of the gelded.

To the winds, the Powers, he addressed:

"Move and Appear! Unveil the mysteries of your creation, for I am the servant of the same your God, the true worshiper of the Highest."

Winds rang throughout the vault. Angelus bells it seemed, and Julian trembled with feverish illusions, of Gabriel coming and announcing another Incarnation, of the Divine embodying within him. But the winds rang not with bells, but with whirling swords.

Its stone vanished, the ceiling turned clouds, both bright and dark, above their heads, and the blue lightning of swords flashed within the clouds. Riotous noise rumbled in the manifested effulgence of sky.

War chariots and drums, the charge of Cherubim, Julian thought, amazed that even his bones thrummed with their thunder.

He groaned, feeling his joints ache arthritic. His brethren were afflicted too and buckled in weakness, not of body but mind, still afraid of the bodily death. But Julian enjoyed it. He yearned for the end of this profane and vicious life, of stupidity and ignorance, and the beginning of the next life of virtue and knowledge.

Even if his blood boiled, he welcomed the Cherubim, guardians of all knowledge.

And here they came, unbridled upon a beam of glory, the shining path between heaven and earth.

The *Shekinah*.

It arched beautifully down, a curved pillar of polished star, gleaming beryl, and Julian gasped as the ray of his dreams alighted the crypt.

The *Shekinah* emitted an aura which clothed the men as if in sapphire robes, and a sense of peace and triumph enveloped the men, not broken at all, even when the Cherubim placed burning coals into their hands. Instead, the men saw bright lumps of gold and rejoiced.

Julian felt lightheaded—his lungs were filled with nitrous perfumes: wishfully, the breath of the Majestic. Perhaps, standing before him, were nothing more than Ezekial hallucinations.

The throne-spirits numbered four, but each had four faces, of man, lion, ox, and eagle, and four wings spread, the sounds of mighty waters rushing forth from them, roaring with prophecy.

"Sacrifice the children to the dark beast . . . "

Countless eyes glimmered with twilight wrath.

"Sacrifice the dark children . . . "

Grins of blood-stained teeth showing, the *hayyoth*, the holy beasts, hungered for justice which only angels served, raw and swift.

"Sacrifice . . . "

The holy beasts, who guarded all temples and Edens, who terrified Adam and all his descendants from entering paradise, may not have given Julian the celestial records, but the *Shekinah* guardians gave him a key.

And its shape was that of a scythe.

The perfect key for unlocking the gates of iniquitous wombs . . .

CHAPTER THIRTEEN

Come seeling night,
Scarf up the tender eye of pitiful day,
And with thy bloody and invisible hand
Cancel and tear to pieces that great bond
Which keeps me pale! Light thickens, and the crow
Makes wing to the rookery wood;
Good things of day begun to droop and drowse,
While Night's black agents to their preys do rouse.
Thou marvel'st at my words, but hold thee still:
Things bad begun make strong themselves ill.

Shakespeare, Macbeth

I.

Snow swirled upon her, beside her, all around her. The air seemed filled with dancing ladies with their gossamer gowns of diamonds and icy ribbons streaming from black as night hair. Delicate ladies of white lace who kept touching her with their cold hands, who kept linking their cold arms around her to pull her into their despairing waltz.

As if her nakedness was not enough, Rani wanted to strip her skin from her bones, her cage of bones from her soul, so that she too could discard the burden of life and dance in morbid mirth. Her spirit, beautiful like a spring azure butterfly, silver-dusty blue finally dancing upon the flowers of the earth, or so she had dreamed. But, overly weighted with sorrow . . . no, she admitted, depressed . . . pretty dreams were crushed into something ugly, and she didn't believe she'd be anything but the shit which the flattened cocoon of her body would expel.

Abnormal bereavement reaction, the doctor said. Something definable, something treatable.

She was an architect, not a doctor, but she knew an unstable foundation of the spirit led to the irreparable ruin of the mind. The stones of stability had fallen long ago, perhaps even before her birth, when her embryonic self floated in the distant darkness of creation's womb. Everything thereafter though aided in her destruction, like pre-placed sticks of dynamite, carefully blowing holes in the structure without bringing the whole thing down at once.

Whole but broken still.

Naked as Eve, she stood in the street, feeling abandoned and punished beneath the darkening heavens, and listened to the winds which smelled of angels whisper . . .

" . . . *you are dust, and to dust you shall return* . . . "

" . . . *but first, in sorrow you shall bring forth children* . . . "

" . . . *our children* . . . "

And, amongst the thorns clawing heavenward, buds formed, swelled and burst the deepest red, like cysts blooming with blood. The winds carried its strong fragrance. Rich, almost sexual, rose musk enveloped Rani, and the child within her moved downward, pressing upon her cervix in a rhythmic manner, almost creating a sensation of sex, though backwards, of being fucked from the inside out.

Blood trickled down her legs.

"Not in sorrow," she told the child, her hand resting reassuringly on her slight mound of belly. On the budding rose and thorns growing within her.

He was the flower for a special kind of butterfly.

Winged death for all those men who murdered children.

For the first time since Stephan's death, Rani smiled a genuine smile of a mother anticipating the birth of a child, the embodiment of love. No matter the child would hunger for marrow and milk; no matter the child would clean the earth of all its blood and bone.

Love never came without pain.

II.

" ... the gates ... "

His scars and wounds, hinges of his flesh, split open.

Beneath his fissuring flesh, muscles murmured in their stretch and bones shifted and popped. The stolen souls whimpered in horrible collective voice then cried.

"Wings of the Wind, answer the cry," Michael spat off. "Aid in the Keep of the dark beast. Harken his coming, the rider on the thunder."

He pushed his thumb through the flaps of a left-sided wound—*black heart, black art*—and ran it along the fascia, scraping viscose fluids off the fibrous sheath. *Ointment for anointment*, and he smeared his forehead, making his third eye rheumy-red.

"Wings of Wind storm upon thunder and hail."

The house groaned, its walls harboring the telltale coming of the Aires, that first inanimate breath, that pain of awakening pounding like a skull-rush of blood. Other noise mingled. Beastly and windy howls. The ripping chant of his scars.

He was better prepared this time for the coming of the Aires, for their ashy yet putrid expulsion from the walls, as if they were made from all the states and matters of the dead. Again, he stank of their septic airs. Again, he lay victim beneath the hovering slate clouds, their black shining eyes boring into his and blinding him. He waited then for their true coming.

The clock in the bedroom ticked. *Tick . . . tick* of dangerous time crawling forward. *Tick . . . tick* of talons along the wall. *Tick . . . tick* of their descent.

Tick . . . tick . . .

Vicious alarm upon his flesh, the buzzing of their breath in his ear, his shrieks as the talons of wind carved into his raw cuts.

Pain exploded across his abdomen. His skin shattered in frag-ments of flesh and shards of blood.

Wings whispering for flight, the Aires licked the salt-offerings from his eyes. Sight returned, though blurred as if his eyes were covered with blood-speckled contacts.

Silver tongues spoke in the old language.

"*Zbh*," they said.

"Sacrifice," he heard.

On his abdomen, another theurgy gleamed. It was a symbol of the dark beast, round and red like pomegranate fruit, with rays shooting from its sun-center.

He was marked the sacrifice.

"*Qtr*," they said.

"Burn incense," he heard.

With difficulty, Michael raised himself off the ground, his body agonizing as if plowed by a speeding car, and slowly made his way to the dresser. Each step left a bloody footprint. But there were bloodier imprints in his mind.

... *fingers shredding against the stones* ...

... *hands heaving against the stones* ...

... *bodies clothed in sweat and dust toppling the temple* ...

... *and the stones fell* ...

... *and the people were crushed by a dying, falling god* ...

Michael pulled open the drawer, and the sticks of incense rolled toward the back. Scattering bones, treasure of pyramids, he thought, and then wondered why he would even think such a thing. Withdrawing the incense and matches, he moved toward the center of the room and reclined at the foot of the bed. He inserted the stick into the heart of his latest theurgy, the insignia of a fallen god.

More than one voice filled his cry.

Lighting the match, he watched the flame wiggle upon the head like some sun-serpent swallowing a man, and the limbless effigy burned the richest gold.

... *casting stones upon the priest until his robes tattered and fell away in strips, until his flesh tattered and fell away in strips* ...

... *torch-lit procession for the dead enemy* ...

... *his body burning on the altar, the burnt offering of meat and incense* ...

... *his sacrifice melting with the sacrifices of all the children who came before* ...

"Fuck ..." Michael shook his hand, waving away the flame which bit at his finger and thumb. He examined his finger— smarting skin, yellow-scorch nail, bitter incense.

He struck another match, ignored the mesmering flame, and put it to the wick. Instantly, smoke drifted upward with a pleasing odor, until the Wings of Wind fanned the incense into a faster burn and then the burn was inside him, creating foul odors of his fat.

"*Wrqtr't `ltw w't mnhtw*," they said.

"Burned his burnt offering and his meal offering as incense," he heard.

"*Zbh.*" And the Aires retreated into the walls, taking all the ashes, smoke, and burnt incense with them.

Taking all but the odor of jasmine, which strode into the room tailored in shadows and manicured in dynasty blue, which lingered over him and whispered of sacrifices.

III.

The house howled.

Howled and brayed as if the brownstone had morphed into a black hound hunter, its door hollowing into a hell-piping mouth. *Dogs ripping into him, quartering him.*

Stephan came the hysterical thought.

Listening for a moment, she realized the pitch matched neither dog nor child but man.

"Michael . . . " Her heart beat wildly hard, almost as if it would pump through her sternum and pull her toward the house by its pulsing strings.

Oh how she imagined such things inside the house. *Dogs ripping into him, quartering him.* His shrills peaked, heightened by torment that all would end but desperately hoping his voice—knocking, pounding thrashing wailing like fists on a prematurely sealed coffin—could thwart death.

Then the force of noise stopped.

Hopes ended??

Shaking off the silent shock, she ran up the walk and steps. Every vibrating flick of soft sound invaded her sensitized ears. Rani heard the wind-troubled thorns scrape the brick, like nails digging behind layers of wall. She heard the dust flow across the threshold and settle upon the floor in bone-clattering clarity, as well as the sun crawl down into the dark well of horizon with the deepest, most forlorn sigh.

The quiet within the house unnerved her though, not a single bit of human stirring, only the faint breath of empty rooms and settling walls.

Her own breath ragged and loud, Rani entered the door and walked across the snow-dusted floor, thinking that the snow was but skin flakes fallen from heaven. But then that would mean God was there. No excuse for His absence or His allowance of suffering.

Suffering was the travesty of life, that which subtends the soul and makes man so wholly aware of the happiness he cannot reach. Which also makes man hope for the other side of life, that the one he didn't have on earth could be lived in heaven.

Thy will be done, on earth as it is in heaven . . .

Death of her only child. On earth. As in heaven.

Suffering on earth as in heaven. Redemption, the terrible, terrible lie of religion uncovered, and Rani rued the day she was born, the worst thing that had happened in her life. Without this, she would never have suffered at all.

The house contained only a fading whisper of Michael's presence—the diminishing smolder of incense.

"Don't let it be symbolic," she said as she watched the last of the wan smoke, the impression of a dying spirit, drift upward and dispatch into empty air.

Empty air, but not the ceiling.

Velvet stain of a blood-drawn emblem spread upon the ceiling, obscene in her eye, of the simultaneous quadruple rape of a monstrous vagina. Its medium dripped down upon her, raining warm and scarlet upon her lifted face. She tasted fertility.

. . . Priests bowing on parched land, tipping bowls of blood onto the cracked, weathered ground.

. . . Mothers weeping for the babies, their babies who had been turned into scarlet waters.

. . . The land sucking sacrifices down and sighing green.

Her symbiont sighed, its half-formed flesh slushing within her womb as if performing the sacrificial dance, as if thirsting for the red, red rains.

Flood of blood . . . tides and tyrants of red. What did Michael know? Where was Michael now?

"The gates . . . unsealed . . . the dark beast . . . " His last gasp, full of mystery and meaning.

And, in her tilted gaze, was that the unsealed gate? Something about it stirred familiarity, and, the longer she stared, the more she realized she had seen something like it before, in a dream where men towered bones into a temple, where men carried golden staffs blazing with this sigil. Except it was more of an eye radiating light.

A woman's burden of dreams, her mother had whispered once as she had kissed Rani's nightmare-damp brow. Of dreams not content to stay dreams.

Especially dreams linked with moon and menses . . .

#

. . . midsummer winds rattled through the blinds; nightingales trilled in the night canopy. Beautiful, haunting, enchanting as the eerie light of the blue moon.

Although alone in the bedroom, she heard her sister breathing as if she'd never gone. Haunted by habit, Rani rocked with the pillow hugged against her face and wept soundless. She endured the cramps. The *Curse of Eve* came as a blood-skinned demon, with claws ripping into her pelvic region, with fists pushing apart her sacrum.

She cried until exhausted, finally overcome by restless sleep. By even more restless dreams, where men were walking on the dead. Squelching plod and cracking tromp of many men on the many more dead. Putrid flesh buckling under the weight and organs spilling outward at the same moment the blood discharged between her legs.

Hands digging into bodies, pulling bones away with ligamentous snaps and grinding them into mortar. Mortar for the humongous skulls being stacked into a wall.

Blood discharged from the mouths and ran down the walls, same as it ran down her legs.

With screams . . .

#

Unbearable silence drove her into the shower. At least the rushing stream filled her ears with something real, drowning out all the wispy whispers of wind and memories. She wished though she could wash away her fears and pains.

Funny, but it was probably her life washing down the drain.

Slippery thumping in her belly reminded her of the twisted hope she carried, and she was determined to shake the despair, such a hard habit she wore. As long as she recalled, she had wished she were dead. But she was too afraid of dying.

Unlike her sister.

She'd always wondered if heartache rotted away with the flesh, or if death carried that pained spirit on forever and ever. If the hereafter promised not oblivion but another life, she feared it was hell. Stephan knew this well enough, right?

Toweling off water like tears, Rani wondered how she could make it all right.

#

She walked toward the Sheridan Square station with the wind bristling against her. Darkness came early in winter and lacked the languid sunsets of summer, without pretty stretches of light's myriad of colors, but merely with bleak and heavy nightfall. Much like her mood. And like scores of others who felt the sad pull of winter on their hearts and minds.

This season came like the postman, through sunshine, rain, sleet or snow, and left dark messages behind, that death would eventually come pick up the package of the body and deliver the soul. Only a matter of time.

Time, Rani snorted.

Little pedigree dogs, all bred of money, yapped at her, perhaps thinking her some hairless wolf sniffing for them, and their Versace-clad owners lazily tugged on the multi-colored, multi-tangled leashes. Again she snorted.

She caught the tail of their conversation as she breezed by.

"Dolce Spina?"

"Dolce Spina, Italian for Sweet Bone, our latest dog bakery venture. We'll send invitations for the private gala before the public opening."

"Grazie."

"Prego."

High-class giggles rang like toasting champagne flutes, and Rani hurried away from the laughter and the dogs and the idea of sweet bones.

Despite the weather, throngs of people attacked the sidewalks, their steps as brisk as the air, their eyes equally grim. Few in the Village strolled in late winter, especially in early evening when the cold seemed to dig deeper into the flesh. Rani didn't break hooded-ranks and dashed along the sidewalk, head down, weaving through the spaces between the crowds, avoiding contact as if maneuvering by thermal radar.

The snow had turned to gritty slush on the concrete. Dirty snow, sullied, corrupted, fouled by man. Dirty snow, she identified with it.

Snow was like the soul, pure until fallen.

Sliding her feet through the slush, she winced at the sound of her steps, perfect mimic of the men walking upon the dead. She ducked into the subway, and her heels slapped on the wet stairs. Images of blood splattered corridors plagued her. The railing beneath her gloved hand could have been smooth bone, and the walls' tiny-tiled mosaics could have been made from millions of painted teeth.

And every man in this Subterrania could be murderers and bone builders.

She fed her subway pass through the slot and pushed through the turn-stile, averting her eyes from the group of construction workers loitering in the passageway. Quiet whistle. Eyes burning at her back-side.

"Hey baby, where you been all my life? Been looking for a pretty girl to be my wife."

Chuckling.

"*Bello chica,* come back. I just want to talk to you, know your name,

98

play a little *chocha* game."

Rani turned her head. The worker had cupped one hand on his crotch and held the other up to his chin, fingers in V formation, his tongue wiggling between.

Automatically, she flipped her middle finger at them, but, feeling perverse, she also licked the length of it. The men cheered and the cat-caller dropped to his knees, placed his crotch-warmed hand over his heart, and beckoned her with the other offending one.

With a coy shake of her head and pursed-lipped smile, she turned her back on them and headed for the uptown platform. Always make them want you but never give them what they want, she thought.

Sometimes a girl had power over a man.

"You shouldn't give 'em the satisfaction of your attention," an old lady said as she sidled beside her, her crone eyes flicking up and down Rani, her matron-wrinkled mouth in tacit disapproval of her hip-hugging leather pants. "Gives 'em more dirt for their minds. Gives 'em reason to come after you."

"I doubt it."

"You're one of those, always asking for trouble." Smug gray eyes brightened. "Don't doubt your body will be gutted by 'em, but we'll give no sympathy for whores."

The old woman's lips drew back into a snarling grin of blood-stained teeth.

"They and the beast will hate the whore; they will make her desolate and naked; they will devour her flesh and burn her up with fire."

Beneath Rani's feet, the platform rumbled, and the train emerged from the tunnel, pushing hot howling air forward.

"Jezebel," she redly spat.

. . . *her son's murderer looks to the window and calls for her eunuchs to throw her down* . . .

Then the old lady laid her claws onto Rani's shoulders and pushed her . . .

. . . *from the window* . . .

. . . from the platform.

CHAPTER FOURTEEN

The desire of power in excess
caused angels to fall;
the desire of knowledge in excess
caused man to fall.

Bacon, Of Goodness and Goodness of Nature

From morn
To Noon he fell, from noon to dewy eve,
A summer's day; and with the setting sun
Dropp'd from the zenith like a falling star.

Milton, Paradise Lost

I.

Falling.
Hands stretched out, grasping fumes and air.
Mouth shrieking yet silent in the train's roar.
Falling.
Into the lights of the train.
But darkness seized her.

II.

The Fallen swarmed upon her in darkened layers, wrapped their
wings around her, and yanked her from the screeching worm of steel

and across its tracks. Nanosecond later, the train barreled by and rocked even the air about the Grigori. Brakes sounded off with an ear-shattering whine.

Doors hissed open, and unloading passengers forced through the converging mass of gore thralls. Windows filled with eager-aghast faces. Peckish eyes roved the rails below, searching for signs of splattering.

Cradling her in his arms and wings, Shemyaza shielded her from witnesses, who saw only shifting darkness. The stink of their disappointment seeped into the stale-electrical air, but someone in their midst had the sight of angels and reeked of hidden knowledge.

Her decrepit womb drew his attention, the smell of it like blighted fruit from the Tree of Life, and he caught her gaze. Her eyes rayed in anger. Her mouth spewed biblical curses.

"The dogs shall eat Jezebel within the bounds of Jezreel . . . "

Her bony fists struck the window, and her bloody sputum smeared the glass.

"The mother of abominations shall be fodder, and her sons shall be slaughtered again . . . "

The train pulled away from the station, and her voice warbled in echo, amplified by the tunnel.

"You will weep and wail forever . . . "

Perplexed, Shemyaza followed the train with his ears, listening to the rattle of its departure and its wake of subtle hum. Darkness never did reveal much mystery. But, then, the dark of the tunnel spoke with a different voice, deeper, older, familiar.

"Here I stand, Azza. Death on delicate wings."

One hundred and forty wings of delicate down.

"I shall rip your haughty wings off . . . " Shemyaza growled.

"No, my sword shall cut your legs short until you bow at my hems, and you shall cleanse the blood of your sons from my robe."

Shemyaza held his rage, violent-trembling as he stayed his ground, ignoring the rash impulse to confront Gabriel.

. . . Gabriel, his taunts thunder-rolling off his tongue, luring them into the umbrageous woods . . .

. . . dominions snickering in the shadows . . .

. . . from the trees, rains of blood, blood of dark angels slaughtered, falling as hot as the burning waters of the pit, and torching their wings, their means of flight . . .

. . . of escape . . .

. . . Raphael and other Seraphim springing from Gabriel's trap in the dark, surrounding them like a wall of wrath, overpowering them, trussing them, and hanging them upside down between heaven and earth . . .

Whimpering, she stirred in his arms. His talons had pierced her tender flesh during his fugue, and her blood splashed onto the track constructs, reddening the black crud of dirt and oil. Fumes of her fear wafted from her wounds.

He walked her to the platform, laid her gently on a bench, and kissed the crescent-shaped punctures until all that remained was the tint and taste of her blood on his lips.

"Azza, why waste primordial spit on the whore?" Gabriel sneered. "She will not survive—-she will be thrown down and her flesh will be devoured by beasts. But not before they empty her womb of your son."

Dominions snickered in the shadows.

"Face the cycle of life, Azza. The Wheel always comes around again."

"Broken Wheels overturn Chariots," Shemyaza countered, but his voice quavered in a whisper of conviction. His hand rested upon her budding belly, the cycle of life warm against his palm, the mystery of it cold within his heart.

Creation had one true meaning and one true purpose: *evolution toward extinction.*

In the early days of Earth, the mountains had towered into the heavens and their peaks were as sharp as the angels' teeth. But, the Wheels of God's Chariots could only run over it so many times before the mountains flattened into the sands.

That which changed no longer existed as it was, and that which changed over and over until exhausting change itself simply no longer existed at all.

Except the Power which turned the mountains into sands and the living into dusts.

"I am what was, what is, and what will be . . . "

The Alpha, the beginning which made darkness into light.

The Omega, the end which will make light into darkness.

The cycle of life, the beginning when nothing became life and the end when life becomes nothing.

Waves as high as mountains rolling in toward the crimson-black shore . . . winds blown from the mouths of Cherubim ripping across the lands, uprooting trees and fields, stripping away the soil . . . waters shed from their infinite eyes falling in a deafening and depressing deluge . . . the waves of dark magnitude finally crashing upon the lands, sudden and terrible liquid fists pounding weak flesh, sudden and terrible liquid arms embracing all, crushing breath and wiping out everything . . . except the screams of their sons which would not drown away with their bodies . . .

"Broken Wheels overturn Chariots," he repeated, his voice resonating now, and a grin cracked his stony-sad face.

Pressing his lips against her ear, Shemyaza whispered a secret of old and then drew himself tall and mighty and walked into the tunnel.

Cata-collision of light and dark, and the tunnel seemed to explode.

III.

Opal and onyx light pinned her to the bench. Ethereal swords sparked within the tunnel, cracking the dark as though lightning had struck underground, and Rani feared her legs would fail if she tried to stand. Awesome, this flickering of the fight that roared along the tracks.

She worried for the father of her son; she prayed for him. But then she choked on anguished pleas, realizing the absurdity of praying for an angel exiled from grace.

The platform rumbled, with battle, not with approaching train. Rumbled as if some leviathan-warrior had fallen. Dust even sprinkled down upon her.

What if . . . ? She shook her head, refusing to entertain the thought further.

Hands clasped and cupped on her belly, she prayed again, not caring if the Father in Heaven listened because she did not beseech him. She cried for the Mother in Heaven to hear her: from one mother to another.

The glory of his breath still warm within her, Shemyaza had hinted as much.

" . . . Yahweh is a warrior. He who creates the heavenly armies, Yahweh is his name. May Yahweh and his Asherah protect you . . . "

His Asherah.

Rani didn't know why, but she knew *his Asherah* referred to an immortal woman. Not an army. Not a weapon. Another thing she knew without reason—-Asherah was not his.

A woman's burden of dreams.

Because the angel's secret had her dreaming while awake.

#

The walls of gold glimmered in the lamplight, and the sapphire eyes of the gilded winged creatures sparkled as if with life. Gold chains placed across the entrance to the inner sanctuary chinked together, disturbed by spirit rather than wind.

Robed in the finest purple linen, a man paced the gold-covered floor. Raven-dyed ringlets clung to his sweaty face. Fear wetted his brow.

A dead priest stood at the altar, his hands melded into the glistening-gold lid of the Ark. Gilt flames consumed his face.

Worse, the two golden cherubim atop the Ark were moving.

Beyond the chains, in the temple sanctuary, sacrificial blood splashed onto the floor, overflowing from the forty-thousand liter tank.

And the emeralds set within the temple's column pulsed with living light and dying sound.

Winds called and complained. *"And now, no house has Baal like the gods, nor court like the children of Asherah. The dwelling of El is the shelter of his son, the dwelling of Lady Asherah of the Sea."*

Winds pled for him. *"Solomon, King of Judah, flee from the false temple. The emerald pillar no longer shines for Asherah. The gold pillar no longer is precious for Baal. Solomon, King of the Semites, flee to the grove where the true green pillar stands."*

Pushing at his back, billowing his robe into royal wings, the winds ushered Solomon from the temple, and vociferous outrage of the two golden cherubim echoed behind him. He dared a backwards glance. Shining-feral wealth of sharp wing and teeth charged from the temple. Heaven thundered hoof on the earth; heaven would fast gain upon him and his tender-skipping feet.

Solomon ignored the rocks which speared into his heels and ran. For his life, he feared.

The angels, coming in a brilliant amber, coming in a brilliant anger, narrowed the distance. Their rich light engulfed him. His back blistered, and his shadow screamed away.

Stumbling over the tangled terrain, he wept for his slow progress and quick-seeping pain as razors of feathers shaved against his pustulated flesh.

Tendrils around his ankles yanked him to the ground.

Stars spun in his vision when his head hit the turf. In supine-resignation, he waited for world to settle, for the mortal blow to settle upon his skull, but the woody tendrils dragged him away from the descending blaze of Cherubim, across the rocks, the grass, and the roots. His body bumped and bruised.

But he laughed, lunatic-loud. Laughed until the sled of his body stopped, until the vines uncoiled and loosed him within a circular grove. He stared in silence at the center-standing pillar of a magnificent tree which sang with the chimes of Cherubic teeth.

The sky of black satin and silver studs draped down upon him, and the belly of earth undulated with dirty giggles beneath him. Winds with gossamer wings tinkled about the silver chimes.

And the tree sang in hungry, high-spirits.

Solomon, King of Judah, stood and bowed before the tree. *The Tree of Life*, with her ever-engorged breast mounding from the bark, with her fat nipple enticing and glistening with milk-sap. *The Tree of Life* opened her canopy. Fruity perfumes whispered along his senses. *"Come to life."*

He did. Solomon fell into her wooden arms and buried his face against her breast, shuddering as the first drop of her milk touched his lips. His tongue circled her nipple, savoring her sweetest taste, like honey warmed in the sun. But the tree was hungry for him and pushed her nipple into his mouth, filling him. The tree suckled him and sang her wisdom into him.

Beyond the shelter of her branches, Yahweh's warriors watched with golden eyes while she fed her lion and then snuck away, clicking their teeth, reassuring themselves that their weapons did not hang on Asherah's pillar. *Lost in war.*

#

Clicking of teeth . . . clicking of a million teeth . . . gold radiance brawling from the tunnel . . .

Rani started from the bench. Fright jammed in her throat, she gasped without breath, and adrenaline pain shot through her chest. Her eyes felt like they were rolling in their sockets. She tottered, off-balance, disoriented.

A hand held her elbow, steadying her.

Dizzy-turn of her head, she saw a silhouette stretched between ceiling and ground.

"Your body disagrees with the child within you."

Gentle voice, rough hand.

Gentle voice howling.

Rough hand pulling her into a hissing gap.

"How you'll suffer your parasite . . . "

Fingers sliding up her arm, nails pinching into her biceps, grip of vertigo bringing her down.

She slumped in the hard curve of a seat and threw her hands at her temples, nauseously riding the revolving mind-attack, merry-treachery going round on the grue-painted backs of satanic stallions which pranced to the music of slick-drumming skulls and clicking teeth.

"And I feed off exquisite suffering," her captor breathed in her ear, minty malicious.

Disorienting-dream fog faded, bringing brutal sight as if her eyelids had been stripped by clear-cutting scalpels. Light was exacting in its pierce.

"Pretty pain," the blue-eyed silhouette sighed, leaning forward, dropping her shadows. Light glittered off her long, foil-false lashes and off the diamond rings through her shaved brows. Beneath oriental slanted eyes, garnets glistened like bloody tears.

"Pretty pain," she repeated and kissed Rani's eyelids. "But give me your heart, your sweetest misery."

Harsh fluorescence dissolved into a sunlight wash of pale lemonade, and drowned her in this soothing shimmer. Her sight transmuted. Auras radiated off the other passengers, rhythmic pulsing as if to the beat of their hearts, expanding as though with breath. Fickle of color, the life-lights changed too rapidly for Rani to pick a dominate hue. Except, the longer she watched the colors shift, the more the auras looked like black iridescence.

Like dark shining angels entombing the passengers.

And cords of this chamelionic light connected all the men, women, and children together.

Like chains.

In the dark-view of the window, her reflection frightened her, with her skin of illuminated silver, eyes of bright coal, and mouth of bloodlight. With her reflection of another woman.

Jezebel, her memory murmured, and hands were upon her again.

"Give me your misery, kiss me. I want to taste it on your lips."

Rani turned her attention to the beauty, her face and manner strange poetry. No light danced from her, but her aluminum-veiled eyes seduced with the glitter of stars, silver rays coming off silver-blue eyes, wickedly promising far out and extreme delights. Celibacy was alien in those eyes.

Enravishing, ethereal, that scarlet-black mouth. That stunning mouth which wanted to kiss her, and Rani was shaking as those gothic lips parted because the Asian Aphrodite had a mouth designed for devouring, not love.

Would her lips taste like her breath, like peppermint and euphoria? Would her kiss liberate her in the rapture or deliver her into the soul-raping arms of death?

Rani glossed her lips with her tongue. Heat of breath and desire touched her lips first, and then full contact surpassed every dream and nightmare. Soft lips sank against soft lips, silk crushing silk. Tongues teased and tasted luscious ardor, slowly exploring more than mouth. It was as if the hollows of their mouths held the primeval substance of spirit, and they exchanged not only saliva and breath, but soul. *Heart.* The essence of her heart, its sweetness and light, its blood and thunder. Its sweetest misery.

On her tongue, blood dropped like acid, warping her perceptions, and Rani saw her delusive self, kneeling before a truncated woman, sucking one of her pendulous breasts. She fondled the other breast and pinched the already hard nipple. Dots of blood squeezed through the tiny ducts.

Greedily, Rani swallowed the blood filling her mouth, thinking she drank the milk of the Mother of God and of the sons of God. A sweet burning, like the myrrh of angels. A sweet revolting of her stomach as she consumed this mind-altering ambrosia.

Mouth open and eyes closed, she saw leaves fall from a tree and stand an angel of jade. Mossy breath fumed from its gnarled mouth, and she heard it whisper, *come to light.* And then the angel of jade punched through the earth and pulled out shiny bones. And the bones of dead sons rolled in the mud and stood with blood-battered flesh and cried, *come to death.*

She tore her lips away and broke the seal of the kiss, and the Goth, her eyes and cheeks glowing with rosy secrets, smiled a cloy smile. Rani felt faint again.

"My blood sister . . . " Her smile widened and revealed filed teeth. At least Rani assumed they'd been filed, ignoring the quibble of her belly that she'd been born with those points. "We're sisters of the blood and the moon. Sisters of death."

Her eyes glazed with cold mischief as she placed a card into Rani's hand.

"Sometimes we must destroy in order to create new life," she said. "Something your sister knew well."

Head thrown back, she laughed.

The train reached the 42nd Street stop, and, seizing her opportunity, Rani hurried off and up the stairs. She exited at the corner of 42nd St. and 5th Avenue, turned and ran toward the Main Library, her breath held as phantoms and laughter pursued her.

Twilight streaked with flurries charged the sky like wild piebald mustangs and carried the mad rider of her sister's screaming laughter through the streets. Stinging, tail-lashing winds brought tears to her eyes. *Quiet, do not disturb . . .*

Huffing for breath, she bounded up the courtyard steps. Icicles of air speared into her, and the blood in the back of her mouth tasted sharper because of it. Her feet crunched on the salt rocks thrown upon the steps, and she couldn't help but think of bones between jaws, her bones between the jaws of the lions guarding the entrance of the library.

Every muscle tensed as she passed the stone lions.

Ridiculous, she scolded herself, but she couldn't shake the unease that something would happen. Nothing of course happened. The two inorganic beasts remained lifeless. Only her breath steamed the air; only her heartbeat drummed into her ears. Only the heavy child of a stone-hearted angel in her belly moved.

She walked over to the Venus fountain and spat into its basin, *sacrificial blood splashing*, dirtying the snow collected within. One red spot, enough evidence on the white sheets to disprove virginity.

Jezebel, the old woman had accused. *Whore*, she had meant.

And here she was giving blood gifts to the venereal goddess.

Rani read the fountain's plaque, "Beauty old yet ever new/eternal voice and inward word."

In her hand, the crumpled card compelled her. She opened her fist and stared at the words as if at any moment the elegant script would pull away from the paper and wrap about her like barbed wire.

The ice hanging from the devil-headed spout glinted silver then gold then red like a vomited stream of frozen blood. Cold as this ice, her sister's face flashed in her mind, blood spilling from her mouth too.

Another drop of blood landed in the fountain.

Rani shook her head, chasing away phantoms and phantasms, and stepped back from the Venus-basin, afraid of some impossible thaw. But no more impossible than angels escaping heavenly penal colonies and fathering a giant of a son.

Without further incident, Rani charged into the beautiful library, more of a castle's interior with its grand halls of marble and rich woods. She half-expected wall tapestries of unicorn hunts and suit-of-armor guards would appear, and at the end of the hall she'd find long banquet tables of roast boar, blood puddings and overflowing fruit bowls. And, at the bottom of these stairwell mazes, dungeons of tortures and screams. Places where her sister would haunt.

Her footfall echoed in the vast corridor, and she instinctively tiptoed, backlash of all those years in her childhood home, when she was warned about making any sound so as not to disturb her sister.

Do not disturb the disturbed.

Unless you cherished the deranged thrashing and frothy tirades. But Rani hated her sister's episodes, always wondering if the screams that bombarded into the walls and into her would eventually come out of her own mouth. She tried extra hard, being well-mannered and quiet, very much mousy, to show the world she was not her sister.

She was not a bipolar schizophrenic with psychotic tendencies.

At the moment, Rani had her self-doubts. Her fingers tingled again as if with some violent nervous tic.

Sometimes we must destroy in order to create new life. Something your sister knew well.

What wisdom drove her sister to whittle the bone into a stake? What truths drove her deadly aims?

Satrina, her red-dripping arm extended, offering the bone . . .

Her temple throbbed with pressure, and she worked the tension with her fingers. The card in her palm brushed against her cheek, the papery kiss tantalizing her with the linger of mint.

Unable to dampen the lure, she read it:

Come celebrate the reanimated beast of Gomorrah
An untamed event
Come surrender flesh to her worship

Come, it read in gothic-noir ink and script, another dark beckoning, and she knew she would come, too far drawn into the shadowy passage to turn back and find her mundane way again. She'd taken up her sister's bone.

#

Seated at a long table, Rani scoured the stacks of books the librarian had pulled from the storage shelves. Old books mostly, smelling of dust and, regrettably, of mold. Her sinuses ached as much as her back while she sat in the rigid chair, reading sentences until they blurred into strings of black instead of words.

She absorbed what she could. Exhaustion muddled her concentration and her mind reeled as theological dichotomy bombarded her. All the sundry names of God in the Bible correlated to other, older gods—El, Elyon, Elohim, etc—, all except Yahweh, and, according to one source, Yahweh was a young god in the mythological scheme, the son of El, rising in supreme power as the Semites rose in political power.

These volumes illustrated a crude point, she realized, that religion seemed little more than a pissing contest. Muscle-swelling, wrath-ripping gods greedy for world domination—*let us make humankind in our image*—and, as god defeated god, man defeated man. Or vice versa.

Elijah had murdered the four hundred and fifty prophets of Ba'al and the four hundred prophets of Asherah who ate at Jezebel's table. He had challenged them. Two bulls chosen; two bulls cut into pieces and set upon the altars. The people would call upon their god and Elijah would call upon the God of Israel, whichever god answered in fire was God. Even after the people had cut themselves with swords and cried aloud, Ba'al held his silence. Elijah had goaded the worshipers, mocking their silent, obviously meditating god. Water had been poured upon the wood, a measure to insure Yahweh's superior strength. And, when he had called, his Lord had answered swiftly in fire. Then Elijah had Jezebel's prophets seized and killed by swords, making them skeletons of the wrong faith.

At God's bidding.

111

Yahweh is a warrior. Yahweh is his name, he who creates the heavenly armies.

Merely a war god, and victorious.

Still she chuckled at the irony of what she learned.

When the Christians prayed to the Lord (long rooted in the Semites fearing to speak God's name), they prayed to Adonai, Saddai, Ba'al, etc, all terms found in the Bible, appellative to Yahweh yet deities on their own. Phoenician gods of vegetation, reproduction, and life. Phoenician gods who consorted with Yahweh's wife.

Asherah . . . Asheroth . . . Astarte.

Jezebel's goddess.

A whore.

IV.

"The whore will come?"

"Yes," she said, pulling off the false foiled-lashes and false skin.

"Collect me a sample of her vaginal fluids because I cannot send the assassin without it."

"Of course." Then Lilith licked her wicked lips with her forked tongue.

CHAPTER FIFTEEN

Come not between the dragon and his wrath.

Shakespeare, King Lear

Behold a pale horse, and his name that sat
on him was Death, and Hell followed with him.

Revelations 6:8

And ye to woman's—beautiful she is,
The serpent's voice less subtle than her kiss,
The snake but vanquish'd dust, but she draw
A second host from heaven, to break Heaven's law.

Lord Byron, Heaven and Earth

I.

Michael knelt on the bamboo floor, his arms and legs tingling from pinched circulation. They had pulled his arms behind his back and bound his wrists to his ankles, and the stress of his weight settled on his knees and toes.

Sweat rolled along his body. The air within the room—a square of three-foot wide bamboo walls—steamed from ceiling vents and down upon him like a feverish dew. His florid skin glistened. His eyes watered, but his tears were feckless against the salt-sting of sweat.

Salt for such wounds. His sight *was* sore, as if with bruises, his cell reduced even more into a livid, hurting haze.

Pops and clangs of valves echoed behind the wood-rodded walls, and the vents hissed with the rush of outputting air. The atmosphere became less humid as thin ginger-crisp air filled his cell and breath. His lungs cleared of the stifling moisture, but the relief was temporary. The ventilation system pumped gallons of noxious green vapors into the minuscule space. Michael thought he would die.

Sacrifice . . .

Gulping air of camphor and hellfire, he shuddered violently with the ordeal of breathing. The pain was unlike anything he'd ever experienced, chainsaws in his throat and exploding shrapnel in his lungs, hot-metal air melding his insides.

"You like my breath of dragon?"

Hidden speakers rasped with Jichun's leprose voice.

"Amazing thing I saw—ginseng smoke turned into *hsien*. The Immortal had voice soft as smoke and skin scaly as ash. She tell me, 'This man is a sacrifice.'

"She mean you, Michael. She tell me she take mercury from your woman, if I take scars from your body."

Surgical air and anaesthetic darkness probed into him, preparing his body to let another darkness out.

Raise the dark beast . . .

And, with the last of their voices, his scars screamed . . .

II.

Scratchy strike of matches shocked the preternatural quiet of the crypt. The match heads flared with flame, touched as if with the fiery gold tear-drops of angels.

Angels cry fire, his daddy once said. And saints and martyrs weep in blood.

Once the four priests relit their candles, the crypt again wavered in gold and shadows. No physical sign remained of the *hayyoth*, only the metaphysical, as the wax of the white tapers dripped cardinal.

Julian counted his steps to the door, seven points between the entrance, where the soul would reenter the dead body, and the exit, where the reanimated would reenter the living world. Seven steps, seven degrees from death.

Turning clockwise until he faced his brethren, he held a brass key in front of him at arm's length. Candlelight flickered in the toothy grooves, but their eyes were shaded with kohl-dusted arcana and roving, unable to focus on the building energy. Bilious spittle ran from the corners of their muted mouths. Perhaps the *hayyoth* had reached into the priests and pulled out visceral gifts, but he'd worry later about restoring their wits, if he bothered at all.

"As we unlock the gates of the tomb, so may we unlock the gates of death itself."

Julian completed the circle and returned to the door. Inserting the key, he gave three ceremonious twists, six clicks which sounded much like the beating of a mechanical heart, and the door parted ways, its iron hinges swinging wide with rusty retort.

"Come ye winds through open gates."

Although the golden incandescence barely arced two feet beyond the front steps, the graveyard took on a numinous glow of silvered mists rising from the cemetery mounds, as if the diaphanous shrouds were the new skins of the spirited dead. The mists lightened the pithy sky. A gray lumen, but brighter than night nonetheless. It seeped across the death-keeper grounds, a filmy curtain fluttering in the breeze, toward the crypt, and his heart fluttered as well.

Believe in God, in His power over the enemies of Devil and Death.

Believe, abandon your body as God's vessel, abandon your heart and let the Holy Spirit in.

Believe, the power of God is within you, preparing you to serve His will.

He snapped his fingers, and the rote-wired Brothers hefted the coffin lid aside.

"Come ye winds, ye spirits, through open tombs."

Lazy flowing winds entered the crypt, tussling his hair with loving, breezy fingers, and the oily fragrance of bodies in decay-bloom clung to him as the winds brushed by and through him. Inside, the winds lost their silver-gray coats. Warm-blooded breath colored them wine-dark.

Except in the space above the corpse. The winds were as black and still as the death which possessed the body. Slowly though, like oil bleeding down a canvas, the suspended airs dropped onto the corpse.

The crypt smelled of more than dust and wax and sour men. Like decomposing serpent-breeding balls in a stagnant pit.

Julian gagged on his breath thick with this coiling reek.

Hoisting himself into the coffin, he lay upon the corpse, head to head, foot to foot contact, and gripped the brittle wrists. His nose touched the exposed nostril septum of the corpse, and its dry musk filled his own cavities. The jaw hung slightly ajar, the flesh and tendons which once held it shut resembling brown tatters of moth-eaten linen. Julian pressed his mouth against what remained of its mouth. Incidentally, he tasted the old parchment of its flesh, and a savage thirst struck him.

Julian breathed into the dead mouth.

. . . *When Elijah came into the house, he saw the child lying dead on his bed. So, he went in and closed the door on the two of them, and prayed to the Lord. Then he got up on the bed and lay upon the child, putting his mouth upon his mouth, his eyes upon his eyes, and his hands upon his hands; and while he lay bent over him, the flesh of the child became warm. He got down walked to and fro in the room, then got up again and bent over him; the child sneezed seven times, and the child opened his eyes* . . .

If you are Jezebel, so I am Elijah, Julian thought.

And the dead man stirred beneath him, squeezing his hand seven times.

III.

White drafts blown by the wind, snow cascaded downward from the tops of the buildings instead of the clouds. Her world, her faith and hope, shaken as if within one of those globes. If she stood on the side-walk, would the cold swirls accumulate upon her and bury her? Would she then find her son in that icy death, where he waited for her arms?

She longed for his weight in her arms, her kiss nuzzled against his warm silken crown as she swayed to some unrecognized symphony playing on the radio. A habit she had complained about because after awhile his weight would wear her down. A habit she'd take up again, even if her arms tore from her shoulders, even if her back broke.

Her miserable sigh puffed into the air as she stepped forward to hail a cab.

Step on a crack, break your mother's back.

Step on a line, snap your father's spine.

Hand in the air, eyes upon the ground, Rani planted her foot on the center of the sidewalk square.

"Step in the middle, kill your little," she said hauntingly, her voice a deep mockery of his murderer. "Your little Boy blue . . . "

She waited a long time for a vacant taxi, and the night cold seemed to replace the marrow in her bones. Even the unborn shivered in her womb, jiggling her belly.

She had waited, and still waited, an even longer, colder times for her wounds to heal. Would time ever ease the pain? Bury the grief, her friends had said. But how could her grief go any deeper? This ache went to the core of her being already.

And time only reminded her of how long he'd been gone, of how short his life had been and how unfair it was. Time didn't heal her wounds at all.

Time was the absolute executioner.

And she wouldn't doubt that Time would eventually see every angel fall.

Finally, a cab pulled to the side and stopped, and she ducked into the back, telling the Pakistani driver, "Evergreen Cemetery in Queens . . . take the Queens Midtown Tunnel. Head out to Glendale. Either Forest or Myrtle Ave will get you in the right entrance."

"This is far?"

"Yes . . ." *But not as far as Satrina's grave, tucked in a private grove on the family's sprawling country estate two hours upstate.* Rani had been afraid to bury Stephan there because her sister's remains had disturbed the serenity and sanctity of the ground.

. . . her spirit laughing moonlight and wandering with weeping shadows . . .

. . . tapping at the window, hushing her with a wild-flowing grin and finger . . .

Rapidly rushing slender fingers through his greasy hair, the cabbie grunted in response and turned on the meter. Crimson glow of numbers clicking, clicking like teeth . . .

She leaned back into the seat, closing her eyes, ignoring the meter and the dark littered view of the brick-walled streets. Exhausted from lack of sleep, she dozed during the ride and shallowly dreamed of Shemyaza and his sword. Warmth chased away the chills.

And their son blew bubbles in her womb waters as he clenched and unclenched his tiny fleshless hand, strengthening fingers for his own hefty blade.

#

"This is good?"

Rani rubbed her eyes and leaned against the window. "Can't you drive in?"

"No, I don't drive in." The driver threw the car in park and printed the receipt from the meter. "You must forgive me, but I don't go into places of the dead. Especially at night. Bad feelings. Perhaps you'll change your mind, and I'll drive you back? Free of charge."

Astonished at this unlikely generosity of a NY cabbie, she handed him forty dollars and fled the cab before she did change her mind.

The cold braced against her and chewed away every scrap of heat from her. She stood, with the wind tearing at her hair and coat, watching the rear lights of the taxi disappear down the deserted street, shivering again. At her back, the magnetic pull of the cemetery beckoned.

Rani waited at the gate for the guard to come around. These locked gates and iron bars, prisons for the dead, keeping them secluded from the living when darkness came. Because darkness always reminded the living of death, and the living preferred not to be reminded of the inevitable, preferred to keep unsavory things locked away.

Amber light bobbed along the path toward the gate--the guard was coming.

"Evening, Ms. Izhar. You come so soon after the last visit," the guard said, swinging his flashlight at the ground.

"Unfortunately, Manny. But I couldn't sleep," she said, slipping hundred dollar bills through the bar, which he palmed.

"I understand." Manny unlocked the gate, turned his back, and walked away from where he knew she would be heading.

Oil lamps glowed along the paths, but the darkness pressed from every direction, the sky, the sepulchral earth, and the freezing spaces between, and diminished the brassy light. The dark came as if a snuffer poised inches over candle flames.

She headed down the path, knowing, despite the maze of darkness, which way her Stephan lay. Devastatingly cruel, that she'd traveled this path more than the one to his crib.

But then, she had not come through during the day since his funeral. Somehow the night lessened the stark impact of his grave, as if she could pretend the endless rows of headstones were nothing more than temple ruins, only broken columns, and her son was an ancient god, simply lost until faith brought him back.

His soul waiting in darkness, in agony.

Within minutes, Rani had her night vision, and the cemetery loomed a forest of marble. The place was massive, dense, and gloomy, with foreboding airs which trebled through the natural wood and unnatural stone. Airs which hovered on the verge of assuming solid shape.

She folded her arms, tucked her hands in her armpits, and crept off the path, scattering the flecks of gold and diamonds glittering in the white, the enchanting snow shushing beneath her feet. *Hush, hush through the haunted wood.*

Statues of cherubs glared at her for disturbing their silent playground. She felt their hard eyes following her. She heard their giggles ring upon the wind, bells of ice and imps, and chills took its toll on her flesh. From the corner of her eye, she saw shadows move.

Howling ripped the dark, as if the night-fiber of sky had come alive and was hungry for the hunt.

The sound pierced through her. Then, like a knife hitting bone, it stopped.

Her body rigid, she listened. Panting of wind-stirred snow, huffing of her own breath, otherwise an eerie quietude descended as if the cemetery hid a harrower in every hollow.

Rani walked with trepidation, shaking as darkness stalked her. Incredibly, sweat dampened her underarms, and her fingertips throbbed with heat. Only her lips were numb, cold with fear.

Shadows of the shade fleeted through the monuments. Soundlessly. Menacingly. Circling her.

Round and round, she turned, hands pushed outward in defense. Nothing but darkness, and she wandered if her mind played tricks.

But darkness breathes here, her sister had said, after showing Rani the empty well. *And what breathes must feed.*

Irrational or not, she ran. Her feet beat the ground as quick as her heart beat in her chest, and slipped in rhythm as much. Hounds on the hunt barked behind her. Darkness on the hunt made no more sounds behind her.

She reached her son's memorial with a strangled shrill.

A guardian angel stood upon her pedestal and tended watch on his grave. Her downshifted eyes would never waver from her vigil. She would always look forlorn upon the buried child.

She arrived and now what was she supposed to do?

Instinct told her to dig. His body lay in the darkness, in agony as the darkness fed upon him, and she would dig him up, bring him into the light.

Howling shadows surrounded her again.

Hurry, hurry, her mind whimpered, and she dropped to her knees. She brushed the snow away in two furious sweeps. She clawed at the frozen grass, and clawed, and clawed, crying, screaming, as her nails tore away instead.

Hugging his stone, Rani wept hysterically. She failed as his mother. She hadn't kept him alive. Couldn't even take care of the dead baby.

She heard the howls, but she didn't hear dogs. She heard infants wail.

Lifting her head, she stared into the woeful eyes of the angel.

"Help me," Rani said.

Darkness buckled around the stone angel, like an oily halo falling to the ground, and winds surged upward, raising great clouds of snow upon her. Ice crystals stung into the skin of her face.

Chin lifted, she accepted these glass-cut kisses and waited for the Grigori to come.

But it wasn't the Grigori who came.

A figure of fire, burning of cool cobalt and myrrh, struck to the earth and became a figure of flesh. He towered above the guardian but stood there like it, wings folded down, head bowed, regarding her with the same sad eyes.

In solemn silence, he went down on one knee and touched her shoulder. His eyes burned of that cool cobalt and brimmed with feeling of the unfathomable depths of sadness, deeper than any she had ever known. She had to turn away from him before she forever fell into his weeping wells.

"Dig my son up." Command was absent from her voice, lacking that demanding zeal of her first request. She didn't expect him to obey.

He kneaded her shoulder with one hand and lifted her chin with the other.

"I have not fallen," he said.

Confusion crossed her features, and he noted this, nodding.

"I am Araqiel who has dominion over the earth and judgement over man. I am without sin, without the corruptibility of the flesh." He paused and leaned close, his head against her head. "But the blush of your blood . . . "

His velveteen lips pressed lightly against her cheek. His nettled tongue explored a cut.

Rani shivered in a swoon of desire.

" . . . so warm, where I am so cold."

In a rash gesture, she kissed her blue-voiced beauty as if he were a man of flesh and blood, holding his lips captive against hers. Her hands slid across his cheeks. She pressed her mouth firmly against his mouth until warmth filled his lips. Then she licked the bow of his sweet-myrrh lips, and his mouth parted for her tongue.

She unzipped her pants and guided his hand between her legs. He responded with a moan as his fingers found her inner warmth.

Picking her up with one hand, he pushed her against the statue and, with the other hand, stripped off her pants. His cobalt eyes burned into her, not at all cool but fervid, as he surveyed the Eden he'd been forbidden to enter. His breath alone made her quiver. His tongue stoked her arousal, and she believed the world would end in cataclysm of their fire. But he was gentle and slow, keeping the intensity of feeling without a frenzy.

He pulled his wings around her, nestling her as if within sun-warmed clouds, caressing her as if with the down of the sky, soft-tickling every inch of her, even under her arms and behind her knees. Araqiel showed her the softer side of time and of love.

#

The voyeur angel had regarded them with the same melancholic expression, but a crack had appeared along the polished-stone brow, as if the guardian had frowned. Rani stepped behind the statue, avoiding her derision.

Seducing an angel to fall.

Whore.

Shame seethed beneath her satiety.

Araqiel fashioned a spade and parted the earth as easily as her legs, and she swore the ground sighed. Dirt piled at his feet. She would pile at his feet if he asked.

When he reached into the grave, she held her breath, not wanting to see his coffin again, so tiny, so abominable, and she didn't release her breath until Araqiel opened the laquer box.

Her breath came out a scream.

Because Stephan's coffin was empty.

CHAPTER SIXTEEN

Under the debris, in this "High Place,"
Macalister found great numbers of jars
containing the remains of children
who had been sacrificed to Baal.
The whole area proved to he a cemetery
for new-born babes . . .

> Halley, archaeological excavations notes of
> a temple of Baal and Ashtoreth at Gezer

And now, behold, the souls of those
who have died are crying.

> Book of Enoch IX

I.

An autumnal midnight, the round harvest moon hung low on the horizon, heavy with the reaper's blood-orange light, and the fickle winds, not attached to any certain direction, frisked the trees and stripped the leaves. Russet and gold carpeted the ground. His steps crunched and crackled as he walked deeper into the rot-fragrant woods.

Old rot of wood and fallen fruit, of meatless birds and rodents, their feathers and fur mere rugs upon collapsed frames of bone.

Wrapped in a chambray bandana and carried Tom Sawyer-style on a stick, the cabalic matter soaked into the fabric and through, scarlet-black and seeping. Drip-drip *onto the leaf litter like death-textured rain.*

Michael entered his rock-studded circle, cast anagogical charms, and untied the ill-conceived bag. Airs of corpuscular ruin and vinegary albumin of the secreted contents rushed into the winds, emitting the distressed cries of a newborn into the swollen night.

In his hand, the umbilical cord of his first born son writhed, a serpent of viscose scales and sorcerous venom, which Michael milked out by squeezing downward.

He rinsed his hands in the blood.

He washed his hands in the ropey gore.

Mimicry of thunder, he shouted and rumbled off his magical liturgy into the swirling winds. Mimicry of lightning, he lit a match and held it beneath the umbilical cord. He caught the symbolic ashes of his son, half he mixed with his spit and used as ink for the letters of the offering, half he pocketed which he would later bury near the foundation of their home in order to bring good luck and prosperity.

But the Thunderer didn't want symbols. Baal wanted sacrifice.

Storm clouds raged above Michael, and the black leviathan of sky swallowed the egg of the moon. He instantly remembered the myth cycle, the benevolent, life-giving earth becoming malevolent, destructive, demonic. Cataclysms of fire, flood, and earthquakes as the cosmos turned against life.

He had to prevent another disaster; he had to feed the fertility gods, Anat-Tanit and Baal Haman, with blood.

Blood he didn't have to offer, except his own.

He didn't have a sacrificial knife, not even a Swiss Army pocket knife; instead he picked up a stone and gauged his old scars along his forearm. He raced to break his skin and draw blood before the sky birthed doom.

Too soon, Nature unleashed her fury, of death bent and thundering toward sterility. Leaves became spears, thrown by furious winds, and he crossed his arms before his face, shielding his eyes from the stingy points. The trees hurled brittle branches at him.

He bled finally, thankfully, flesh unknotted and red ribbons running down his arms.

Wolfish winds fought over his blood, snarling, biting, and the force knocked him to the ground. Old scars splitting apart, he shrieked and instinctually rolled away from the ravaging winds. Sandy dirt stuck in his sticky tears. Salt for such wounds. The blood mixed with the sands, a visceral medium for mud, and aided in sealing the gross gaps in his flesh.

The blood didn't flow.

"No," he cried, digging at the clumps imbedded in his wounds.

The winds didn't blow.

"No . . . " *His voice, his desperation stifled in the leaden, phlegmatic dark.*

An owl dropped from flight, body cataleptic in air, not a flutter of wing, only that plastic stillness which didn't change even as it slapped onto the ground. The wild lights in its eyes were the only signs of life.

Nothing moved in the woods.

Yet, Michael felt it coming. The whole wood felt it coming, reacting in rigid terror and dead silence. Waiting, waiting in queasy inertia like calves bound for slaughter.

The darkness assumed weight, obese with malice, and crushed down upon him.

A rib cracked under the pressure.

Blood-shiny eyes appeared in the gloom and fixed upon him. He tried to squirm away from the glowering face of night, but only his piss escaped, a wet warming beneath his immobile body, an action he neither controlled nor was conscious of doing.

Wet drops struck his face. For a moment, he thought it had begun to rain, but the spoil of hot, gamy air meant only one thing. The bestial dark had opened its mouth.

Slimy chunks of saliva plopped down on him, and Michael cringed inward, unable to rouse even an eyelid to shunt the spit away. His insides quaked with fear and hurt as if the black claws of Baal were scrambling his organs.

But the blood-skinned lord of the dead hadn't touched him yet. Merely tortured him with the thought of his macerating touch.

Baal uttered his demand.

"Sacrifice the child . . . "

His child.

Stephan.

His mouth in rigor horror, he couldn't say no, and Baal put the mark of blood-frenzy in his heart.

#

Michael opened his eyes. Granular shadows caroused in his monocular scope of morphine-laced vision, silhouetted parades of raven-headed men swooping upon him and pecking at his suspended body. Chains rattled as his body swung in the assault.

"You like my breath of dragon?"

"You like my bite of dragon?"

Besieged by tooth and claw, by scalpel and forceps, his scarified wards wailed. Their horrifying stridor echoed in his head, of broken men trapped and dying beneath broken buildings, of war-time children being yanked from their mothers arms, of mothers strapped down and forced to watch the enemy drag their children away.

As they peeled the skin from his back and dug out the magical cords of tissue beneath, Michael writhed in anger. Not because of the pain, but the lack thereof. He wanted the pain, wanted to experience the horror of being dismantled. His life-long sought magic destroyed in seconds.

But he merely felt the vapid tug and pull upon his flesh, his body anesthetized with dragon-serum.

Grainy indiscernible images and soupy thoughts even dragged his mind away from the theft of his scars and wards.

He heard the buzzing of flies and wondered if the flies had come from his body or for it.

Swarms of darkness crackled and buzzed and popped into the room, and then the screams began.

Someone cursed under his dying breath. "Damn the *hsien* . . . damn us too for what we've done . . . "

Michael shut his eyes.

II.

"Where's my son?" she cried.

Tilt of his head, Araqiel regarded her with anguished eyes but said nothing. He stood statue-stoic.

"Where's my baby? Where's my baby? Where is he?" she wailed, ruffling through the white satin, bunching the snowy cold of empty in her fists and ripping the luxurious fabric from the coffin.

Rani clenched satiny bouquets in her hands. Her hands shook; her shoulders shook.

Even through the blur of tears, she spied the terrible nothing which should've been her son. She expected the shock of his decomposed body. She had expected anything gruesome but this.

"Where?" The tiny squeak of her voice belied the sheer intensity of her emotions.

She sobbed into the torn satin.

"The dead are countless like the stars." Araqiel knelt beside her and placed his marble hand upon her shoulder. "I cannot know where the dead lie, any more than you can know where every star shines."

"But you're an angel . . . "

"Angels have not been given the keys to all mysteries."

She stared at him, mouth agape, all questions stumped by this confession.

Helpless and hapless, she thought, pitying herself, all hopes degraded. Her son would stay in darkness, in agony.

Not unless . . . *not unless she came to light . . . came to death* . . . whatever that meant. Helpless and hapless as ever.

A deep sharp ache spread from her heart into her belly, and Rani doubled over, clutching beneath her pregnant swell, rocking in hopes to soothe her body as well as her unborn. She felt him roiling within, turning as if away from her threatening pains.

Between her legs, something wet trickled. Rani reached into her pants, dipped a finger in the discharge, and withdrew her finger for inspection. Silvery mucous. Shining like star-dust. The angel's semen, not blood.

Relief that not all hope had gone.

"How will I find my son?" She looked to the angel, the sky, the moon, the stars, searching for an answer.

The heavens were ignorant.

His brow withering in shame, the Watcher shifted his cryptic eyes from her and crossed his hands over his hardening member. In a damning grimace, his teeth showed in deadly points. "I fear the stars can't help you, nor me."

She bit her gums in frustration, chewing, sucking, tasting the tang of the gothic kiss. *We're sisters of the blood and moon. We're sisters of death.*

"Sisters of the blood and moon . . . of death . . . what does that mean?"

Disgusted with enigmas, Rani threw the scraps of satin at the incompetent guardian, stood and paced around Stephan's hollow coffin and grave. She avoided Araqiel's arms.

"Sister moon, brother sun," Araqiel said, standing, spreading his wings, trading his flesh for fire.

Clothed in blue molten veils, he danced. Lissome spine contorting and coiling, smalt rippling torso and hips in sinuous shimmer and shake, arms and legs wavering in a sapphirine-torched arabesque. His sun-bright eyes begged her company in his lonely, cold minuet. But she backed away from him, averting her eyes in shame now, unwilling to fall for him as he had fallen for her.

The air thrummed with the music of his screams, and she choked on the sulphur of his song. He ended on a note of despair, in dying embers and ash, as he burned into the ground.

But from his exit came gifts. His screams had been a call . . .

The earth grumbled, and winds of decay bristled from the gaping grave and wired around her as if the cemetery had let loose dreadful breath.

Other foul things loosed from the quivering pit.

Bone pushed through the deep dark dirt as if being birthed, crowns of misshapen skulls erupting from syphilitic and seismic holes, litter of grand-malformed bones piling out, an afterbirth of blasted-trench carnage spurting and pooling beneath the bones.

This gutty soup which filled Stephan's grave slushed with the anguished echoes of long dead children.

A heartbeat skip later, the winds blew with the sounds of stillbirth. Of fathers crying in deep-raged voices.

Unbelievable but lightning flashed in the sky, a web of silvery light strung through the night clouds. Rani couldn't help but think of Araqiel, if he was being taken back up to heaven and punished. Lightning of God's switch flicked again. And the bones thundered.

In her mind, the sigil flashed, the radiating eye carried on golden staffs, carried by men who would build a temple from bone and blood. She had her answer, staring her in the mind. The eye of the sun.

Sister moon, brother sun.

Brothers of this sign.

CHAPTER SEVENTEEN

I saw the key-holders and guards
of the gates of hell standing,
like great serpents, and
their faces like extinguished lamps,
and their eyes of fire,
their sharp teeth . . .

Book of Enoch XLII

For the souls that are filled with
much evil will not come and go
in the air, but they will be put
in the places of demons,
which are filled with pain, and are
always filled with blood and slaughter.
And their food is weeping, mourning, and groaning.

Hermes Trismegistus: Asclepius

I.

Lost in the dark, down some abandoned unfinished shaft, the two great angels came together in explosive blows. Swords had long since been abused and broken, and were tossed aside. The air in the tunnel reeked of cordite and methyl amine, the charge of their fists and breaking flesh.

Gabriel struck Shemyaza squarely in the chest.

Breath and blood pushed out of his mouth, and the impact bruise looked as if his onyx heart had exploded against his chest. He staggered backwards. Gabriel lunged and followed through with another strike, hands grappled on his neck, his weight of force toppling them both to the ground.

They rolled along the tracks, thrashing, gnashing, slashing, a ferocious train of teeth and talons. Gabriel roared as Shemyaza ripped into the sockets of his left wings. Amethyst tendons sprang from torn flesh and snapped. With grisly *pops*, several wings separated from the shoulder joints and hung precariously from meaty-pink cartilage bone.

"Next, your feathers," Shemyaza wheezed against the vise of Gabriel's fingers.

On his back, with Gabriel straddling him, strangling him, he pulled out handfuls of feathers . . . *the mother of his son pulling out handfuls of white down . . .* and stabbed the arrow-bunches into Gabriel's sides. His blood fell in golden showers.

Burning like hot cinders, this was the waters of the burning lake of hell, the blood of fallen seraphim.

Satanail, his body chained at the bottom of the pit, ravenous hooks splitting his flesh and draining his veins for thousands of years, his blood filling the pit and overflowing into magmas rivers.

Blood scorched his throat. His own blood as Gabriel pierced talons into his throat. Breath turned to liquid gold and curses bubbled out in gory glimmers.

"Azza, the wheel turns again."

Quick as light, Gabriel jumped off of him and looped a hand around his ankle, yanking him off the ground, hanging him once again upside down.

Gabriel pinned him to the ceiling with an old rail spike rammed through his foot. He writhed, twisted, bucked, and swung in old agony anew. Blood from his throat punctures pumped from his nostrils and tear ducts, and dust and tarry grit billowed downward, but that was all that fell.

"A poor prison, but it will hold you long enough." The Archangel grinned wide, garish display of sadistic glee, and, from Shemyaza's angle, his mouth stretched a hideous scowl on a hideously arranged face. "By the time you break your bond, your son will no longer have the safety of the womb."

Shemyaza raged and spat frothy words.

"And the dogs shall eat the flesh of your Jezebel."

Wings spread in a cacophony as if hundreds of doves alighted the midnight sky, ravaged wings disjoined in wet rustles by the forceful display, the dark antagonist bid Shemyaza a laughing farewell and disappeared into the chasm between earth and heaven. He fouled the air in his wake. Sulphur and brimstone. Roasting meat of the dead.

Scent induced nostalgia . . .

#

The damned sat on the crackling crust of cooled lava, feet crossed and tucked beneath her legs, hands resting on knees, her sex exposed and mutilated. The inner petals of flesh and her clitoral hood had been shorn off. Puss outlined the gross vivid frills of her sex-wound, and blood drained in gourd-sized clots from her butchered hole. The long, bone-deep slashes on her inner thighs though were bloodless, rift with tiny gluttonous demons.

Surrounding her, a mote of flowing lava swept along carcasses dumped in from the crag above. The dead burned, blackened, and bubbled away, only to resurface further down, newly fleshed and screaming.

She watched the other damned burn in the river of fire, blinking only when their screams ended, opening her eyes when their screams began again. Her pupils were large like those of a bird of prey, but she did not see him standing beside her.

Like the rock upon which she sat, she was still and silent, her face hardened against any emotion. Suffering eluded her. She picked at the scabs which continually formed on her brutally circumcised sex and threw the flecks into the molten river, as nonchalantly as feeding black swans at some park's stream.

Her skin reflected the amber of the lava, giving her the appearance of a low-ranking angel rather than the damned. Golden-toned and serene upon a rock, an impervious judge, without empathy or genitalia.

Shemyaza knelt beside her and razed a talon along her ruined sex. Her gaping wound quivered, and the effluvium of her arousal puddled beneath her.

Eyes rolling backwards, moaning, she turned her head toward him and stared with the whites of her eyes, watching him as if through the clouds.

"I slept on the edge of the sky," she sighed. "Hiding under the blanket of night, listening to the angels fall."

She pulled his hand to her lips and licked her coagulated fluids from the chalice of his talon, then rubbed her cheek against the points, adorning her cheek and lips with keen rosy color. She smeared her excrement upon her eyelids. Strange and frightening as ever any human had ever been, but he also found her beautiful.

And irresistible.

"I danced in the garden," she sighed. "Twirling in my gown of moon beams, listening to the sad angels sing."

The Ophanim called down from the crag, their anger rattling the rock upon which she sat, and Shemyaza fled before they recognized him and demanded he come forward for judgement.

He never learned her crime against heaven, nor the reason why she alone didn't weep, mourn, or scream. But the mysterious allure of the daughter of man had fermented in his heart, and he was drunk on their beauty.

Perched on his mount at Hermon, he watched, and watched, and watched the comely daughters of men until he could no longer rein in his lust.

#

The seraph-foul air dissipated, and he caught the human odors trapped in the bottled tunnel. Urine and feces dominated the smells; however, he sniffed out the presence of a ripe daughter of man, her womb a cache of fertility and sweet disease.

Faint perfume, strong ache of desire.

Straining against his inverted crucifixion, Shemyaza searched the dark choke of the tunnel for signs of the humans. He saw nothing but the hulks of debris. Their smell intensified. Seen or unseen, the sons of Adam were drawing near.

He arched his nailed foot and felt the flesh give way but not the spike. Pulling himself up by using his leg as a rope, he studied the large stud in his foot and determined that, if he reached his hands to the floor and pushed against the ceiling with his unfettered foot, then he could either rip the spike from the ceiling with his strength, or rip his foot from the spike.

Where's my son? Shemyaza heard her call from faraway, and his bruised heart lurched. She needed him. Oh how his son needed him.

Upside down again, he wrinkled his nose. The stealthy company of man had advanced, lulling now only a few feet away, and they stank of forty Cains.

His fingers dangled inches from the floor, which stretched a black wrecking yard of construction discards. Which became hunting grounds as figures who looked like the roasted damned crawled toward him, their bellies growling with untamed hunger.

II.

The spirit of the corpse felt the call from the other beyond as his hell-body waded in the worms. The worms waded within him as well, squirming nests in his eyes and mouth, in the pulp of his heart and lungs, and in the bowl of his cranium. His thoughts were wormy.

Feed . . . feed . . . feed . . .

Vocal chords eaten, he couldn't scream and suffered his pain in wracking silence. Horrible, horrible pain within a pause, without the relief of a single scream, and he envied the other damned with their endless wailing and their piercing agony. He felt like a balloon inflated beyond its limits, grotesquely stretched, on the brink of bursting, of letting loose all the tension with an explosive sigh.

But his hell-body kept filling with worms without a break. Many, many worms with many, many teeth.

Feed . . . feed . . . feed . . .

Cannibalistic silence. His punishment for telling all those lies and interrogating all those dead.

He felt every bite, every single ring of teeth of every single worm cut into him. Tens of thousands upon tens of thousands to the nth power of infinity. Afflicted with such tiny, tiny bites that brought much, much pain.

Not to mention the incessant vile squirming within him . . .

Tugged from the other beyond, the spirit of the corpse rose from his hell-body, the body he'd had for years, how many he did not know because time meant nothing in Hell. Seconds held all the torturous measure of eternity.

His soul traversed the cold darkness once again, breezing through all the pitches of black and purple and blue, without his worms in tow.

How he'd forgotten he ever had another existence beyond that execrable place of worms.

Then the spirit of the corpse came to the end of darkness and heeded the call of bones, settling in his old dead body, hurting and silently cursing. The worms were within him again.

Feed . . . feed . . . feed . . .

And another voice whispered in his ear, "We will feed you the blood of the Jezebel and you will abort the abomination in her womb. God will absolve all your wrongs with this right and you will enter the Kingdom. Acknowledge this."

Snapping rotted ligaments in his neck, the corpse nodded, and his decimated lips crumbled as he smiled.

CHAPTER EIGHTEEN

Anything fallen again?
nay-—what was there left to fall?
I have taken them home, I have number'd the bones,
I have hidden them all.
What am I saying? and what are you?
do you come as a spy?
Falls? what falls? who knows?
As the tree falls so it must lie.

Tennyson, Rizpah

Flesh of my flesh was gone,
but bone of my bone was left--

Tennyson, Rizpah

I.

With shaking hands, Rani gathered the bones and dumped them into her son's fancy box. She pretended the clatter-rattle requiem of the skeletal instruments were hollow sticks knocking together. She pretended the skulls didn't stare at her with ghastly sight. She pretended not to hear the childish weeping.

Muffling the haunting sounds with the lid, she cradled her body against the coffin and rested her head on the cold varnished wood. Her heart pounded on the lid.

"Let me in," she whispered. "I want to be with you, my sweet little boy."

A single tear rolled down her cheek and into the crease of her mouth. *Salt for such wounds.*

"My lost boy."

Snow flurried down again, beautiful as if heaven cast glittery white jewels upon the cemetery, and the winds were breezy sighs of wonder. Rani pretended her son played in the enchanted forest, hiding like an imp among the trees and graves, giggling, tempting her to follow him deeper into the marble grove. But she knew in the heart of all magic was darkness, and horror, and evil.

Where the witches always ate the children.

As she dragged the coffin from the cemetery, she pretended not to hear the cackle of her sister.

#

Love NY, she thought. Where else could she travel with a coffin without raising much more than an eyebrow? Pity that same indifference applied to random acts of petty violence as well, and she hated to think that her city had a heart of stone. Hardened perhaps by all that concrete.

But then she knew best that stone, with the right force, could crack and crumble away and show all its vulnerable spots. Beneath the hard facade, she knew her city had a soft heart. As soft and hurting as hers.

People like her had too much heart and too much feeling, and the only defense was to turn it all off and feel nothing. She always wondered if she allowed herself to feel fully, would her heart beat itself to death?

Rani walked up the steps to her brownstone, laboring with the coffin which followed with heavy thumps. With groaning.

Throwing open the front door, she dropped the box over the threshold and pushed it with her foot into the corner, beneath the coat rack, and it seemed Michael's sable trench hung like a grim angel above it. The wind brought in the snow, blanketing the floor as if with the white velvet of Stephan's coffin. Very sepulchral, she chillingly decided as she shut the door.

The walls creaked with age and an unsettling echo of emptiness, and she went through each room, flipping on the lights, chasing away the dark but not the darkness of her mind.

Michael had not returned.

She worried. Michael had disappeared like smoke as if some Chimera, drawn by the smell of his blood, had breathed fire upon him and burned him into ash and smoke. He had disappeared as if some *dark beast* had swallowed him whole.

Come celebrate the reanimated beast of Gomorrah.

In the hallway, the clock chimed midnight, the dead of night, the hush of night, the witching hour, the hour of the wolf and all other voracious dogs. Rani shuddered as the wind howled against the windows. She pushed her hands into her pockets, squeezed her elbows close to her sides, and walked to her bedroom. Fingering the card in her pocket, she stared at the ceiling, at the blood-stained eye with its blood-strained sight spreading outward, watching, waiting.

Waiting for her to come . . .

Uptown. For the worship of flesh. Her fingers kinked as if into claws, tense for blood. She'd find her son by any means . . . *sometimes we must destroy in order to create new life.*

Shrugging out of her pants and sweater, Rani stood in front of the antique floor-mirror and surveyed her body, the changes subtle but warming in their fuller promise. Her breasts were small but plump, with nipples blushed dark-rose as if blood-milk filled the ducts. She traced the veins, the blue lifelines for her half-breed son, showing beneath her olive skin. Fingers going down the slope of her breast, palm tickled by her erect nipple, she sighed as she remembered Stephan at her breast.

. . . her aureole and nipple sucked into his warm soft mouth, squeezed between eager-hungry gums, stroked with his tongue. His small hand cupping and massaging her breast. The tense surge of milk flowing through. The dreamy-drowsy bliss of being in this mother-child coil . . .

Rani circled her hand over her belly. Unnatural child, unnatural growth, she thought, staring amazingly at her budding reflection in the mirror. She looked four or five months pregnant after only . . .

. . . *yesterday, her flesh pillaged by midnight rogues and peril eyes* . . .

"A day," she said, incredulous because, at this frightful rate, the child would break her pelvis and be born tomorrow or the next day.

Her heart leapt; her belly leapt with the unborn shifting and stretching within. She touched the protruding bump of him, hard and round like a head. But unlike any human head. Too round, too large.

Through her very thin, stretched layer of skin and fat, the cream of his flesh showed, if he had flesh yet on his bones, which he should if he would enter the world soon. But then Rani had a disturbing thought—what if the children of angels had no skin but were creatures of malformed bone, huge lumbering sticks of meat hungering for flesh, forever dripping red slime as if newly birthed?

She glanced to the doorway and thought of the skulls within the coffin, misshapen, craniums bulging as if two giant brains were housed inside, eye sockets as large as fists, crocodilian teeth. Skulls of predators with sharp minds and teeth.

The unborn moved again, settling deeper in the womb, pressing against her sciatic nerve. It felt as if electrified pins pricked her upper leg.

"Little one, ugh, get off my nerve." Rani pushed upon her lower belly, prodding him to a higher position. The electric-pain seized from her pelvis down to the back of her knee, and she cringed to think how it would feel if she tried to walk, her weight bearing upon her nerves like shocking bolts.

Obeying either her word or her hands, he turned upward and nestled beneath her ribs, beneath her heart, his ever-wound music box.

"Thank you." And she patted her belly, caressing him in the only manner she could until he was born and she would cradle him in her arms, flesh to flesh.

Her cheeks warmed and her heart pounded at the thought. Jittery smiles played upon her mouth, and she felt giddy and sick all at once.

Soon, in her arms, she would hold the Fallen Seraphim's son. Her son, with whom she had already fallen in love.

"My son," she whispered, tears dribbling from her eyes for both sons. Part in sadness, part in joy.

Wiping her eyes, Rani stared at her reflection, at her puffy eyes, and wished her doppleganger would step from the mirror and walk the miserable world for her. Then she could slip into the silvered world and live happily ever after. A queen with her little princes.

The wind bawled in white noise. The lights flickered, connection breaking in the old wires, and in the momentary blink of dark came the rickety sound of walking bones.

She held her breath and looked to the hallway. Nothing but drunken shadows wobbling along the floor and walls as the lights continued to falter.

In the flickering light, she caught the surreal reflection of the other woman. Eyelids colored with the flirtatious night. Lips with the shine of a bloody sunset. Winter sadness in her eyes. Midnight delights in her smile.

"Jezebel . . . " she began, but the face wiggled away like a whiff of smoke blown away by the wind, by her voice no doubt.

Rani crossed the bedroom and slipped around the corner into Michael's study, an idea burning the way. On the right, a hand-hewn bookshelf of black-stained walnut covered the entire wall. The shelves had been devoted to metaphysical studies, which included Bibles. She pulled down an annotated bible and flipped to the back index, found references to Jezebel, and rifled through Kings until she found what she was looking for. She read:

"When Jehu came to Jezreel, Jezebel heard of it; she painted her eyes, and adorned her hair, and looked out her window."

Eureka. The painted lady in the glass.

Intrigued, she continued, "As Jehu entered the gate, she said, 'Is it peace, Zimri, murderer of your master?'

"He looked up to the window and said, 'Who is on my side? Who?'

"Two or three eunuchs looked at to him. 'Throw her down.' So they threw her down; some of her blood splattered on the wall and on the horses, which trampled on her. Then he went in and ate and drank; he said, 'See to that cursed woman and bury her; for she is a king's daughter.'

"But when they went to bury her, they found no more of her than the skull and the feet and the palms of her hands.

"When they came back and told him, he said, 'This is the word of the Lord, which he spoke by his servant Elijah the Tishbite, 'In the territory of Jezreel the dogs shall eat the flesh of Jezebel; the corpse of Jezebel shall be like dung on the field in the territory of Jezreel, so that no one may say, This is Jezebel.'"

Jehu, the murderer of her sons.

Elijah, the murderer of her priests.

Brothers of the same faith. Murderers for that faith.

Thoughts in a whirlwind, Rani sat cross-legged in the middle of the room and read all the Jezebel passages. The wood flooring was cold against her bare bottom. The scriptures were colder.

Israel against one woman. One woman whose husband, Ahab the seventh king, couldn't deny and built her temples for her Phoenician gods, Asherah and Baal. One woman who commissioned the death of an innocent man. One woman who defied Elijah and threatened the worship of Yahweh.

One woman who painted her face and adorned her hair, stood a beautiful pillar of dignity and strength, and looked ruefully out the window and down upon her son's murderer, who was uglier than any demon of death.

Instead of cowering before the general in charge of her execution, Jezebel hurled insults upon him. *Is it peace, Zimri, murderer of your master?* Zimri, the name of the unscrupulous predecessor of her father-in-law, the king who ruled seven days after murdering the king and usurping the throne. Unlike the meek and mute biblical woman, Jezebel had a tongue. And she wagged it like a sword.

Whore? Rani disagreed, smirking.

Jezebel was an idol herself, symbolizing the fertility of womanly power, something men had to degrade or destroy in order to perpetuate male dominance. Someone men made into a false idol, same as her goddess.

But what connection did she have with Jezebel?

Besides unscrupulous men who murdered their sons.

141

II.

And unscrupulous dead men who would murder another.

The corpse shifted in the coffin, turning his head toward the voice, unable to see his necromancer because his eyes had collapsed into crusty detritus within the sockets. But it mattered not, his eyelids had been sewn shut with fine black threads. The longest lashes he'd ever had.

In his dawn, he had the sight which needed no eyes. The Dreamer, he'd been called, and, later, The Harrower. How it all came back into his mind, his memories like dust within his bones and stirred by his unsettled spirit.

He lingered on the disjointed memories, his fondest and his worst . . .

#

The garden path narrowed into a single strip of stepping stones, and thorns of the overgrown rose bushes plucked and snagged at his linen sleeves as he made his passage through. He tasted the roses upon the humid fragrant air. He tasted Isabelle as well.

Beneath an arch of white climbing roses, she waited for him, and his heart swelled with lusty blood. For she looked herself a pink flower, adorned in nothing but her lacy gloves and ivory stockings. The wind teased her buttery hair, slyly fanning strands upon her nipples.

Isabelle smiled. Her lips were dewy petals, and this he spoke breathlessly as he drew his face near hers. But she tipped her head away, her coy mouth widening.

And he, a mandrake in this cornucopia of blooms, grabbed her soft hair and dragged her to her knees. With one hand, he unbuckled his britches and dropped them. His cock leapt out straight as an arrow and pointed at her mouth.

Rubbing the head against her lips, he whispered all the naughty things she had dreamt, how she was his milkmaid and sucked his cock dry, how she was his flower and spread herself for him, and so on until her cheeks blushed. Until her mouth parted and softened into a supple opening.

He maneuvered her head back and forth by using her hair as reigns and bucked into her mouth. Isabelle grunted her pleasure. He grunted as well and matched his thrusts with the rhythm of her middle finger as it pumped into her rosy hole.

His senses abandoned to this frolic, he never noticed her choking, not until he withdrew his cock and splurted his cream onto her bluish face. Still a flower, a morning glory.

In shame and disgust, he released her hair, and Isabelle's body slumped to the ground. He buried her as the sky darkened into a funeral purple and the shadows came to mourn.

His dreams were of nothing but death after that moment, and every night, he screamed, so as not to hear the bones calling him. But he was not strong enough to ignore the bones.

With his axe and spade, he wrecked the garden. With his hands, he tore through her grave and dug her up. He carried her through the swinging gates of the garden and laid her corpse upon the ruined bed, which used to grow dahlias of every shade, her favorite flower. Flowers like her, pretty and showy, but needing lots of care and attention.

She rested upon the dirt, above the grave, yet covered with the grave. Blues and grays mottled her skin, and the expression on her haunting face was that of someone unable to wake from a nightmare.

Tearless, the well of his eyes run dry, he cut into the hollow of her throat and dragged the blade down her chest, in the valley between her once magnificent breasts. The worms had fed upon the firm fat of them now. He watched the skin part, bloodless, gaseous, and felt as hollow as her veins.

The Dreamer tossed away the divining rod of dreams as he reached into her vivisected abdomen, and became the Harrower, awakening the dead and inquiring of the future and of the world beyond this world. He burned her body when he was through. Although her corpse yielded gems of secrets, her bone powder failed to yield silver and gold.

Thus became his passion. The bones. The ashes. The alchemy.

And when he had raided the cemetery of all its corpses, he, enacting as the town's midwife, told birthing mothers that their infants had died in the womb and then bundled them away, smothering their first breaths.

#

What his necromancer asked of him was a task he knew well.

His memories, his talents, his madness, it was all coming back with a vengeance.

CHAPTER NINETEEN

"Do you call it peace while your mother
Jezebel keeps up her obscene
idol worship and monstrous sorceries?"

2 Kings 9:22

There is a kind of pleasure,
which comes from sacrilege
or the profanation of the objects
offered us for worship.

Marquis de Sade, 120 Days of Sodom

I.

Image of Jezebel, her hair in licorice-twist braids, her eyelids smoky
and alluring, her lips nearly drinkable in a deep claret.

As if drifting in a dream, lazy moving as a gentle stream, Rani
dusted body glitter under her eyes and at the crest of her cheeks, and
her image, sparkling and wavering as if viewed upon rippling
waters, mesmerized her.

"Jezebel," she whispered, and her lungs filled with more than air.
She inhaled lilies and dreams . . .

. . . *desert dancers in robes of dust drawing enigmas with their feet
in the sands* . . .

. . . *winds of sands and devils billowing into the angry sky, raised by the yells of prophets, by the hisses of the deadly snakes held in their hands . . .*

. . . the burning tree in the oasis looking like a blood-engorged penis . . .

. . . the unwashed, pleasure-loathing Levi priests taking the fire from the branches and making burnt offerings from the worshipers of Asherah . . .

. . . air reeked of death and god . . .

. . . desert evils soaking in the blood and melted skins, sighing in ashes, and swelling into the night . . .

. . . beasts of prophets hunting the last prophet of Asherah, impaling the rod of his idol into his stomach, gnashing the soft semen-bloated sacs with teeth, their mouths red from tasting sacrifice, their hearts afire with tasting the impotence of their enemy . . .

. . . and their hands ached for another holy massacre as the sun, the eye of God, lighted upon them, pleased . . .

Her hand tingled. Jezebel in the mirror, Jezebel in her heart.

"Stone him to death," her hand seemed to murmur.

Sunken deep but rising like a gas-riddled corpse in sewage-piquant waters, the cries of her son resounded in her mind, and the skulls hidden in his coffin shared his pain, of falling prey in infancy and growing old in tortuous darkness.

If only her eyes had an aim.

II.

Waltzing in through the door, spying the carnage art upon the walls and the exotic rugs of human flesh, Lilith smiled, her eyes and teeth in their natural reptilian shapes, her body pasted with human skins and curves. Her dragon-smile complimented the Oriental meat-flair of the room as she stepped through the origami of organs and muscle-matted bones, wetly crumpling the designs.

Flies and maggots crawled through the dismembered bodies. Through the fertile clays of decay. Sacrifice drawing the Lord of Flies and his plague of minions.

The Mao Shan master huddled in the corner, mummy-wrapped in white worms and flies. His long nails, the color of the deep-sea, had been turned upon him and were imbedded within his throat. No voice for magic or screams.

The disinfected host swung upon his chains, the hooks pulling the flesh of his shoulders and thighs like scarlet dough. She sniffed his eviscerated wounds, strong with blood and dead oracles.

Other smells interested her. Within his gaping chest, the lingering odor of filth, of the Lord. Lilith placed her hands on the chains and pulled herself up onto him, straddling him, lowering her head until her mouth hovered an inch above the bloody sun dawning on his chest.

With flickering tongue, she tasted the peels of flesh.

Metallic and salty. Pure human meat, without the flavor of gods. Disappointed, Lilith lapped at his cut flesh, and her spit, primordial and celestial, worked on closing the wounds and bubbling away the nephritic bacteria.

He moaned beneath her quick-forked tongue, and his eyelids fluttered with the struggle of waking. His cock had already awoken.

Grinning bright-red teeth and situating herself further down, she licked his cock, the split tip nearly wrapping around the shaft. She licked and sucked, enjoying the salt and throbbing velvet of his engorged cock, until she nursed a pearly mouthful. Lilith swallowed and felt satisfied, finally tasting the god in his seed. Sweet pomegranate.

No son of Adam, this one, she thought as she teased the last glistening drop from his cock. Garden descendent though, with the flavor of his father within him. A distant son of Eve and her Eden-seducer.

Before he strutted about with the title Baal, he had been called Enki-Sammael the serpent, son of Apsu and Tiamat, brother-husband of Lilith the Snake Demoness.

She remembered . . .

. . . being handed over to Adam as his wife.

. . . Adam attempting to force her to assume the passive position in sex.

. . . refusing and, in a rebellious fit, fleeing Eden with Sammael, mating with her brother, and subsequently birthing all manners of serpents and demons.

. . . slipping into the Garden upon her belly, with Sammael following, and, in an intimate slither, seducing Adam and Eve to eat the apple from the Tree of Knowledge.

. . . the good apple being toiled by worms.

She remembered it all but especially the hatred between the sons of Adam and her sons, and, in retribution for their heinous cowardice murders, Lilith crouched between the legs of mothers and ate of those red fruits.

By then, the god he'd become had left her and took other wives. But she had taken no other husband, wanting and waiting for only him.

The Freemasons believed by mating with their wives that they vicariously mated with her. Laughable in the least, but the dark goddess found her way through the moonlight, blood and semen, and, through moonlight, blood and semen, she would draw her Lord back into her schemes.

Unhooking the son of Eve, Lilith carried him out of the charnel-stinking room and headed for the club, The Cutting Room. The show was about to begin.

III.

Rani tucked her burgeoning figure into a lightly tied, high-waist, pink-brocade corset and a long, loose side-split skirt. Advertizing her sub status, she strapped on a leather collar and bracelets with nickle-plated rings. She bent over to lace her five-inch heel boots and regretted having put the corset on already as the steel boning pinched her rib cage.

In the mirror again, without the phantasms, she nodded her approval, and a hint of normalcy crept into the image, her familiar night-image in fetish gear. Nothing more unusual than that.

Quiet bones, quiet wind and snow. The house was static, empty, unlike her heart which thudded anxiously, full of angst and fear, and Rani felt as if she crossed a threshold into a different world, where the creeping cold was more than air but famished denizens waiting in the dark and stalking her.

Somewhere in this world Stephan endured the dark and cold, the utter loneliness, the agony, and called for her through the years, through the winters of midnights. His call going unanswered thus far.

Horrible, horrible, horrible, and her breath whistled in her tight throat. She had no tears, but she was crying as she walked toward

Christopher Street. She couldn't imagine how horrible it must be for him, an infant accustomed only to the pains of birth and hunger but having always been comforted by his mother's presence, arms, or milk.

"Stephan," she whimpered, hugging her arms about her body, aching for even his bones to dispose the void.

"Shemyaza," she called, looking toward the sky.

Only snow swirled in the ebon sky like icy ashes of dead angels.

"Shemyaza," she called again, this time with fear fiddling with her vocal cords and butchering the sounds. Her body shook as she thought about him abandoning her in her greatest time of need. When she desperately needed to find Stephan and with the imminent birth of a son who may split her in two.

Even minutes after leaving her brownstone, her belly felt fuller and strained her skirt. Walking would soon be an ordeal as the unborn took up all the space in her pelvic cavity and pressed her hips outward. She had the beginnings of the waddle already.

She tired and hailed a taxi as soon as she could.

The driver stared at her through the rear-view mirror, his eyes seemingly disembodied, darkly alien and sinister, hovering in the glass. Watching, waiting.

"24th Street, between 6th and Broadway, please," she said, clenching and unclenching her hands. Her hands were like her sister's hands, aching for the knife or bone.

"Do you need hospital?" he asked, his voice thick with Middle Eastern accent.

"No, why?"

"You look in pain. Like my wife who had tumors growing in her belly."

Coincidentally, the fetus rolled in her belly. The feeling, slippery, solid, punchy, and turning as if she were swinging high and soaring down. Sickening and thrilling all at once.

"I'm fine and in a hurry," she stressed, waving her hand for him to move on.

Maternal murmurings of her wishes and promises surged through her veins, soothing her anxious son and her own unstable impulses. She caressed her abdomen, calmer, confident of her survival. Such was the power of the angels within her, of bringing the indefinable, boundless laws of spirit into the physical.

Goddess-like, with her rotund belly and globose breasts, with her nipples tingling with abundant milk, Rani acknowledged the pride and the beauty of the womb. The beauty of life, its creation-energy churning within, the stuff which made the stars and moon and all the celestial horizon.

Warmth spread through her because she shared a connection with Jezebel beyond murder. Their bodies were forever linked with the Mother of gods, birthing as Asherah birthed, legs opened, slippery life shooting from the blackest hole, where nothing lives but which gives up all life.

The angels had touched her, corrupted her, but did not damn her after all. Shemyaza, fallen Seraphim, had lifted her into transcendence, bestowing the gifts of the divine within her. Seeds of creation grew inside her. She glimpsed the world before the world had a sun, darkness all around, lifeless. But the Grigori gave her a son, and the darkness will fade, and life will reign.

And this son will feast upon those who had slaughtered her firstborn.

Rani leaned back in the seat and smiled.

#

Without electric or gas lamps, 24th street was a dark slash between the brighter avenues. Winds swept snow through the cleft of buildings, and the darkness swallowed the twinkling white like a child sucking down sugar. As she departed from the corner and its safe bubble of amber-glow, she too felt like she was being swallowed, slipping deep into the belly of wind-mewling darkness.

The lock of buildings created a wind barrier. She walked without winter tearing icily at her face and shearing through her coat, clothes, and skin. But other things chilled her to the bone.

Her heels clicked with the beat of her heart, and, when she stopped, it felt as if her heart did as well. Heavy and aching in her chest. Shocked into stillness by what she saw.

There, the sign of her dreams, the sign of murder. Inconspicuous, spotlighted only by the beams of a passing car, a sign of the radiating eye stared down at her. The eye was inside a triangle, a pyramid she gathered, and lines like shooting rays of light emanated from the pyramid. Another sign, depicting a square and compass, hung on the door. It simply stated: Masonic Temple.

The building looked nothing like a temple, without religious adornment or symbol of denomination, without any iconoclastic characteristics in the structure. She scanned the five stories of rust brick and barred windows, thinking it looked more like a warehouse. Or a seedy meeting place for a seedy Brotherhood.

The mysterious sign captivated her. The eye, watching and waiting within the pyramid, the tomb of an ancient pharaoh, the symbol of death. But also of the life waiting beyond. Those rays of light spoke of hope, triumph and glory over death.

Come to light, come to death, it spoke as well.

Rani put her hand upon the door knob and jiggled it, half-expecting it to open of its own accord like some kind of haunted abode after sensing her presence. But this was New York City, and the lock didn't budge.

Accepting the futility of breaking in, she walked away from the Masonic Temple. Its eye followed her. On the other side of the street, a few places down, The Cutting Room waited. Without a sign. Only the address and a beefy bouncer standing in front of double black doors clued her in.

"Invite," he growled, holding out his large, potentially skull-crushing hand.

She handed him the card, and then he smiled, bowed, and opened the door for her, waving her through with that awesome hand. One swat from that hand would cover her entire ass.

Ushered inside, she walked through an empty bar area. The liquor bottles, infused with the glow of bar lights, looked like bottles of liquid gems, garish treasures of intoxicating topazes, diamonds, rubies, and sapphires. Treasures guarded by the goat-heads craved into the wooden columns of the old-fashioned bar.

Smoke drifted at the bar as if cigarettes had been left burning in ashtrays. But the ashtrays were as empty as the stools and tables.

Perplexed, Rani crossed the room until she reached the far wall, the wall being a black velvet curtain instead of drywall. She pulled on the folds, trying to find the separation of fabric and the dark entrance of Gomorrah. Muffled voices guided her.

She found the break at last and slipped between the curtain and into an unlit hallway. Hands outreached, she felt her way down the narrow hall, and her head began to ache from straining her eyes in the deep unforgiving pitch that smelled of sex and death.

The voices intensified, not in sound but in number, as if a horde of demons crawled along the ceiling and whispered excitingly, breathlessly, about meat.

Arms grabbed her.

Arms came out as if from the black velvet, pulling her into an assembly of desperate fondles. Like jilted lovers in the throes of raw reconciliation, her handlers sighed and wept, and kissed her intensely upon the mouth. Hand after hand, mouth after mouth.

Rani suffered the salt of their tear-wet kisses and the disorienting turn of their arms. Swept in this weird dance in the dark, *tangled in the ebon ribbons of death's ladies,* she felt frantic and terrified.

But suddenly she stumbled into a theater room, the stage lit by torches, the audience awash in soft flickering golds, their bright eyes rapt on the show. Someone helped her to a seat. She glanced around. Behind her, the curtain hung without ripple or sigh of the groping chaos.

"Next up, a Blue Angel original, hot enough to make this Jew turn Catholic in a heartbeat and hard-on," the barker on stage announced. He breathed heavily into the mic before he rolled it down his chest, down the red tattoo of the vampire-like Devil, and rubbed it on his groin.

A broad, nasty smile cracked his chiseled face as a diminutive girl in a nun's habit shuffled onto the stage. He feigned wiping sweat off his shaved head.

"You don't know heaven until Mary's knelt before you."

Demure tilt of her head, with the wimple falling across half of her face, Mary folded her palms as if in prayer and smiled. Dainty, teasing, erotically mysterious.

"Say a little prayer, because Mary will bring out the horny devil in all of you."

The speakers piped a melancholic symphony, and the violins and clarinets reminded Rani of human cries. Mary danced slow and sultry, her habit sweeping across the floor as her hips swished to and fro beneath it. She pulled off her wimple and loosened her sandy tresses, which were long and tasseled as if she'd spent the day rolling in bed with her dead husband, Jesus.

Fingering the cross, she raised it to her luscious lips and licked the tiny figure of Christ. Deftly, she undid her habit. The black stiff fabric parted to her navel, giving surreptitious peaks at her breasts, girlishly small with pointed nipples begging to be sucked.

Mary, in sinuous motion, shirked her habit.

To the left of Rani, one man found religion in the palm of his hand as he ogled her petite body and her seemingly juvenile triangle, the pubes waxed off, leaving her looking very nubile and chaste. Corruptibly enticing.

But her body belonged to the savior of the church.

Stripping off the crucifix, she kissed the length of the chain. She dangled it down her sternum, and the figure of Christ swung across her pubic mound. Her hand slipped between her thighs. Fingers trailed upward and inward, and the Christ made tiny little circles as she rocked her hips slightly. With the heel of her palm, she pressed the cross against her clit and rubbed.

Mary dropped to her knees. She drew the cross between her thighs. The length of the chain disappeared between her puffy labia like a long metallic tongue. Seductively, explicitly slow, the chain sinned back and forth, all glistening gold and divinely naughty.

Mouthing *oh god*, Mary leaned all the way back until her shoulders touched the stage floor. Her legs were still bent at the knees and spread wide, providing such an intimate view of her sacrileges self-pleasure. The son of God was born again in pink wet flesh, incestuously incarnated.

Rani could almost smell the musk, like altar incense, sweeten the air. Her chair thrummed with the clit-titillating bass of the music, and she bent forward, taking vibratory advantage of her seat.

Quivering rapture of her buttocks, and Mary finished her act. The audience, shock-delayed, didn't applaud until after she scampered naked off the stage, the black bundle of her habit in her arms, the crucifix returned to her slender neck.

Mary then made rounds through the crowd, extending a brass plate for an offering. Those gratuitously grateful handed over their monies.

Mary stopped beside Rani.

"Jesus loved the whore," Mary whispered in her ear, her soft voice sending tinkling bells down Rani's spine. "The gods want to love all whores, all the Magdalenes and the Jezebels. Downstairs, sister, you'll find Gomorrah. Through the door behind the stage."

Then she skipped away, blessing the eager audience with her kisses and her uplifting presence.

Rani was nervous about wandering around the place, leery of what lay in wait for her, all of seeming like some elaborate scheme. She sat in her chair and stared at the stage, unable to see the door. It meant she would have to traverse the stage, in full notice of every watchful eye. Perhaps if she waited until the next performance, then she could escape attention. Deciding this, she moved from her seat and waited against the wall across from the right side of the stage.

From this vantage point, she spied the girls and the transsexuals behind the stage getting ready for their stints. Arabic sheers and finger cymbals for belly dancing. Gowns of beads with butterfly wings made from razor wire and vivid silks. Feather boas and boa constrictors. A platinum blond with platinum-credited breasts practicing fellatio with her sword, her mouth and tongue sucking in the tip, her throat convulsing as the three-foot blade was swallowed down.

Rani watched, sickened, mentally gagging and holding her throat, as the lady, head back, arms and mouth extended wide, spine straight as the blade, danced with her sword. Only the hilt showed, the silver stuck deep inside.

"Another Blue Angel original will come on stage for you. She's all hardcore and punk-anger. Naamah, the bride of Satan, the seductress demon, the mother of divination. She comes hot in your dreams, steals your desires, then leaves you for dead. Very nice, ain't she? Let's welcome Naamah, my promiscuous wife, who comes with a flute made from bone and a knife made for bones." The barker tipped his head toward the shadows of the stage and retreated to the side with a half-smile on his lips. A smile which read: *I like to watch, the bloodier the better.*

Naamah crawled across the stage, not on her hands and knees, but with her entire body wriggling on the wooden-acoustic floor and propelling herself forward with her elbows. Hissing and snarling along the way.

Beastly looking too, with her feral yellow eyes and wildly dishev-eled hair as if she hadn't washed or combed her straw-blond hair in months. Naamah reminded Rani of her sister, maddened and darkly sadistic and completely alluring.

She wore a simple dress of thin white cotton, which, as she stood, showed all the dust of the stage and the carnations of her nipples.

"My song for all the dead boys," she said with husky voice.

Lifting the hollowed-tibia flute to her generous lips, she blew a screeching note and then played the most beautifully haunting song. Rani found herself enmeshed in the flute sounds, exotic like warbling birds or melodically weeping angels.

The virtuosa told a story with her flute of bone. One laden with bruised skies and battered flesh, with ill-fated lovers decaying as licentious tangles in black sands, with the Fallen in sad watchful chorus. Rani saw and felt it all in her mind and heart. It seemed as if some of the notes were drawn from her, her sorrow flowing through her flesh and into the air. Sharply.

Her hypnotic flute ended. Rani lost her balance and fell against the wall like a puppet whose strings had been carelessly dropped. She had been entranced, held up by mere harmonious airs.

And then knocked down even further by Naamah's song of oper-atic screams. Rani covered her ears and watched in morbid curiosity as Naamah raised the knife and brought it down upon herself.

In a frenzy, she cut away her dress. Cutting, slashing, slicing, shredding fabric in psychopathic abandon. Cutting even after tatters were strewn at her feet like crushed white roses and she stood naked on the stage.

Silver flashed again and again into her. Her screams pierced into the audience again and again, and everyone flinched with each strike and sound.

Naamah cut her vanilla cream skin. With artistry and madness, she created red graffiti on her round breasts and belly, all soft and budding like a prepubescent girl's. The man beside Rani giggled quietly and rubbed himself. *Rubbing, rubbing.* Old George had taken her hand and made her feel his erection, running her hand as if up and down a broom handle. *Rubbing, rubbing.* Acid burned in her throat. Her hands trembled for the knife on stage, itching for her own performance and force her urges on any pedophile.

But the knife stayed in Naamah's hands.

And then stabbed into her genital slit.

The audience cowed, heads turned, arms thrown up, gasping but watching with peripheral and stolen attentions. Intensely, with carrion decadence.

Naamah masturbated with the blade, ramming it back and forth as if trying to saw herself in half. With furious thrusts, she fucked her nine-inch cock of steel. Crimson cum snaked down her thighs.

Instinctively, Rani cupped her hands between her thighs and squeezed her legs together, cringing as she imagined the keen pain. Near impossible to turn away, but she couldn't continue to watch. Too interested in the knife and the sex and the blood.

But, after exiting her voyeuristic chair and slipping behind the door and down the uneven stairs, she saw men and women engaged in another rollick of knives, sex and blood.

Rani walked as if through a libidinous temple of ritual sodomy and orgy. She reeled in the heavy scents of sweat, juniper-oiled bodies, cum and blood.

Men fucked women in the ass. Women, with the use of strap-ons, fucked men in the ass.

"Give praise to Asherah and Baal," they moaned.

One man laid upon the bondage bed, pulling tight on his wrist and ankle straps, while his lover made razor cuts on his twitching cock. She sucked the gushing cuts, and, arching his back, he gasped in desirous pain.

"Blood sacrifice," he said, eyeing Rani, breathing hard as his lover attended to his scarlet-shiny cock.

In a festal circle, one beautiful woman handed a polished cylinder of wood to another.

"The Asherah will bless you," she said.

And the recipient inserted the pillar as if it were a dildo, moving it in and out, bucking her hips and deeply accepting the idol. She fingered her clit as she thrust the idol.

Enthralled by her rapid breathing and aching moans, the women who knelt by her side served her pleasure as well, running nails along her smooth back, nibbling the curve of her neck, fondling and sucking her porn-ample breasts. The Asherah worshiper shuddered. She pulled out the twelve-inch pole and offered it to her neighbor, who smiled and licked the whitish fluids from the idol, partaking of sacred communion of the womanly fruit before paying the same homage to the Goddess of sex and fertility.

Round and round, in and out, the Asherah went. Blessing the circle, and adoration glowed on every face, cheeks rosy from vigor and arousal, eyes sated but sparkling with lust renewed.

Rani continued through the flesh-banquet of Gomorrah. She had been feeling the vibrations of the tribal techno-trance drums in her feet since she stepped in the room and expected the floors and walls to shake apart as the ancient city had for the shameless debauch.

In the back of the fetish temple, a statue of Asherah sat upon a sphinx-flanked throne, nude with prominent breasts and a bloodied pubic triangle.

. . . the lurid womb and the waste she birthed . . .

The Goddess likeness held bowls under her pierced breasts, which fountained with cardinal milk, and the bowls spilled over with this ever-flowing, life-promising drink. Beneath the bowls crowded men and women. With upturned heads and opened mouths, they caught the overflow, and their faces were beastly with red-splashed chins and hungry eyes.

Rani gasped. *Michael.* In the feral midst. His head being forced under the rich-bodied spills by her gothic sister of the moon.

Her heart jerked into her throat. With jerkier steps, she drew closer to the fountain and smelled the pungent copper of the milk. *Blood*.

"*Taste*," the shadows of unseen angels hummed in her ear. "*Taste the milk of the Mother of gods and of the sons of gods.*"

And invisible hands of talons hooked into her and lowered her into bloody shower.

Rani tasted myrrh and meat.

Someone took her hand and held it gently, and she turned her head from the warm intoxicating flows. She locked eyes with Michael. He looked at her as if his eyes were sponges and soaking her in, as if sight alone could bring her soul into him and make them one.

Pulling her against him, he kissed her. Their tongues touched and explored all the copper in their mouths, and Rani felt the kiss ignite all the way down to her belly, breathtaking butterfly-fires.

She felt every beat of his heart, every ounce of his breath and love, in that kiss.

Other hands besides Michael's stretched her waistband over her full-moon belly and tugged the skirt down her legs. Reluctantly, Rani pulled away from Michael and glanced at who undressed her.

The glitter-eyed Asian beauty winked.

Then lowered her mouth and breathed onto Rani's pussy, warming it with the lightest of touches.

She whispered, her voice soft like the hissing fountain, "You've heard of the 'Vagina Monologues,' the play?"

Rani nodded as Michael nuzzled her neck, kneaded her swollen breasts, and scratched her sides. She arched her back, turned on by his attention and her fascination with this girl.

"Well, I want to have a dialogue with your vagina," she said, grinning with that mouth made for devouring. "I will be the man."

She kissed Rani's labia, then licked between the lips.

Rani flinched in surprise but recovered quickly, spreading her legs for her, utterly curious and wanton.

Teasingly, the darkwave girl parted her pussy with her fingers but licked in the sensitive space between leg and labia. Rani giggled and squirmed.

"Such pretty pain, you deserve romance and poetry recited

from *Jezebel A Norman Latin Poem.*" Her words were hot upon Rani. In a man's deep-vibrating tone, she spoke. "What do you seek constantly?"

"To be mounted, pressed down," she answered in a husky mimic of Rani's voice.

Her hands pushed her legs as far apart as the bones and ligaments would allow and held her open. She plunged her mouth upon Rani, her tongue stroking her clit with small, softly pressured circles. Rani succumbed to the little twitches and twinges in her groin, moaning. Not wanting to be left out, Michael gripped her hair and crushed his lips against hers, as if his mouth were mounting her and pressing down. She was held at both ends, dominated top and bottom. She shivered in delight.

Her body flushed excitedly, and her nipples sprang hard and tingly. Between her legs, that tongue flicked with the surging beat of her heart, then worked faster and faster like some kind of organic vibrator. Rani was on the quickened edge. Losing control, unable to stop the orgasm that was starting.

"Tell me: why commit adultery?" Again, the man.

"Let the fire of the vulva respond to that."

Something thick, long and slippery pushed inside her tightening vagina, stretched her vaginal opening until the stinging nerves numbed, and rammed against her G-spot, unrelenting and hyper-stimulating.

Something alive, with teeth.

Rani shrieked as this something ravaged inside her.

Still, her cunt muscles quivered and coiled in climax as her blood sister kept at it, lips locked, tongue performing deep cunnilingus torture. She came in blood. Streams of it spilled from the corners of the girl's wicked mouth and down Rani's legs.

Then the mysterious girl withdrew and walked away with twinkling eyes and a red mouthful. Shedding skin along the way from the light of the room and disappeared into darkness.

CHAPTER TWENTY

A sad tale's best for winter.
I have one of sprites and goblins.

Shakespeare, The Winter's Tale

At round earth's imagin'd corners, blow
Your trumpets, angels, and arise, arise
From death, you numberless infinities
Of souls.

Donne, Holy Sonnets

I.

Advancing within a foot, the faces of the dark dwellers showed the grime of the rails and hardships, not the char of another underworld's fires. These were not the peckish eyes of the damned but the phlegmatic eyes of the despaired looking for the angel of mercy.

Anguish emanated from their bodies as if someone had torn open their chests, cracked their sternums, and aired their hearts of their sicknesses. Anguish which smelled sulphuric because of pain-rotted insides.

Bodies of earth, souls of hell, Shemyaza mused.

The sons of Adam approached him first, prodding, poking, pulling like curious children encountering a new insect. He endured the cruel touches. Man had ways of tearing things apart, and he felt the flesh of his foot inch away from the bolt as they piled their weight upon him. Blood bubbled and boiled in the wound.

Shemyaza shifted, using the torque of the men to assist in freeing his foot from the railroad tie.

Scampering beneath his swinging form, the daughters of man swung their heads and followed his face with theirs, tongues licking cankered lips, fire in their eyes they had thought had long ago expired, in the days when they had homes and beds instead of streets and sewers to roam. The Fallen Angel, despite their fishy wombs and lice-matted hair, found himself desirous of their banal charms.

One mite of a woman snatched a feather from his wing. She grinned a mouthful of plaque-black teeth and held up her prize, a peacock plume of pure white with a dazzling sapphire eye.

"It winked at me," she said, her voice pneumonic.

"Look . . . tears," another woman remarked, pointing. The scabious skin on her fingers, hand, and wrist made it seem as if silvery barnacles had grown upon her.

Like ink on a quill, a single drop of gold lingered at the shaft tip, waiting for the trash-bag bohemian to pen a flagrant ode into the greasy parchment of flesh.

"Nope, looks like piss."

"Piss off, ain't piss. Angels don't piss . . . "

"Sure, the rains . . . the Old Man is snoring, it's pouring, it's pouring . . . "

"Tears then, you pisser. Rain's angel's weeping."

The woman with the quill shrugged. "Water's water." And sipped at the needle-hollow shaft until the whites of her eyes were marbled with veins of gold. Immortal blood poisoned her mortal body. Her skin rippled as if marbles were boiling under her skin, and, from her eyes and nose, viscid fluids streaked golden-red down her smudgy face.

In seconds, her flesh alchemized into bloody-sunset slime and then evaporated into old-gold flecked clouds.

"Oh, Jasper," the barnacled lady mumbled, her flaky skin all speckled silver and gold, her eyes without a single sparkle. "You's right. Was piss. Bad piss."

She pinched the angel's lips. "You's been drinking gasoline?"

Shemyaza grabbed the diseased daughter, hugged himself against her and twisted, using her as a brace. Her spine twisted as well, and she screamed, blasting breath and blood that smelled of rotting apples and worms.

Pieces of his foot flesh plopped onto the ground, sizzling. The rest of him fell with an earth-cracking thud. Drawing his knee, he held onto his ankle and hissed because it felt as if he had dipped his foot into the shallows of the lake of fire. Throbbing sine waves of pain coursed through his lower leg as the injured flesh burned away and new flesh formed.

Unfortunately, the Fallen Watcher, in the earth realm, needed some earthen time to heal celestial wounds. He watched the azure fire smolder and waited for it to cool into flesh. On an astral level, he watched the mother of his son, her belly round as the earth, her legs spotted a disturbing red, and sweated his wait.

II.

The rustle of dead flesh reminded Julian of the mountains, of the vapid snap of fallen pine needles underfoot. He missed the piquancy of the pine forest, the way it made him feel, lightheaded, lighthearted, as if his body was but a vessel of prayer to be lifted from the mountain's steeple and carried by the sweet-wood scented winds of angels into God's golden kingdom.

But the wind carried only the smell of winter and decay into the crypt.

However the wind was not as silent as winter or decay. Julian smiled at the hissing and rattling winds, at the song of snakes, at the coming of Lilith.

He walked out of the vault and embraced the sibilant winds, feeling Lilith within, the demon of chilling wind. She returned his embrace and laced her etheric fingers against his nape, then icily tickled down his spine. Shivering and tight-lipped, he shrugged the cold of her off.

The wind flurried about and away, and the shade of Lilith appeared.

"You brought me the blood of the Jezebel?"

Dropping the darkness from her like a black negligee, she sidled up to Julian, wrapped her arms under his arms and around his shoulders, and pressed her awesome nudity against him. Lilith squeezed him and her soft breasts yielded to his taut muscles, and he found himself yielding to her as well, unable to pull from her embrace, an embrace that felt like it went beyond flesh, which would make them one. He reeled in her intimate presence. Because she wore the perfume of pine and the face of his dead wife.

"Of courssssssse," she slurred in his ear, brushing cheek against cheek.

Elise's cheek, silky warm again not clammy cold.

No, he told himself. Don't fall for the demon's deceits.

But he had forgotten how good it felt to hold his wife, and he didn't have the will to give it up so soon, illusion or not. It would be as real as he wanted it to be. The ironic power of the mind.

Tender ache in his heart, Julian encircled one arm around her waist and held her head against him as if enfolding them together. He felt the skin shift beneath his fingers as Lilith conformed herself to his memory of Elise, the unique silk of Elise's skin, softer than any other woman he had ever known and as unblemished as her soul.

She too sought the divine.

And, on a summer's night, with the moon and stars as bright witness, with the dark pine woods in protective attendance, they had sought to bring the divine into the child they were trying to conceive.

#

Facing the Qabalistic cross set in the east, with the dagger in his hand, Julian touched his forehead and said, "Atoh."

He touched his heart and said, "Malkuth."

He touched his right shoulder and said, "Ve Geburah."

He touched his left shoulder and said, "Ve Gedulah."

Again he touched his heart and said, "Le-olam."

And pointed the dagger inward, saying, "Amen."

With the dagger, he traced the banishing pentagram into the earth, whispering the consonant name of God, and thrust it into the heart of the five-pointed star.

He turned south and thrust the dagger into the air.

"Adonai."

He turned west and did the same.

"Ehich."

To the north, he honored Agla.

Returning the dagger to his breast, Julian imagined a flaming circle of four pentacles spinning in the air around him, fiery wheels as if from cherubic chariots. He stood with his arms straight out, his body like a cross on Golgotha.

"Before me Raphael. Behind me Gabriel. At my right shoulder stands Michael, and, on my left, Auriel stands."

"Before me flames the pentagrams. Behind me shines the six-rayed Star."

Julian faced the Qabalistic cross and recited the call of the 30th key, "Madrariatza das perifa TEX cahisa micadazoda saamire caosago od fifsa balzadizodarasa Iaida."

Then he knelt in front of Elise and touched her radiant face, marveling as he always did at the softness of her skin. Her eyes sparkled like blue stars. She wanted his as much as he did, and it excited him even more to be here with her performing the ultimate sex ritual.

Gently, he kissed her lips. For minutes they stayed like this, lips barely touching yet trembling, eyes closed yet envisioning the Shekinah, the manifesting light of God which they would call into their union.

Julian and Elise breathed as one. Deep breaths of spirit, of energy, of their power combined and doubled, because magick was synergistic and the power conjured up was geometric.

The wind became like a third pair of hands, caressing and teasing delicious shivers along bare skin, and he was chilly and hot all at once, feverish with desire. His fingertips flowed where the wind had aroused, circling her hardened nipples, tracing the curve of her firm breasts and the goose bumped trail down her velvety belly.

He stroked her downy labia. He thumbed the nub of her clit.

Her breath quickened, became more shallow, and the blue of her eyes deepened in their star-fire. The look she burned into him quickened his breath as well, and he inserted a finger into the core of her heat, deeply, roughly, coyly shocking her sensitive G-spot and withdrawing.

Elise gasped, then kissed him hard on the mouth. Her hand slid up and down his erection, stopping at the head, squeezing, tightening her grip as she thrust her hand downward again. She pulled on him as if she were trying to pull him into her.

Groaning, he felt the head of his penis rub between her warm wet labia. She tortured him this way, using his penis as a masturbating tool.

Julian felt the tension build as his testicles drew up and balled. Blood pounded through his groin, and all he wanted was to thrust into Elise and ride the rocketing explosion, but it was too soon. Before he backed away, he teased himself by pushing into her, only the head, only inside an inch, but that inch was moist, warm, tight. The perfect ring for friction.

"I love you," he murmured, pulling from the quiver and clench of her.

"Mmmmm, and I you."

He showered her angelic, moon-illumined skin with kisses and touches, and her giggles flirted upon the night winds. Hours passed as they explored and exhausted themselves in sensual drama. Their bodies ached for release, being brought close so many times only to quell the genital-coiling tension.

The night, breathing hard winds, watched on, and the moon hung low on the horizon, flushed bright and swollen as if with excitement.

In his mind, he pictured the daughters of the moon, carefree and celestial, carried down upon its silver-white rays, enamored with his Elise, their sister. Touching her secret places with borrowed light. Blessing their union of darkness and light, of feminine and masculine, of yin and yang, of all opposing yet balancing and perfecting elements.

He bowed between her legs, licking, tasting, toying with her, and her arousal struck him like an open lotus flower, heady and wanton. Elise spread her thighs, opening herself further for him.

Drunk on her, Julian lifted his head and brought his body upward, mouth pressing upon mouth, heart beating against heart. He held her as he rolled onto his back.

Without prompting, Elise drew herself up and straddled him. She lowered herself onto his heaven-pointed penis, slowly taking all of him in, making a face as she did, as if it pained and delighted her at the same time.

Neither moved.

No rocking of hips, no thrusting.

Nothing, save the powerful throb of their blood and energy.

The wind wisped through her hair, and she looked down upon him an angel, with her golden halo of hair and her moonlight-banded eyes.

Behind her, in the backdrop of the heaven-dark, the stars shifted like scintillating spiders of light crawling across the tangled black web. Weaving round and round. Spinning shrouds of chaos. Whirling down, down, down.

Like chakras of the world, he thought.

Julian gazed into the empty space of the spiraling light, into the humming dark vacuum that was descending upon them. Hairs stood upon their ends. The air crackled and his skin tingled as if he'd run his whole body across a static-hot television screen. A screen as wide as the sky.

Hypnotized by the show of whirling light and white noise, he hadn't noticed the rhythm of their hips. Quick and swirling like the light. Controlled by a higher force, the same invisible force that directed the winds and the stars.

The light whirled down upon them.

Whirling in white and then in all the colors of the earth, sea and sky, and of all the living creatures within.

Elise's flesh reflected the light and its heat. Julian gasped in the pain of coupling with her.

But he climaxed nonetheless.

"Madrariatza das perifa TEX cahisa micadazoda saamire caosago od fifsa balzadizodarasa Iaida."

And the whirling light sucked in his seed and went utterly black.

Black as the burns on his hips and thighs, as the burns he didn't want to see on his penis.

Black as death.

Black as the primal face of God.

Transcended into another state of mind, each dwelling on the obscure light and its rapturous grin, Julian and Elise collapsed into each other's arms, curling together within their protective circle, and slept with open eyes. Cool dew blanketed their fervid skin. The mountain breeze chilled them further, but neither budged in their loose embrace. Too shocked, too exhausted in mind, body, and soul.

Breath and heartbeat were unperceivable, their bodies entranced by the transfusion of otherworldly energy. *The Shekinah.* Surging through their veins, making them sluggish, nearly comatose, with the peace of heaven.

Immobile and feeling buoyant as if cradled in the womb again, Julian listened to the voice and the commandments.

And Jephthah made a vow to the Lord and said, "If you will give the Ammonites into my hand, then whoever comes out of the doors of my house to meet me, when I return victorious from the Ammonites, shall be the Lord's, to be offered up by me as a burnt offering."

So Jephthah crossed over to the Ammonites to fight against them; and the Lord gave them into his hand.

Then Jephthah came to his home at Mizpah; and there was his daughter coming out to meet him with timbrels and with dancing. She was his only child; he had no son or daughter except her.

When he saw her, he tore his clothes and said, "Alas, my daughter! You have brought me very low; you have become the cause of great trouble to me. For I have opened my mouth to the Lord, and I cannot take back my vow."

Julian felt a heart-hiccup within his chest. A bubble of fear.

The spirit of the Lord came upon you and has delivered his peace into your hand.

For your own lifeblood he will surely require a reckoning: he will require a reckoning for human life.

By morning, in the golden dawn, the voice dissipated with the dew. Elise had gone as well. At least in spirit, because her body lay stiffening and cold to touch.

He removed his hands.

But her neck still sported the bruises of his fingers.

#

Tightening his hold on the Lilith-Elise, Julian wanted never to lose the feel of her silken skin again. Too long the cold, clammy horror of throttling . . . *reckoning* . . . her flesh haunted his hands. He buried his face in her nape and smelled the odor of reptiles, and his breath hitched as if he would weep, knowing the illusion would not hold.

"Husssssh," she said, lifting his fallen face.

And then again, nightmare ever-repeating, Lilith was kissing him and spitting the blood of another into his mouth.

III.

The necromancer cut into his abdomen. At first, the knife merely pulled upon his leathery skin, and he felt nothing more than if the necromancer tugged his shirt tails from his waistband.

But . . .

Then the knife cut deeper and hands tore open the flaps of his dead flesh, and hands hollowed out the filaments of his entrails. Blood, by the smell, was spat into his body cavity. By touch, it was worms that seeped into his dry decay and fed frenziedly on what was being made wet again.

"Accept this blood of the Lady Babylon, Ancient One, Chaos, the All-Father. Accept this Cup of thy servant."

The strike of a match made the corpse tremble. All those times he struck the match and laid the flame upon the dead. *Ppphhhttt* into screaming ashes.

He grunted as the necromancer stabbed the knife into his chest and rotated the blade, sowing a hole for the worm garden. Hot worms, smelling of wax and sulphur, spilled into his abscessed rock of a heart. Writhing upon the slab, the corpse choked on the waxen plug poured down his mouth and throat. Without screams and infested with wormy torture, he hadn't left Hell at all.

Liar, liar, necromancer.

Oh, but didn't he know the lies. The damnable lies.

"By witness of the Powers of Air, I mark upon the seal the sign of the Brotherhood."

His third eye spied the burning pyramid and sun in the ether spinning down upon him. Spinning so fast it looked like the six-pointed star of David. The sign struck him with all its points of teeth and zeal.

"By the power of the sign and seal of the Brotherhood, I, Master of Magick, hold thee, Jon Weir, bound in slavery and agony. From the darkness I brought thee and to the darkness shall return thee, if thy fail my command."

The necromancer crowded his mind and his body, leaning in as if to examine him, as if to dissect him even further. Instead he threaded yarns of darkness through his wrists and ankles, around his neck, and connected them with this leash.

"Arise by the blood and the bone."

Bones were dumped into his vivisected gut, clattering like strange hard laughter.

"Arise by the froth of a rabid dog."

Upon his mouth, the necromancer smeared the bitter, burning poison. He shook in agony, ghoul-rattling the bones within him, the steam of silent screams rising off his grotesquely stretched mouth. He was a kettle without a whistle.

"Arise by the sloughed scales of the snake."

His skin crawled and itched as if covered with snakes and worms. There was no escaping Hell.

Needles and thread crawled through his skin as well.

"By the grant of the Prince of Powers, I command thee, Jon Weir, arise. Arise a darker dawn and eclipse the Lady Babylon's son."

The corpse rose. In his hand, the necromancer placed the key, which he traced with his thumb. No grooves along this key, only the curve of a very sharp blade, which sliced into his bloodless skin.

In a rattle-lumber, he exited the crypt, every step causing pain as the bones in his foot loosed from rotted ligaments speared his soles. The necromancer's spell pulled him onward and faster. Faster and faster, until he was running as swift as the Powers of Air.

He ran with furious pain. He ran with the wrath of a rabid dog, mouth foaming blood and froth, mouth in feral need to rip into meat and tear it apart. Grabbing at his wiry tufts of hair, the corpse pulled and yanked and tore in soundless snarls. He looked a whirlwind of dementia, his legs pumping, his arms flailing, dust and rot wetted with her blood arcing into the air.

But it felt better for him to tear loose, to destroy.

Faster and faster, he ran. Spurred on by the nearing scent of her blood and his pain-relieving need to rip into her.

CHAPTER TWENTY-ONE

And All shall be smitten with fear,
And the Watchers shall quake,
And great fear and trembling shall seize them
Unto the ends of the earth.

Book of Enoch

I.

Rani stared dumbly at the black space where the . . . the . . . she had no idea what . . . disappeared.

"She wasn't human," Michael whispered in her ear, nuzzling into the crook of her neck.

"What then?"

But before he could answer, others had gathered round the fountain, eager for the drama and the blood of her cunt.

Her crimson sprinkled thighs were still spread as if she was offering communion.

One woman dropped to her knees and crawled toward Rani, sucking on her lower lip. Cat-o'-nine-tails marked her back in a splay of sordid crimson whip-scratches. Beneath these marks, old bruises of yellow beatings faintly showed.

"He comes," the woman whimpered. "We've been neglect in our sacrifices."

She greedily eyed the mound of Rani's belly.

"I smell him, the sweet fruit of his loins. I hear him, the buzzing of his anger."

Backing against Michael, Rani scrambled to shift back into her skirt. The woman stopped short of them and cocked her head.

Others in the room followed her lead, dropping in supplicant poses, listening for something inaudible to Rani.

"The Dark Beast," Michael groaned.

"The Lord Ba'al," the woman corrected him. "Ba'al zebub, the lord prince. He comes. What has been sown in his name must be harvested. She warned us."

Tremors passed beneath the floor.

The electricity was cut, and a hefty draft blew out the candles, throwing them all in the dark. Someone tittered, and a buzzing treble rode that giggle. Indeed, her skin vibrated as if static bombarded her. Or flies, the way the air buzzed, the way it crawled across and creepily tickled every inch of her flesh.

Something howled. Something that cut the stifling, static dark and seemed to fill the entire room and more.

In her womb, the unborn kicked and kicked, running from the terror felt in every ounce of her blood.

Then screams filled the room, and Michael gripped her arm and dragged her away. Somehow he found the exit and pushed through, and she couldn't help but glance back.

Even in the sliver of light, the slicks of gore were oily-black. But the shadowy loom of that terrifying something was bloodier and blacker.

Rani squeaked in fear.

Michael looked back, his face glistening with sweat, his eyes glistening with terror.

"Let them be enough as an offering to Aliyan Ba'al."

Up the narrow steps, through the door, and around the stage, they ran, both imagining the Lord storming upon their heels. Nothing but darkness and screams followed. The audience assumed some hidden act went on, another illusion of some horror being played for their shock and benefit, and they relished their goose bumps. Such gruesome promise in those screams, screams which punched like a fist against their sternums and nearly stopped their hearts. With mad-touched grins, they perched upon their seats in anticipation. Only the barker and the true performers looked concerned.

One security guard stepped in their path.

"What's going on down there?"

"Sacrifice," Michael shouted as he tried to push the block of muscle out of the way.

The beefy guard roughed Michael against the wall. "If you hurt anyone, I'll smash in your face."

Michael laughed, which earned him an elbow under the chin.

"I hurt them all by failing to keep the gates sealed and released the alter ego of a god."

"You're fucking whacked."

"Yes, yes," Michael laughed again.

Tears of tension slipped from the corners of his eyes, and Rani placed her hand upon the security guard's chiseled biceps and said, "Let him go."

Perhaps something in her voice or eyes persuaded him to let Michael go.

But then perhaps it was the way the air thickened about them, smelling of sweet smoke and hissing.

The bouncer flinched and ducked as if something swooped over his head. Rani thought she'd heard the ring of a sword.

Behind them, the stage door splintered apart. Bits of wood propelled into the audience, though hurting no one. The people sat stunned as darkness strode onto the stage. Darkness which flowed like robes in the wind about a massive man.

Several bold women approached the stage, eyes mesmerized by the strange man's unearthly beauty and palpable sexuality.

" . . . as an offering to Aliyan Ba'al . . . "

Rani noticed his feet and hands weren't human but like lion's paws, and his teeth were fanged and dripping. A dark beast indeed. The prince of beasts, with the prince of all erections.

No doubt why the women were drawn to him, that bull-huge cock bobbing before them and needing *an offering to Aliyan Ba'al*.

Nudging, hands inhuman and unseen ushered her from the club. Even in the stale cold, she smelled the presence of the Grigori and waited for them to appear, but only the swirls of snow paraded before her smoke-stinging eyes.

"Why don't they show?" Michael asked, clinging close behind, his finger still hooked through a belt loop.

"I don't know." She felt their eyes upon her though. Watching and waiting.

Cupping her belly, she knew what they waited for. Already, the seams of her skirt were spreading and thin-bare, the same as the skin of her belly felt. The unborn had dropped into her pelvic region. A little quirk of panic jittered in her mind because the head was humongous, bigger than a bowling bowl between her legs. He would split her in two.

At the thought, her pelvic bones ached. Images of her sister snapping apart her Barbie dolls' legs scared into her mind. Always, only one leg could be torn away, and her sister would cry and rail, all the while hammering the one leg, with its white socket plug like a disc of hip bone, against her head.

"Sometimes we must destroy in order to create new life," she had said. "Something your sister knew well."

Winds hustled through the street and carried away the scent of myrrh. Cold nipped at her again as if with the teeth of angels.

Rani wrapped her arm around Michael, snuggled against his emanating heat, and walked to the corner, glancing warily at the Masonic Temple, feeling a deeper chill, as they passed.

"What do you know of that?" She pointed to the sign, the staring pyramid.

"Well, I believe, in Freemasonry that the glowing pyramid and eye stands for the 'Great Architect of the Universe.' The eye in the pyramid goes back to ancient Egyptian times—the all-seeing eye of Horus. It's like some kind of warning, 'The eye of the world is watching.'"

The wind shivered down her nape as the eye watched them sweep by.

"And, as God watches man, the Freemasons strive to behold the glories and splendor of heaven with unveiled eyes." Michael spoke as if reading from a recruiting pamphlet, his voice theatrically poised. "But the Brotherhood is blind to their greed. Many of the power-hungry, well-heeled politicians in Washington have taken their masonic oaths."

"And then you have the famous Freemasons who were versed in matters of the occult. John Dee, with his Qabalistic and Rosicrucian arcana, served as Queen Elizabeth's astrologer and spy—signed his correspondences 007. With Edward Kelley, a grave-robber, necromancer and alchemist, he immersed himself into Enochian magic. Together they extracted the alphabet of the angels and inspired a new Hermetic order in their wake. Once, and this if funny, Kelley informed Dee that the angels had visited and told him they should swap wives. Dee actually went along with this." Michael chuckled.

"I think they killed Stephan."

"What?? Dee and Kelley?"

"No, this Brotherhood." She pointed back to the foreboding sign.

"Why, Rani?? As far as I know, Masonic rites don't include child sacrifice. They don't worship olden gods like Ba'al who demand blood tithes." His voice trembled.

"No, the Brotherhood didn't sacrifice our son for any god. They have stolen his body—I have found his coffin empty——and hold him like a prisoner in darkness under some horrid ransom until I concede to them."

"Concede how?"

"His murderer has told me, 'Come to light, come to death.' Where I should go, I have no clue, but I am sure has something to do with this light." Rani pointed to the sign of the glowing pyramid. "I dreamed of this sign before, and it was carried upon golden staffs by men who built temples from flesh and bone."

Brushing both hands through his hair, Michael stared at the sign and frowned.

"Long ago, I met an initiate of the Brotherhood." he started, chewing on his lips as he spoke. "At the time I thought he was tripping on acid, the way he babbled on about the Masonry, how man was a living stone, rough and unhewn, but through death would be polished and made perfect, and how from the material of the physical body they planned on building the deathless body. What they called 'Solomon's Temple.'"

Strange jolts of images ran through Rani's head. *Demons, flying sands, gold, stones and bones and a king commanding it all.* Temple of Solomon. Temple for Asherah.

"Oh damn." He gripped her shoulder and turned her toward him, his face snowy-pale. "They're necromancers. When you 'go" to death, they will cut you open, pull your organs from your body, and study your inner light, your wisdom which radiates in your flesh."

"But what knowledge would I have? And why not stick me with sodium penthanol?" she asked.

"The power to call the angels who know the secrets to all things. And these things can only be gotten from your dead body, not your mind." Michael hugged her tight against him and kissed the top of her head. "But will the angels keep you safe from them?"

"I don't know. For all the power and wisdom I supposedly have, I don't know much of anything."

Except that enlightened men and darkened sisters kill.

II.

Glass shattered.

His pain shattered.

Reaching through, the corpse unlocked the back door of the brownstone. He pushed open the door and stepped inside, broken glass crunching under foot. Slippery glass.

As he stooped, the bones sewn within his abdomen protested with a clatter and poke through his skin. He swept his hand along the floor, and the point of a large shard stuck into his fingertip. This he palmed and put to his eyes. Severing threads of those funeral lashes.

The corpse blinked. Empty sockets filled with conjured sight.

The floor looked littered with ice, with the footprints of winter, with the footprints of something cold and deadly.

Within the kitchen, the moon cast bluish and hoary light, and he lifted his hands. He flipped them over and over, aghast at the appearance of his flesh, of what could barely be called flesh at all, more like the dry mold of compost.

The key he held in his hand glinted savagely. He had a mind to raze the horrid flesh from his hand and whittle the phalange bones into points. At least then he could pick the pain from his flesh.

Following his instinct and the necromancer's command, he moved toward the back room, where her smell permeated all the way down to the fibers of the carpet. He liked her smell. Clean, healthy, somewhat floral like his lady. But it intensified his pain. The smell, the memory.

He clutched the key so tightly a few knuckles cracked open.

How long would he have to wait? He couldn't bear a long wait because the pain would drive him to destroy himself before long.

The scrape of a key in a lock answered him.

The corpse wouldn't wait long. Soon he could rid himself of the pain.

And he tucked himself into the closet, hiding within the folds of her fears and the dead butterflies he sensed in there, waiting in rabid tension, much like the sister she feared.

III.

Thorns from wind-blown rose branches shrieked along the brick as Michael carried Rani up the steps. She had fallen asleep in the cab, and he hadn't the heart to wake her. The skin beneath her eyes had grayed since he'd last seen her, only an afternoon, which felt like an eternity, and she had an aura which weighed upon her, no doubt anchored down by the impressive weight she bore.

. . . the offspring of flesh and spirit . . .

The sound of the thorns reminded him too much of the sharp whispers of his scars, scars silenced forever now by sharper instruments. He was abandoned again, left alone to face the empty chimes.

His hand shaking, he struggled with sliding the key into the lock.

"Come on," he hissed, and then his hand obeyed and inserted the key. He pushed through the unlocked door, wincing as the door banged against the wall. With a downward glance, he checked to make sure Rani hadn't woken, but she slept on, not even stirring as he juggled her weight in his arms.

Michael hurried down the hall. His muscles were tiring and turning rubbery. Too much stress, too little food. He couldn't remember having eaten at all today, and he staggered into the bedroom, elbowing the light switch before collapsing with her upon the bed.

His arm draped across her abdomen, he laid there with her, staring dizzily at the crimson-spoked circle upon the ceiling, at the bloody wheel of life turning in a deadly evil spin. He thought of sacrifice and slaughter, of the angel-hybrid child that now knocked within her belly. Wanting out. Wanting the blood of all the men and women of the earth.

Rani groaned in her sleep and absently placed her hand upon her stomach. *Tic, tic* of her flesh as the monster within shifted. *Tick, tick,* only a matter of time before the rains of blood would begin.

He sat up. Her belly was a globe of the earth, terra sienna skin, blue-jade rivers of veins, fertile with expanding and evolving life.

Flood of blood . . . tides and tyrants of red . . . god dead, dead, dead . . .

Tentatively, he touched her belly that would birth nothing but blood and death.

He felt her heartbeat in his fingertips, rapid and strong, of blood raging through arteries and veins like pre-flood waters surging through channels.

And he understood his dreams finally. It was not the dark beast of Ba'al that would explode from her stomach in showers of blood, but this giant of an infant. And all the death it would bring.

But then the mercury of her womb and the silver of the child could bring immortality.

Standing, with bed springs complaining, Michael walked toward the closet and scanned the floor for the syringe. It had rolled into the corner, its needle pierced through a ball of dust. He picked it up, blew the dust from the tip, and stared at the steel promise of turning jade dreams into gold.

He patted his pocket. Paper crinkled, and his mind crumpled in conflict. Here, in his pocket, he had a page from the *Pao_p'u_tzu*, the formula for the *Chin-tan*, courtesy of the *hsien*.

There, on the bed, the magical harvest awaited.

Her expanded belly rose and fell with her labored breath. His doubts followed suit, pitching his mood up and down, and Michael twirled the syringe in his hand, same as he rolled the thoughts in his mind. *Would she survive it? Could he survive forever without her if not?*

Again, the dark beast called for a sacrifice. But this time the dark beast was him.

Sacrifice.

Once upon a time, he had stood within the nursery, the mark of blood frenzy upon his heart, the iron knife tight in his palm. He had watched Stephan sleeping, his little chest rising and falling, expelling milky breath.

Sacrifice, sang the winds and the shadows.

Sacrifice, he had repeated, stealing himself for the act, for the strength to make that fatal offering to Aliyan Ba'al.

He had raised the knife above the crib and struck the mobile, sending the stars and moon in a chaotic spin, disturbing the heavens. And he knew the only sacrifice he could make was himself.

On his chest, he had drawn the circle, the symbol for the gate, for the pomegranate and Ba'al as well, and called the red lord into him. As a gift for possession. Then he had raised the knife again, cutting wards and signs upon his back. Sealing the circle, the gate, the lord into him. And, by the power of the dead he raised again and again like the knife, he had kept the dark beast within.

But now, standing again with blood frenzy marked in his heart, Michael knew, even if he reined in the dark beast of the god, he would not be saved from himself. From the dark beast that he was. Hungry for sacrifice and immortality.

The needle was pointed at Rani, at the target of her bellybutton.

He took three steps toward her, hunting.

Scars or no scars, his skin itched with the voice of angry Watchers.

Sweet smoke came for him as the fallen angels drew the salts of the earth and the dust of the air to manifest bodies. Michael turned heel and ran from the room, and kept running from the house with the Fallen right behind, closer than his shadow had ever been.

IV.

Time was against the nature of angels.

And Time was against this angel.

There were no torrential rains and winds this time to drown out Shemyaza's cries, which circled the world seven times over.

V.

Of thundering torment and dark waves of bloody waters, she dreamed.

She lay beneath a yellow sky, on the shore of white sands of ground bone.

The children of the angels gathered around her, chests shrunken and showing prominent bars of malnourished cages, starving mouths and eyes agape. Darkness poured forth like tears, like screams. Like blood, filling the sea beyond the beach of bone.

"Open wounds never heal," the voice of midnight and murder murmured.

He was the wind. Cold and brutal.

He was the eye of the sun. Watching, waiting.

Waiting for her open wounds to shed light. Like blood.

Storm clouds break from the sky and fall in ashes and ashen butterflies. At the sight, her tongue cleaved to the roof of her mouth and her breath went away. The butterflies floated upon the winds of murder, their wings broken and still. They drifted and tumbled in the coiling winds, and wailed with crazy laughter.

As they landed upon her, she screamed.

Because the dead butterflies had millions of mouths with millions of teeth, and they were feeding upon her.

#

Waking with screams, Rani thought the nightmare had ended.

But the teeth still fastened upon her flesh. Tearing, it felt, through her abdomen.

She looked down, and her jaw worked up and down in noiseless terror.

A dead man perched on her lower half. A dead man, with empty eyes and rotten grin, was hacking at her stomach. Blood sprayed upward like little scarlet butterflies.

Shock obliterated any pain, and she watched the tiny brass scythe rise and fall with paralyzing idle torture, watched it cut away her flesh, her womb. Her baby.

He might as well as cut out her heart.

The son of the angel squirted from her punctured womb, sliding from his red sac in redder skins. The dead kept hacking at the aborted infant until only pooling bits of flesh remained. As red and slick as the satin sheets.

Rani screamed finally. In a pain that only equaled that of losing Stephan.

And the dead man opened his mouth, spilling worms and cries like her son's.

CHAPTER TWENTY-TWO

Regions of sorrow, doleful shades, where peace
And rest can never dwell, hope never comes
That comes to all.

Milton, Paradise Lost

What though the field be lost?
All is not lost; th'unconquerable will,
And study of revenge, immortal hate,
And courage never to submit or yield.

Milton, Paradise Lost

I.

Her screams broke the barrier of the walls and windows and shattered the night in an avalanche of icy horror. Michael froze in the street, paralyzed by the intensity of her screams, by the cold fear in his mind of what could've made her scream like that.

Showers of blood and death exploding from her body.

Winds of angels at his back turned him back toward the brownstone and pushed him forward.

Winds of angels at his back were furious and biting, and he faltered in his steps, stricken with the sharp snip of new scars forming. Scars with many mouths and many voices. Scars with teeth.

Scars of stygian stigmata. Marked, not for sacrifice, but for Hell. And the beginning of Hell was waiting inside.

II.

The slaughtered wasted him, and his frame of decay slumped onto the ground, worms of carrion cruelty spewing from his rot-riddled flesh like seedling masses sprouting from the dirt. Like the worms, his pain exited his body. Exited in an oozing filth, as if an enema had been preformed from both ends, hoses down his throat and in his collapsed sphincter flushing the shit he couldn't endure through his porous flesh.

In short time, the corpse was emptied, emancipated.

Except from the cold, cold corridor light of heaven that burned him into ashes and claimed the dust of him.

His spirit ascended with harps of screams.

III.

"Scream, scream, scream, all you want . . . " someone sang in her ear.

Blood in her throat though stanched her screams. Her diaphragm in tangles, Rani coughed without much force but still brought up more blood.

"Look upon me, whore."

Her cheeks were pinched between inhuman fingers. His touched burned without heat, and that hand with vermillion-tipped talons wrenched her head to the side.

Swathed in gold lumen of cloth and wing, the mighty angel was radiant beyond mere words. The sight of him pained her, as if her eyes would turn to ashes.

"Look upon me, who deals in death and destruction. Your death and destruction. Soon the beasts will devour you until nothing remains, not even your bones, and all who look upon you will say 'there lies the shadow of Jezebel.'"

The mighty angel removed his hand from her face, taking care to drag his talons along her jaw, down the gentle slope of her neck, around her left breast and side, between her mutilated thighs. Bending low, he pressed his jasmine-sweet mouth against her ear and laughed. Laughter that tingled and buzzed like Old George's.

Rani sputtered with semi-liquid breath, weeping, cursing at the commanding soldier of God.

"We give no sympathy for whores," he said.

And unsympathetic light filled the room. Other angelic beasts, with their halos, blood-bright teeth and misanthropic eyes, gathered around her death-strewn bed.

Despite their radiance, darkness was only visible as shades of death drew down upon her. As soul divorced matter and all other physicality.

She welcomed this, the lukewarm ooze of her blood and life, all her pain and madness escaping in succulent sighs. Her oblivion. Plum-dark and sweet.

But then the calm was disturbed by hot-frothy breath and the wet sounds of beasts opening their mouths.

As much as she hungered for the end party, they hungered for her.

IV.

Shemyaza arrived too late. He smelled the salty death of his son and crumpled to his knees, head bowed, unwilling to witness the massacre once again. His throat tightened with garrote-wire breath. His chest tightened with strangled heart. Deep inside his body, the ache of anger and hate intensified until all he could think of was vengeance, of an escalade into heaven and launching another war.

Sounds of feasting drew his attention.

Like pack-feeding dogs, the hayyoth huddled around the daughter who would've been the mother of the Nephilim. Shemyaza reviled the heavenly beasts. The hayyoth turned their heads of four faces toward him and snarled in red fits at the interruption.

Shemyaza thunder-rushed upon the Merkabah Cherubim. Swords sprang from the ether, two in each hand, one carried within his mouth and thrust forward, and he besieged them. Every strike was strengthened with his unbound rage.

Cherubic flesh blasted apart. Smoking bits of meat smacked against the walls and ceiling, and slid down, hissing and steaming in chunky rain.

Other hayyoth dropped in heavy heaps of wet bones.

But all the hayyoth met unpleasantly with his blades, and Shemyaza walked across the fresh cut flesh toward the bed.

Behind him, the other Grigori entered the room, shouts on their lips that made him believe in another war. And in triumph.

He touched the bed and recoiled. Beneath his fingers, the dregs and sludgy residue flowed like some gory stew spilling from the pot of her. Flotsam of his son cascaded over the edge of the bed, falling in loathsome gurgles and splashes, like the bubbling cries of the dying drowned.

Palming his ears, Shemyaza attempted to shun the sound, the sound of megadeath, of all the earth's children rolling under the ruddy waters of the flood.

Waters made ruddy by the treacherous right hands of God.

But he couldn't stop hearing what he couldn't forget.

He brought his hands down and placed them on her listless purpuric body. Her brutally injured womb was birthing blood and clots of her chopped placenta, a gruesome sign that her heart still pumped.

He was not too late to heal her.

Joined in effort by the fellow fallen, he repaired her womb, making her more than whole, making her fertile again. A ripe egg was nestled in her ovary, like a pearl within an oyster. Riches of a promised future.

She woke, eyelids fluttering, pupils dilating to pinpoints of focus. As if accessing her whereabouts, she blinked a few times and then her face withered into a falling mask of anguish. Mirror to his own. Tears rolled from the corner of her eyes. Shemyaza kissed her cheek; stuck out his tongue to catch the tear, her salt of suffering.

"Let me go! You should've let me go!"

She wailed. She pushed and punched with her small fists, and kicked, inflicting little harm upon them. But the Grigori backed away, confused by the chaotic twists of her arms and legs, by the bloody spittle flying madly from her mouth.

"There was no despair. No despair, do you hear me? Let me go. Undo your miracles," she cried, gouging her nails across her soft abdomen.

Shemyaza held back her hands. She thrashed upon the bed, torso

185

wrenching this way and that, head flinging fast and hard, and he thought her neck would soon snap from the force.

Clasping her hands within his as if in prayer, he told her, "There is always despair. Creation of life is but a violent union between energy and matter, a bad marriage rife with unhappiness, bitterness, resentment, and suffering. Not until death does the spirit depart from the matter. Even then . . . through destruction comes life."

She settled upon the blood-soaked sheets and looked into his peril-eyes without squinting, her eyes glazing though with stinging tears as the light of his eyes burned into hers.

"But I felt something waiting in the beyond, something wonderful," she said, averting her gaze. She stared at the Cherubic remains which now burned like coals, the smoke of the hayyoth rising with rumbling growls.

"Don't fool yourself in thinking heaven exists for man. In Paradise, you would stand alone."

"If Heaven exists, then where do all the good people go?"

Shemyaza half-smiled, pinned her arms above her head, and licked the colostrum that leaked from her nipples like honey. She squirmed beneath his razor-sharp tongue, moaning.

His lips wetted with her pre-milk, he said, "The faithful, the pure, the martyrs, and the saints get taken into heaven."

She looked at him perplexed.

"God must feed his children, his soldiers, something. What better than unspoiled meat?"

Her body trembled beneath him as the revelation sank in.

"What are we, fodder served raw or roasted?" She sneered.

Her ripening ovum sweetened the air with the saccharine perfume of a budding flower and its coy nectar, and the Seraphim was sick with desire, his erection sharp as the bee's stinger-barb. Man was meat, but woman was dessert.

"Not all. Some escape the snares of Yahweh and flee into the branches of the Tree of Life, into the arms of the Mother of God and the sons of God. Her branches and her trunk form the circle of everlasting life, and her fruit gives new life. But the tree stands guarded within the gardens of heaven, in the midst of a forest of ever-lasting darkness, and some find themselves lost forever."

Slipping from beneath him, she squatted by the bed and pushed the pieces of fetal gore together as if she were working on some elaborate puzzle. Sobs wracked her body. And, watching her, Shemyaza felt the sorrow well within him and subdue his desire.

He could not take her, not in her miserable state, not in his own.

"What happens to the innocent? Like my son, like ours?" Her voice had taken on a new quality, that of the hopeless, hollow and echoing.

The Fallen ached for her, for them, for all the children gone from the world.

And he couldn't answer her, couldn't voice what would've brought her further down.

With a start, Shemyaza realized he loved this daughter of man, that he cared for her and wished desperately to protect her from harm. He retracted his talons and caressed the soft angle of her cheek. Tears ran over his fingers, and it pained him as if her tears were crystal cutting through his flesh and becoming a wreath of barbs around his heart.

He kissed her forehead. She tilted her head, and her dewy eyes begged for him to *let her go*. How easy it would've been for his talons to spring outward and pierce through her skull, ending her life, her misery of memory. But he couldn't. No more than he could walk away from this room and its carnage, and forgive it all.

Upon her lips, another kiss, and he held the bond of their sadness until her body softened and succumbed to his embrace. She was tender and ripe, and he loathed to depart, but he needed to eradicate the threat to her and the would-be fruit of her womb.

Broken wheels overturn chariots.

Through the first heaven of clouds, through the second of stars, through the spiritual third, Shemyaza led the Watchers. The ether cracked apart, sounding as if glaciers were plowing through tundra. But it was only vengeful prodigal sons heading home.

#

The Grigori loitered in the fifth heaven, in the oily darkness of their prison, listening to the knelling swing of their chains that hung now broken and empty from the gallows of black. Breath shuddered through them. Memories of their dark silence of suffering congested the air.

And the longer they stayed, the more the vibration of the chains sounded like soft tinkling laughter and metallic hisses.

Slowly they moved through the fifth heaven, each of them fearing that the chains would reach down and shackle them again. Not an absurd fear either. All the things of heaven were many-eyed and ever-watchful, even chains, but especially the darkness which was but the pupil of God's ubiquitous eye.

But unhindered, the Grigori made their passage and found themselves shunted from the darkness into blazing light. They stood between the pillars of heaven, columns of fire that no longer seemed as awesome. Shemyaza thought, after coming back from being banished, that the sight of heaven would reduce him into a gibbering homesick child. But he beheld none of the grandeur his memory treasured.

The seven mountains of magnificent stones—pearl, jacinth, and other colored gemstones—were excessive, merely garish crown jewels of a pompous king. The middle mountain of alabaster, of gypsum ice, reached into the heavens, and on its summit of pure sapphire sat the gold throne of God. Of their omnipotent father who usurped El with the army he created and who imprisoned the Queen in the Tree of Life.

Beyond the mountains, there laid a vast region of opulent gardens, ever in bloom, with petals as splendid as precious stones. But none of the flowers possessed a fragrance. Only the Tree of Life gave forth wonderful fragrance, and it grew at the center of the gardens, its leaves and blooms and wood never withering. Angels guard it to keep mortals from the fruit, which once eaten, the fragrance would be in the bones, and there would be no sorrow or plague or torment of calamity on earth.

Shemyaza entered between the pillars of heaven and met with Uriel, the Watcher of thunder and terror, at the gates of the lost Eden.

"You are forbidden," the Seraph who gave the cabala to man said, drawing his fiery sword.

Shemyaza stepped forward. Uriel held his sword steady but did not strike, did not blink his moonstone eyes, did not thrust the flaming tip into his old leader's heart, even though he stood close enough for a ring of diamond blisters to form on his flesh.

"And you are forbidden to slay me without command. Step aside, Brother, for you've no word from our Father."

"I cannot."

"Very well." Shemyaza raised his sword. "Heaven has no command over me."

And swung the blade of mighty fire down upon Uriel's wrists, cutting clean away his hands and the sword he held which smoldered into the ground.

He knocked Uriel aside and walked through the drifts of Seraphical smoke and stench toward the awaiting gardens.

"You are forbidden," Uriel whined, his brow shriveled like the flowers scorched at his feet as he took in the sight of his ore-leaking stumps.

"The heaven which has forsaken me cannot forbid me."

Crushing flowers, he waltzed into the garden with pollen-dusted feet, with the bronzed feet of the Christ. His eyes were shooting stars of anger, and the children of heaven hidden within the plush greenery shuddered for fear of his judgement.

Shemyaza spied the seven Thrones lurking in the woven tendrils, their sad saucer-eyes of blue light looking like luminous flowers among the trumpet vines. They regarded the Grigori with a mixture of trepidation and scorn.

Nimbus-eyed and niveous-skinned, the Thrones were the beautiful forlorn. They cowered much like the pale orphans of earth, desperate for love, their provocative airs of innocence merely nets for vulgar abuse. Androgynously sexed, they appealed to any persuasion.

Bellows and bleats and insidious howls erupted further down the path.

Every shining white face turned toward the noise. Every shining eye shut in resignation.

Jeduthun, leader of the choirs and Master of Howling, stormed down the path, with Chayyliel H', the ruling prince of the hayyoth, in furious tow.

"Come forward," the Master of Howling bellowed, froth of his anger flying as he tossed his head side to side, searching for the urchin angels.

Umbrae of shadows, the Grigori slid into the wood, watching and waiting.

The Thrones flattened themselves onto the ground, but the trembling leaves gave them away. Before Chayyliel H', all the children of heaven trembled because the great Merkabah angel could swallow the whole earth in one moment in a single mouthful. He appeared only to dole out punishment.

Jeduthun charged into the growth that snapped and rustled in salacious sighs. His conductor's baton swished back and forth like a machete, slicing through vines and green-shoot stems, clearing the sanctuary.

Uncovered, discovered, the Thrones bowed deeply, supplicating before the Master of Howling. But, Jeduthun had a taste for cutting and pared the tips of their wings.

Down fluttered into the air. Down fluttered onto the ground, falling like the softest snow. Snow that murmured with tears.

"You who have broken heaven's law, who fled your ministry and failed to chant, come forward," Chayyliel H' ordered, and the Thrones crawled shakily from the thicket.

They kneeled before Chayyliel H', awaiting their punishment with arms and wings open wide.

The great Merkabah angel then flogged the seven with lashes of fire. Fire that whipped from his palms and sizzled the very air. Fire that melted the mouths of disobedient angels.

But from liquefying lips, the holy urchins sang, and all of heaven listened to their glorious voices crackling with heat and fervor and agony. All of heaven rejoiced.

Jeduthun stoked the lyrics within their hearts and led their chorus.

"I love the Lord, and I shall sing his praises.
"For he gave me his rod of power

"And I drank of his milk
"And my mouth filled with glory.
"Through the power of him, I sang
"And brought the clouds
"Which bellowed and belched.
"Through the power of him, I sang
"And brought the winds
"Which wailed from the deep distress.
"Through the power of him, I sang
"And brought the waters
"Which roared from the pit
"And covered the earth.
"Through the power of him, I sang
"And brought death,
"Death which I shall sing again
"Through the power of him."

At first lilting, the Thrones warbled like doves as their lips dripped indigo smelting song. Dominions drawn by the minx-melody gathered in the clouds, swirling in a maelstrom of rapture and rage. High frequency winds ripped through the gardens and shrieked the names of the Seraph-damned.

Eyes of blue flames lit upon the Watchers in the shadows. Shifting blame.

With continued lashing, Chayyliel H' played the lutes of the drones' throats. Torturous music escaped through the burbling burn-vesicles, piercing and swift like madrigal knives. Siren-sharp timbre that cut into the skull, which dropped the Grigori to their knees. Shemyaza clasped his bleeding ears, and the fire of his blood burned his fingers and the velvety carpet beneath him.

Uriel entered the garden, pointing with his stump. Behind him, Gabriel and Raphael stood, their faces smug, their weapons brighter and stronger than all the magnificent stones of the mountains.

"Kokabel, Sariel, Gadreel, Amazarak, Araqiel, Tamiel," Shemyaza called, bringing six Watchers from the shadows, nodding toward the two Archangels.

"Danel, Barkayal, Penemue, Ramuell, Asael, Ertael," Shemyaza called, bringing forth another six and directing them toward the center of the garden.

"Armers, Zavebe, Ezeqeel, Shamsiel, Kokabel, Akibeel." He opened his arms toward the sky and swept a circle about him, indicating these six should engage the dominions and thrones.

"Surrender, you cannot defeat our numbers," said Raphael, the six-winged Seraph who gifted Solomon the ring engraved with the pentalpha, the ring that had the power to subdue all demons, the ring that Solomon used to enslave the demons and build his Temple.

"We do not need defeat all the numbers." Shemyaza smirked. "Only a certain few."

Gabriel stepped forward on the mossed path, and the six Watchers thrust their swords and formed an arc of fiery spikes in front of them, blocking the high-ranking angel. Shaking his head, a little evil grin curled upon his mouth, Gabriel fanned his one hundred and forty wings. One hundred and forty raptorial claws sprang upon the tips of the wings.

In a flash of an embrace, Gabriel had Danel crushed against him, the one hundred and forty raptorial claws gored through his entire backside. Danel's sword and blood fell in ashes at his jerking feet.

"Welcome home, brothers," Gabriel hissed, releasing Danel.

Shemyaza watched the lights in Danel's eyes extinguish, watched the fire of his body turn to smoke, flames blown out by the angel of war, then marched before his archenemy. He threw down his sword.

"Surrendering, Azza?"

"Never," Shemyaza growled, the scarlet images of his sons bleeding into his mind. "I only want to feel your death in my hands."

Gabriel laughed and tossed his scythe as well. "Come forward then."

Dominions, thrones, and seraphim came forward, came together in a luciferous riot, in torrid collisions of light and sound, and the whole of heaven quaked in the math of arms and thunder and trauma.

Amidst the clamorous cut and thrusts, Shemyaza and Gabriel fell into feasts of fists. Rapid-fire punches split windpipes and sternums apart. Beautiful faces shattered beneath slamming knuckles.

Shemyaza sucked down the blood and fractures of his nose while he grappled Gabriel, whose features were gnarled with knotty bumps and bruises as if he was afflicted with ogrish pox. From their punctures, painful light of their beings shot outward like meteors burning into the atmosphere.

Smoke mushroomed from the fallen men of fire and billowed throughout the garden, making the dwelling of God black as the penitentiary of the fifth heaven. Sounds of suffering were as thick and dark as this smoke.

The two mighty angels scuffled in the pitch, tearing and slashing with talon and teeth, slapping with razored wings, pummeling with the stones of their hands. Gabriel kicked him with a cloven hoof, obviously having assumed his guise of beast in the dark.

From the force, Shemyaza stumbled backwards and toppled upon a victim of war. Nothing but a pile of scorified feathers and crunchy flesh.

Gabriel dropped like concrete upon him and crushed him flat to the dead-matted ground. Talons dug into the soft of his eyes, and he gripped Gabriel's steely wrists, frantically trying to hold those talons back from sinking into the wells of his sight. He felt the one hundred and forty claws prick in his sides. He yelled in pain, in wrath.

An errant piece of luck clouted the side of Gabriel's head. The hilt of a dominion-knife, which Shemyaza found by his side and with which he knocked the apocryphal angel off-balance. He pushed Gabriel over and shifted the position of power as he sat upon him.

One hand throttled on the Archangel's throat, Shemyaza repeatedly bashed his flaming fists into Gabriel's face. The structure of his jaw gave way. The molten of his mouth gushed in viscose screams.

"You . . . murdered . . . my . . . sons." Each word was punctuated with a hefty punch.

That haughty face surrendered to his fist. In cracks and snaps and pops, as sabers of teeth broke and ripped from the pulp and bone of the jaw.

Shemyaza gathered the teeth and left Gabriel, toothless and nearly faceless, writhing in the dirt. The teeth were white hot like the stars. They hissed and sizzled into his palm, and he contemplated using them as lit arrows. Scattered along the path, he found plenty of gristle for string and heated bone for the bow, but he had a better use for the teeth of an Archangel. For the pearled power of God.

In the pithy gardens, trees splintered down, felled by Grigorian swords, and flame crackled in the forest of darkness, destroying the very dark and heart of it. He trudged through the meat rubble of war, spying a face or two of the Watchers among it. The air reeked of cordite and ozone, as well as the blossomy fragrance of the Tree of Life. This he followed through the ashen darkness.

The dark and smoke dissipated from the Tree of Life, and she stood with a regal canopy-crown of leaves, all bronzed at the moment from the fiery blood of angels. Her branches, swayed by wind, sang as if thousands upon thousands of cardinals were perched upon the multitude of limbs. She bowed as he approached.

He wondered if he should summon the angel Onayepheton to raise the dead, start a cataclysm of resurrection and fulfill the revelation of a new kingdom and sovereignty. Here stood the Queen. There in the graves laid the subjects ripe for ruling.

But the teeth in his blistered palm chattered for other deeds.

Shemyaza stuck the teeth into the leaves and into the bark. Golden sap, her honeyed milk and soul, dripped down the trunk and onto the ground. Then the amber rose. And the Mother of God and the sons of God opened her golden-lumen arms and offered her breast to Shemyaza.

As she suckled him, she sweetly whispered of infanticide and revenge, of murdering all of heaven.

CHAPTER TWENTY-THREE

In every cry of every man,
In every infant's cry of fear,
In every voice, in every ban,
The mind-forg'd manacles I hear.

William Blake, London

Into each life some rain must fall,
Some days must be dark and dreary.

Longfellow, The Rainy Day

I.

All night, she sat in the grume, weaving her fingers through the darkening muck and drawing butterflies that refused to stay put. Blood kept seeping back into the lines. Please, please, she begged every time, seep back into me.

Rani shed no tears. She tried, tried for hours until the dry-sob strain made her head pound, but she had no tears left, not even the glimmer of teary veils across her swollen eyes. Only the deep emptiness within her.

Dark movement fluttered before her. *Fly, butterfly, fly.*

Lifting her head, she saw Michael at the bed stripping the corners of the red-curdled sheet. Ghastly bits bounced with his effort.

"Don't touch it," she hacked, her voice hoarse from her grief-venting.

"We can't keep it like this. It'll soak through and ruin the mattress." But he dropped the corner flap anyway.

"Ruin," she repeated and laughed harshly. *Ruined*, that was her. But could she be changed?

The soles of his shoes made sick sucking sounds as Michael walked through the mess of child-murder toward her. Balancing himself with a hand against the wall, he knelt beside her, rested his forehead against her shoulder and touched her arm. He caressed her skin with his thumb.

"You're cold," he whispered. "I'll draw you a hot bath, sprinkle in some sea salts filled with the essence of oranges, meadowsweet, marjoram, lavender, sesame, and a touch of saffron, as well as some sweetpea oils. You'll feel better."

"I'll never feel better," she replied flatly, shrugging him away.

"Rani . . . " Michael pressed, his voice soft and breaking with emotion.

"Leave me alone."

But he stayed.

Dismissing him, she lowered onto her side and fetal-curled upon the wet-scarlet satin. His presence didn't alter the fact that she felt all alone in the world.

Rani made circles in the blood, spirals that could have been a simulacrum of her pain that kept coiling down and down until every bit in existence drained into her. She flattened her hand upon the blood-seeping whorl. Then swiped her hand, creating pentamerous lines, and it looked as if headless serpents trailed her fingers.

And these did not disappear.

II.

He waited until dawn crept across the horizon before he left the crypt. The statues were silhouettes in the gray light, an army of black weeping angels and crosses marching on the dead. Snow falling from branches or mausoleum roofs landed with the crunch of soldiers' boots, and the air smelled of crisp cold guns and frozen souls.

Hours ago, the four Brothers had lumbered into the cemetery and found fresh graves upon which to rest. Candlelight had flickered with their images, even after the wax had melted and the wicks burned in the oil, and Julian had looked into the flames, witnessing how the night disposed of the living who slept with the dead.

The wind murmured omens. In the morning sky, the moon was still visible, a canker sore of pus-leaking light, an omen itself of wounds to come.

He hurried through the cemetery, snapping his fingers and muttering about sundown and new moons and the bloody keys of the whore. But first, he had to prepare the call.

#

Julian tapped the padlock against the box and brushed off the dirt from inside the keyhole. He broke the seal of the wards with his blood, only then did the key slide into the lock and turn.

Once opened, a draft of sorrowful air rushed upon his face. He smelled the dust of decay and despair, which intensified as he unwrapped the black funeral cloth and revealed the infant's corpse. Pasty eyes stared at him, unblinking in their terror.

Lilith perched upon the edge of the tub, dusky haunches against her heels, and cooed. Her voice dripped with syrupy malice, sounding the same as a ruffian-child who wiggled his fingers and sweetly called *kitty, kitty*, even though he held the scissors for skinning behind his back.

In her arms, she held another infant, this one living and simpering. Another progeny of whore. Lilith tickled his fat pink belly, and the baby pumped his little happy-jiggly arms and legs.

"Quit playing with it," Julian said as he lifted Stephan from the dark fabric and box.

"You'll be with your mother very soon," she nuzzled into his tiny ear.

The baby grabbed her hair and sucked on a red ringlet, but Lilith untangled the strand from his clench and teased his puckered lips with her studded nipple. Sour milk or not, he was hungry and latched on, greedily pinching the nipple and aureole between his lips. She expressed the other nipple as he nursed, and bluish milk dribbled at first, then streamed down her breast and belly, and over her protruding pubic mound into the tub basin.

"Sweet boy," she cooed.

Then she smothered him with her kisses.

Kisses made mostly with teeth.

Lilith bit and ripped and ravaged. His wails were cut short. His tender flesh tore open at the throat, at the thighs, and at the heart of his fat pink belly. From his bisected jugular and vena cava, blood sprayed and spewed. She had her mouth open and her tongue stuck out, laughing as she caught the tremendous crimson sprays.

"Dammit, Lilith, you're wasting it!"

Redly scowling at him, she held the sponge of infant over the tub and squeezed, and filled the basin with all his blood. Then she chewed the exsanguinated body. She popped the hinges of her jaw and, with wide grotesque mouth, swallowed the infant whole.

"Run the water; make it cold," he told her when she was through.

Through eating, yes, but her meal bulged from throat to navel, making her look as though she suffered from elephantiasis. But within hours her strong stomach acids would dissolve the body, bones and all. An amazing and sickening thing to watch, and to touch. Like gelatin melting.

The knob turned with a squeak, and cold water gushed from the faucet. Lilith added her own cold water as she stood straddling above the tub and urinating.

Julian poured runic oils into the evocative mix of blood, milk, water, and urine, spatting off anathemas and enchantments.

Stephan, in football hold, was tossed into the tub. His grey body plunked into the thick fluids and onto the bottom of the tub, turning upon itself and rising for a moment. His face broke the velum-surface, his eyes like bobbing sacs of gelid screams. Then he sank to soak for a day in the fluids that would freshen his corpse. Which would make him appear like the healthy infant he had been. A sight which would destroy the whore-mother, when, before her eyes, Julian would strangle him again.

"I charge thee, I conjure thee, I command thee, on pain of torments and wandering thrice seven years, which I, by force of magic rites, have power to inflict upon thee, by the sights and groans I conjure thee to utter thy voice."

And rising again, gurgling, clearing the visceral spume from his mouth, Stephan cried. As wretched and haunting as ever.

III.

The serpents in the blood hissed.

The wind beyond the window wailed with the voice of her son.

Wire and hook of his cries pulled her from the blood, and she rushed to the window and pressed her face against the cold glass, searching the air for his tormented spirit. Rani clawed at the glass.

But then the glass clawed back at her. The hands and voice of midnight and murder were upon her again.

"I've woken your little Boy Blue. Hear his cries. I will silence him again in the most awful manners, if you do not come."

Beneath her fingers, cracks formed on the window, webs of crystalline thread and danger.

"Come to light, come to death, and we will release his soul from the darkness, from the agony."

The mournful tune of Stephan's cries rattled the pane, her heart, her mind and all the fragile pieces of herself.

"Where? Where the hell do you want me to go?" she yelled.

"Exactly. Tonight, at the iniquitous cathedral on 26th Street, we will expect you. Come, where fornicators will lie with Babylon, where the great whore will fall . . . "

Rani fell away from the window, away from his laughter of shattering glass.

CHAPTER TWENTY-FOUR

Set me a seal upon your heart,
as a seal upon your arm;
for love is strong as death,
passion fierce as the grave.
Its flashes are flashes of fire,
a raging flame.
Many waters cannot quench love,
neither can floods drown it.

Song of Solomon

I.

Psychic force imploded the window, and Michael watched in awe as the shards flying through the air formed the profile of a face, its mouth open and full of sharp teeth. Its mouth falling upon Rani.

Snapping into stride, he gripped her beneath her arms and pulled her backwards. Arrow-pieces of glass shot down. She cried out as a triangle chunk imbedded into her lower leg, but the rest crashed onto the floor, scratching and chipping only wood.

Brisk-bitter wind whipped into the bedroom, and the sound of sad children struck his ears, of all those children bartered for crops and sacrificed, of all those children unwanted and abandoned on the shores of angry waters. Chimes of his childhood haunted him.

Michael took his boot and, with the heel, smashed and ground the broken glass into white glinting sands. Or salts.

"Wait--don't remove the glass yet," he told her, standing and holding his hands in halt-signs.

In his study, he gathered his mortal and pestle, knife and the note binder, and returned to her side, where he went about digging out the shard. He cut deep, hitting the shin bone. Rani flinched and bit her lip as he scraped the knife against her bone. Sweat shimmered on her forehead.

"Sorry, can't help it," he offered, words hardly a substitute for painkillers.

Glass, bone and blood were put into the mortar. With his pestle, he worked it around until he had a rosy powder.

"What are you doing?" she asked, shakily dabbing a cotton sock against the shallow puncture.

"Making protective salts." Michael transferred the powder into a vial. "Which I will invoke and rub into the cuts of a theurgy placed upon your body."

"Don't bother."

She knocked the vial from his hand, and the salts spilled onto floor and into the grain and grooves of the planks.

"Fuck . . . " he muttered, brushing what remained into his hands, wincing as the fine slivered salts pinpointed into his skin.

"I will trade my life for our son's peace."

Through the hair fallen over his eyes, he glanced at her. Rani's eyes were hard, hard enough to shed stones instead of tears.

"You don't need to die," Michael said, picking at his blood-glittery palm. "There is another way."

"I'm listening," she said.

And, as he described what she must do to release Stephan's soul from the powerful necromancer, she threw her hands over those hard-hurting eyes and wept for the angels.

II.

Behind her hands, cupped in her palms and over her eyes, she spied those formless dark arms that cradled her son and those blind mouths that fed off his soul. Reaching and yawning for her.

Bile burned up her esophagus and into the back of her mouth.

Rani swallowed the acid but her mind couldn't swallow the bilic thoughts of what she must do. She feared finding his body. His animated body, Michael warned her. Her son would move as if he lived and would regard her with trusting eyes as she torched him into screaming ashes.

About her, the air dripped liquid myrrh. It fell upon her skin, oily and chilled like polluted sleet.

"We come for our sons born and slaughtered."

She dropped her hands.

"We come for our sons unmade and waiting."

And dropped her head, shaking it, terrified of bringing another son, another lamb for slaughter, into the world. A lamb, regardless if it had the teeth and claws of the lion.

"Lift your eyes toward me." Fingers burnt and dripping myrrh touched beneath her chin.

Slowly, sadly, she lifted her head.

Shemyaza towered before her, his radiant beauty shadowed with hideous bruises, his posture battered, but his eyes were anything but lackluster.

"You can't stay fallen forever," he said and held out his extraordinary hands.

Rani reached for him, hesitating when her fingers were inches from his. Her fingertips tingled, her hands tingled, her entire arms and body tingled with the heat of longing, and she had trouble breathing. The air seemed charged. Charged with the force and doom of forbidden love.

Her heart thumped turmoil as she decided whether to withdraw her hands or give herself wholly to the hurt he offered.

"I can feel the pain in you, deep and dark as the angels have ever felt. But I shall silence it and you shall cry no more," he whispered, his words breathing down upon her in the sweetest lie.

Succumbing, succumbing because she was only human, Rani placed her hands within his, and the tattered Seraph raised her from the glass-dusty ground. He led her across the room, until they both stood within the eddying womb-waste.

"We are the Watchers."

"We are the Keepers."

And the other Grigori, smaller in number than before, gathered around and knelt along the expanding edges, unfolding their war-gloried wings and laying the tips into the crimson ripples. White feathers soaked in the blood. Keepers of the slaughtered son, like snow keeping the red stains of battle. Indelible if the winter of land or heart never ended.

Shemyaza shed one long vaned feather, which sailed downward and skimmed along the surface. Blood seeped into the calamus, the lower half of the feather, even though the entire feather floated flat and broad in the mess. Like the stern of a ship taking on water, the calamus took on rubious color and sank. The rachis lifted slightly and pointed, but soon its barbs and barbules filled with blood as well, and the entire feather disappeared in the red.

But not for long.

The dark angel fished the feather from the muck and, without shaking it or allowing its liquid color to bleed off, wrapped it about her head, covering her eyes with this sopping blindfold. Fluids drained down her face, ran between her lips. Viscid. Clammy. Tasting of buttery brine and curdled piss.

She was choking on the scarlet waters of her son, wishing she had never slept, never dreamed, never lived.

His pinny tongue prickled across her abortive-smeared lips, scouring the mucilage and the skin on her lips, making her kisses raw and messy. Rani sought his tongue greedily. Sought the lashes of the spikes, the cuts, the flagellating pain. Sought redemption where none could be found.

We've no sympathy for whores.

But that Christ-Fuck had sympathy for the whore, Mary Magdalene. He had loved her, redeemed her, raised her above all women, including his virgin mother. With her tears, she had washed his feet, and he had washed away her sins with his blood. They had shed the salts of suffering.

Where was her savior?

No pretty prince for the Princess of Pandora.

203

And the pain chuckled through her mouth and down her gullet as if swallowed. Crazy laughter rippled through her belly, and she groped for Shemyaza's hands, gripped and pushed them against her sides. His talons pierced through her skin, the five wounds of Christ doubled. Pain like splinters of the cross nailed into her. This was her Golgotha and it had been dark for a very long time.

"Crucify me," Rani said. "Mortify me, torment me. Take my flesh, take my pain from deep within."

Her sister had been her own savior. Through destruction comes new life.

In the other room, the skulls wailed.

In the corner, Michael wailed.

The angel's teeth were upon her throat. His sword was between her thighs, cutting her open from her anus upward. She felt the keen slide of the burning blade, felt her cunt seethe wide and wet and terrible. Shemyaza thrust his cock into her gore-gaping sex. Such ripping agony, tears flowed from her eyes, tears she had thought had forsaken her. She howled laughter. She sounded exactly like her sister.

Images of Naamah ramming the knife in her cunt flashed infrared in the dark of the blindfold. Naamah had the painted face of the harlot, eyes darkened with bruises, lips bloodied by fists. But she smiled as she cut away her clit. As she regained paradise.

"Cut me," she begged. "Cut away my clit."

Shemyaza moaned against her ear and whispered something about the daughter of hell, something wanton, yearning, aching. His hand reached down and fingered her clit as he rammed his knife-tipped cock into her cunt.

She rode the pain, the pleasure, all the hills and dips of mania.

In the dark of the blindfold, Naamah had her arm out, offering the knife in her hand, offering Rani the blood of her womb.

Viscid. Clammy. Tasting of buttery brine and curdled piss.

His talons pinched off her clit.

So much pain her screams were pinched off as well.

She reeled also in a vacuous orgasm, of coils snapping in half instead of springing. It was as if she had woke, sweaty and shaking, grasping at that elusive dream, knowing she had dreamed but unable to recall it. This was the same. She knew she had climaxed—all the signs were there, the trembling, the lax-faint of her muscles. But she missed the throbbing of her clit and core. Now only another phantom of her mind.

Veiled in a cold sweat, Rani nearly blacked out. Too much pleasure it felt like pain; too much pain it felt like pleasure. Too much of it all, and it became nothing. She clung to the Seraph, her body going limp and numb despite his brute thrusts and the brunt of his teeth in her shoulder. Still, she grunted wantonly, rhythmically with his grinding.

Sometimes the act of surrendering mattered more than orgasm.

His semen scalded into her. Her womb burned with his seed, and the buds of her ovaries blossomed orchid petals of tissue and pulpy-pearl eggs.

"The world began in fire," he said. "The world will end in fire."

Behind the blindfold, Naamah drew the knife against her smile, cutting the corners of her mouth broader and broader until the crescent of the blood moon showed. In her eyes were the stars. Unblinking milky light. Stellar corpses telling her in the language of the future she carried death in her womb.

In the other room, the skulls wailed with the voice of her son.

CHAPTER TWENTY-FIVE

These violent delights have violent ends.

> Shakespeare, Romeo and Juliet

'Tis now the very witching time of night,
When churchyards yawn and hell itself breathes out
Contagion to this world.

> Shakespeare, Hamlet

I.

A package arrived. Dropped mysteriously upon his doorstep, wrapped in plain white paper, the butcher's standard complete with butcher odor, his named scrawled blotchily in something other than ink.

Julian pushed the package in with his foot. The contents shifted within, solidly thudding against the side, not the sort of sound associated with pounds of spoiled meat sliding around. He was relieved.

Once inside, with the door secured, the shades drawn, and the lights dimmed, he tore off the paper, reeling as the strong smell of death and oddly of old roses wafted from the wrappings. He recognized the rose. *Rosa sancta,* also called the holy rose because the early Christians saw the five wounds of Christ in its five petals. This was the rose found in the petrified wreaths unearthed from Egyptian tombs. This was the rose Griffin, Hierophant of the

Qabalistic Order of the Rosy Cross, Seer of Eidolons, Magian of the Rosicrucians, tended in his hermetic garden.

The rose has the scent of immortality, Griffin would say, his nose buried in the wound-hued petals, his fingers as wetly red as the dewy thorn-stemmed roses he clutched in his hand.

The package had come from him. Julian needed no airpost from England nor letter to confirm it, only the perfumed message which whispered of the dead arts, of the purloin of those grim secrets.

Beneath the last of the paper, he found a beautiful box. A box of sycamore, an ark of secrets. The nine vaults of Enoch's vision were carved upon the top, and, in the ninth vault, the replica of the golden triangle had been placed. Enoch, fearing the premonitory deluge would destroy all the genuine secrets, had hidden the triangle of purest gold within a sanctuary in the Mountain of Canaan. Upon this triangle had been written the true name of God. The grand patriarch of Noah also had engraved a white oriental porphyry stone with the Masonry principals of science and buried it in the bowels of the earth, and two pillars, inscribed with hieroglyphics understood only by those versed in the Secret Tradition, marked the spot of concealment.

Chills ran along his arms as he opened the box. Dust puffed into his face, and he breathed in the precious spores of a treasure.

Julian gasped.

Within the box, the *Book of Enoch* rested as it had for thousands of years, undisturbed by anything but the fine shroud of Ethiopian dirt. The delta of Enoch glinted even beneath the ancient grime.

Shakily he closed the ark of secrets.

His fingertips were black. Black as they had been when Griffin tapped him on the shoulder and showed him a world where the stuff of light was found in the dark. Where living truths were found in the dead.

#

At the unsanctified church, in the dank basement, Julian unpacked the malformed skulls and traced various sigils and runes upon the cranial tops before placing each within a pentagram of blood-dust. Candles surrounded the pentagrams and burned in different scents. But only the chthonic smell of the *Book of Enoch* registered in his brain.

The tome rested within a chalked equilateral triangle, the symbol of the Divine. Once, the casting had been completed on the skulls, he would call upon the names written in that sacral book and force the spirits into the enruned skulls, other dark prisons.

He ran his finger through the X-carved groove on the top of one skull. Griffin had gifted him this skull long ago, after a failed attempt of opening the gates of the four Watchtowers, explaining the X might pertain to some conjure or curse, or perhaps as a symbol for death or the fear of death. Given the nature of the skull, Julian believed it to be the symbol for death.

In the *Book of Enoch*, in the book of giants, he had read the fragments:

. . . *they defiled . . . they begot giants and monsters . . . they begot, and, behold, all the earth was corrupted . . . with its blood and by the hand of . . . giant's which did not suffice for them and . . . they were seeking to devour many . . . the monsters attacked it.*

. . . *flesh . . . all . . . monsters . . . will be . . . they would arise . . . lacking in true knowledge . . . because . . . the earth grew corrupt . . . mighty . . . they were considering . . . from the angels upon . . . in the end it will perish and die . . . they caused great corruption in the earth . . . this did not suffice to . . . "they will be . . .*

Julian would bring Ohya, Mahway, Hihya, Hahya, Gilgamesh, and the other giants of the skulls before a dream-seer again.

But he wouldn't portend the flood as Enoch had.

No, he would make them wail and roar like the waters which had destroyed them and bring their fathers.

The angels with the true knowledge.

The Watchers who would open the gates for him.

II.

Guided down upon the fetal flotsam, Rani stretched on her back. Her hair soaked in the blood like some kind of emulsive dye, and inhuman hands rubbed it all over her skin, conditioning her with this liquid lust. She felt as if she had crawled back into the womb, covered in visceral albumen and nurtured by chaos and darkness.

Shemyaza stripped the feather from her eyes, which pulled away as if had been attached by sticky tape or clotted glue. Her temples, brow and eyelids were raw with abrasions as the skin peeled away. She blinked, wincing at the brash light of their somber, bowing, crowding faces.

And cried out as talons masticated, made pulpy dough of her flesh.

Epidermis layers, abdominal wall, sheath of muscles, and sinew looking like florid petals opening for the sun. Red-pain poppies bloomed within her.

Bending toward her, the Fallen sniffed her body bearing those flowery wounds.

. . . the heavenly beasts at her sides, their snarls, their maws dripping mercurial froth, their teeth ripping into her. Like feral starved dogs frantic to turn her into bones . . .

. . . into the shadow of Jezebel . . .

But the Grigori reared into mighty pillars of men and stood towers above her. Rani was temple and altar and sacrifice within their circle.

Shemyaza knelt between her legs. His sharp tongue stabbed at her ruined clit, cut circles around the plasmic-shiny sore, and pierced into deeper nerves, deeper darker desires. She shivered and shuddered in orgasmic shattering.

Cocks stroked fast and furious, the Seraphim reeled in their own painful eroticism. Their talons curled into their thick-girthed shafts, metallic flints carving silver-bloody hieratic symbols. Semen shot from their hard hand-pumped cocks.

Rani screamed.

Their silver-fiery spray was seeded with cold matter and melted star dust, and the molten-cum globules sizzled through her skin, her organs, bubbled through her bone and slagged her marrow. She smelled the acrid smoke of her blast-roasted flesh. She heard Michael retching. He sounded faraway, as if he had left not only the room but the plane of existence, another phantom of her life.

But perhaps she was the one who had drifted from the room and into different spaces.

Voices of the celeste, of black static and cosmic-clicking pinwheels of light, like galactic clocks ticking or pulsar-hearts rapidly beating, resonated within her head.

Terrified, awed, humbled, Rani listened. Her heart fibrillated, attempting an in sync marriage with the flash-pulsing voices. She imagined looking down upon her dissected chest in horror, seeing the vermilion bulb of her heart muscle quaking and thrashing between splayed ribs, and screaming. Screaming without affect on empyrean ears. Screaming in the voice of the void, eternally silent, in terror without end.

Voices of the celeste named themselves . . .

. . . *Armers . . . Kokabel . . . Ezeqeel . . . Araqiel . . . Sariel . . . Kasdeja . .*

And, as the Seraphical sperm seeped through her marrow, the secrets of the angels seeped through her mind.

. . . teaching her the solutions of sorcery and the resolving of enchantments.

. . . teaching her the science and myth of the constellations.

. . . teaching her the knowledge of the clouds.

. . . teaching her the signs of the earth.

. . . teaching her the motion and course of the moon.

. . . teaching her all the wicked smiting of spirits and demons, and the smiting of the embryo in the womb, that it may pass away.

Rani fell into a stupor, her mind turgidly digesting the knowledge forbidden to man, her body sluggishly suturing itself with the primal spit and sperm.

"As the apostle Timothy wrote, 'Let a woman learn in silence with full submission.' And so you shall, chosen among women," Shemyaza murmured in her ear, giggling in diabolic hisses.

Her bones, her blood, her gamic-stirring womb thrummed with his voice, with all their voices and secrets. A powerful thrumming throughout her body as if she held onto a frayed wire, as if she were the wire itself conducting power.

Winter invaded her home through the broken window, in frost-winds and cold noises of death. She remembered those hands upon her skull, pressing chiller fears upon her, like the weight of ice crushing what was buried beneath it. But, she had another son within her and another waiting in darkness and agony, desperate for her. Those hands could take her life but not her love. More fierce and fiery than an angel's sword. And she would do anything in her power, borrowed or otherwise, to save her sons from the murderous dark.

"Strike from the heart, into the heart."

"As the Mother of God and of the sons of God does now in heaven . . . "

Teeth chattering, she watched the fathers of giant sons and secrets walk through the glass-less window, into the wind, into the falling night, leaving her behind in this rosy pandemonium. Of skulls squalling for flesh and blood, of flesh and blood weeping for bone.

Fetal bones slid together in the grume and fused into a pentacle. She bent down and touched the tiny bone-emblem of a star.

. . . Solomon standing before the Asherah pillar in pentacle-position, the womb-vessel set between his spread legs, his blood flowing from his cut groin into the bowl.

"Solomon's Seal," Michael rasped. "Don't touch it . . . the angels wait for the rains of blood, and you're their vehicle for the storm."

Rani ignored Michael, ignored his beseeching eyes and arms, picked up the pentacle, and headed for the bathroom. She closed the door on his omening voice.

In the mirror, she studied her blood-painted reflection, her death-shadowed eyes, her death-promising lips, and smiled darkly.

#

On a gloomy path taken days ago, on Broadway with nothing like a song within her heart. Only paradox, of the fear of losing the life she didn't want.

She walked in the gutter instead of on the sidewalk, shuffling through the shin-deep snow, through the soft collection of fallen purity. No *click-click* of her heels, no tell-tale beating heart of stalker Time, only the silken-soothing *shoosh-shoosh*.

Like discards of white tinsel, the snow glittered beneath the sallow light of the street lamps. Rani thought of Christmas, how the tinsels and ornaments and all the bright trappings of magic and miracles were placed upon evergreen trees. An honoring of the Asherah, the Tree of everlasting life, and the adorning of the Queen of Heaven with baubles and jewels. An honoring of the time when the Mother would birth the sons of gods.

Her worship had been subverted, but her symbolism remained.

Rani had slipped the pentacle on a chain and wore it around her neck, and the star of Solomon burned against her chest, a cold burning as if ice had been held too long against a purpling bump.

. . . in the grove, lit only by the engorged moon, young virgins fed cakes to the erect goddess, preparing her for marriage to the god reborn from the grave, then drank from her bleeding breasts.

. . . a woman knelt before the king of Judah, his swollen member in her hand, her head bobbing back and forth, her mouth sliding up and down, her tongue flicking, and Solomon gave her pearls.

. . . the land heaved with verdant sighs as vines and ferns sprouted in twisted and frilly abundance; hundreds of hares hopped into the grove and mingled together, in fecund-frenzied humping until their sweat seeped red in their desert-fawn fur.

Asherah . . . Astarte . . . Oestre . . . Easter. Her angel-touched mind connected it all. The virgin-born son dying and resurrecting; the rebirth of the land, of fertility, of life; licentious veneration.

The cycle of primitive worship followed the course of the moon and sun. In spring, at the Vernal Equinox, man believed the goddess he worshiped would be fertilized by the risen god, and the land would produce bountiful crops. At the end of summer, when the land turned brown and arid beneath the hot sun, on the Summer Solstice, the goddess would kill the god by hacking him into pieces, harvesting him. The goddess would weep on the Autumn Equinox for the dying sun, for the murdered god. At the Winter Solstice, the sun came back to life and the goddess would give birth to the son fertilized at the previous Vernal Equinox, and the god would be reborn.

And here Rani was, sister of the moon and blood, heading for the brother of the sun, where everything between moon and sun had to do with life and death.

III.

In chains hanging from the ceiling, an initiate burned. Fire robed his body and cowled his screaming skull. His skin had bubbled and sloughed like melting cheese off his body, strings of it still dangling from him onto the ground, but what was left of his flesh was crust and char.

The initiate burned as meat to attract the Nephilic spirits.

Julian had persuaded him to offer himself as sacrifice with a story, the same story which Griffin told him the first night in his chaldean-bucolic study, when Griffin offered him as meat to Tzaphqiel, an angelic entity of destruction and death.

#

Memory came so strongly anymore, as if his mind could no longer tell past from present, and shunted him back and forth through these mind-time barriers like water through a sifter.

"Christian Rozenkruez, a Rosicrucian founder, wrote the 'Chemical Wedding' after experiencing a transformation mystery. A glorious lady appears to Christian clothed in the colors of the sky and the splendid stars of heaven and hands him an invitation to the wedding of a King.

"The marriage of spirit and soul, of sulfur and quicksilver, sun and moon, or king and queen, is the central symbol of alchemy, understand. And, in the chemical marriage of the king and queen, the groom and bride would be killed, buried, only to rise again, rejuvenated. The connection between marriage and death is the nature of things. In ancient experience, to dream of marriage meant death, and the dream of death meant marriage, merely different states of spirit.

"After receiving the invitation, the founding of spiritual impulse, Christian travels on the second day, the second stage when spiritual impulse encounters crisis. Four paths confront him, and the correct path proves the most difficult to find. But he finds it by accident, by providence. Then he must pass three gates, giving up his possessions to the porters. His success for reaching the castle is being bound by chains and imprisoned in the hall with the other guests.

"He refers to the third day as the last day of the initial phase of the process. The guests are weighed. Weighed for virtue—wisdom, justice, fortitude, temperance, faith, hope, and love—-,and then the guests are judged and sentenced.

"On the fourth day, he witnesses the king's and queen's wedding/execution. Beheaded, their blood fills goblets, and their heads are placed in chests, and their bodies in coffins. And the Virgin tells the guests that they hold the lives of the king and queen in their hands. 'That this death shall make many alive.'

"The next three days represent the arc of inner spiritual impulse manifesting outward. The guests are now called Alchemists and struggle to bring their work into expression. The adepts are given ropes, ladders, and wings to rise through the difficult levels into the tower and perform tasks appointed them, one being feeding a hatched bird, all bloody and unshapen. If they could bring the bird to perfection, then the ceremony to awaken the king and queen would begin.

"Christian and the others feed the bird blood from the beheaded, and it grows fast before their eyes, becoming wild and black, biting and scratching them. Once more, they feed the bird meat of a dead Royal and the black feathers molt. White feathers replace them, and the bird appears tamer, but the Alchemists do not trust him and feed him a third time. His feathers turn all the colors of beauty. Awed, the men release the bird, and the Virgin rewards their efforts by inviting them to witness the awakening and anointing them as Knights of the Golden Stone."

Griffin handed Julian a silver flute. Dark fluid effervesced within and smelled of roses and runic poison.

"I dreamed of a king, with skin as golden bright as the sun, wearing the mask of your face. I dreamed of his marriage," the Hierophant said, his cockney accent thickened with grave humor, indicating with a nod for Julian to drink.

He raised the flute to his lips and drank. The liquid acted as alcohol, fuming in his throat, intoxicating him, and he staggered on his feet, the sights of the room spinning and moving before him. On the wall tapestry, the stitched lions, unicorns, dragons, Roman gods, and bodies ending in fish tails converged into one horned, clawed, scaled, winged, finned, man-headed beast. It seemed to pull itself from the threads and stand upon the floor.

"The Chosen of the order must either attend or participate as groom in a chemical wedding. Our highest goal is to transform from darkness into light. But first, you must be enshrouded in the dark."

With a Key of Solomon, Griffin chanted an invocation.

"O'h Tzaphqiel, Hidden Voice of God, who bears Yahweh Elohim, I behold the Vision and hear the Voice by thy revealing and concealing."

The beast stepped forward. Changed. It stood a tall man, his black robe flowing shadowy and fluid about him, a blue Egyptian nemyss upon his head, a red amulet dripping about his throat, silver wings spread wide and those feathers glinting like hundreds of knives. In his taloned hands, he carried a dark rod and glowing cup. The mighty man stepped forward again, stepped within inches of Julian, and smiled broadly, showing all his sharp silvery teeth.

"And, before I can raise you, the angel much like the bird must feed upon your blood."

Then it was only darkness and teeth.

#

Crackling shrills disentombed him from that ebon memory, from that echo of rictus-agony.

On the chain, the initiate hung limp but twitching, his body and life exhausted by flames burned out, embers of his eyes dying down. He looked a tar-smeared skeleton, with gummy-masses of carbonized flesh clinging here and there on the black bones.

Julian basked in the heat emanating from him.

"Pray the angels come," he said to the dead initiate, who smelled of meaty incense, who caught in magical compulsion could still hear the living world. "Because I can't raise you if they don't feed upon you."

Ashy smoke of screams poured from his torched mouth.

"Something comes, Magian," John Kirby warned, pulling down his hood. His sky-blue eyes clouded with fear, and he scratched nervously at his beard. "It doesn't feel right."

215

Tilting his head, Julian listened.

Stone walls snickering with old confessional sins; pipes sighing with wasted consecrated waters; the creeping patter of heels on the floor above them.

"Oh, it feels more than right."

Yes, indeed, he thought, nearly tasting the brassy blood of the keys within the whore upon the air.

IV.

Moonlight colored the grisaille windows white-gold and streamed into the cathedral, an aurora borealis of phantom light. With only this eerie luminescence, Rani traversed the aisle, her nerves fluttering on the razor's edge, her stomach under siege as if by carnivorous butterflies. The wretched smell of burnt flesh guided her toward the tribune.

She touched the altar. Felt the dust of skin and dried semen. Felt the memory of rape and the plunder of her womb.

Her fingertips hissed through the dust, moving sinuously and making serpents in their wake.

On impulse, she drew a circle and a crescent—the moon crowning the sun, horns crowning the head of a god. Or goddess. Asherah with bull horns, the sacred symbol of life and fertility, of the waning of the full moon, of the waning of masculine power.

Rani walked on, her teeth chattering from holding such secrets within her body.

An eddy of darkness and death, in sight and smell, waited at the bottom of the stairs, and she hovered at the precipice, gathering other senses to rely upon before she descended into the unknown which howled in dark silent noise to be known. The air could've been his foul breath. She knew he was down there crouched and flexing his throttling hands.

Her hand upon the stone wall, she waited for the vibration of his cold laughter. Nothing but cold silence. Cold breath of stone held in anticipation of blood splattering into the mortar.

One step. Two. Her heart pounding away, giving her away perhaps as she went down the uneven stairs.

V.

Julian motioned with one finger at his lips and another pointing for John to follow him into the other room. The door creaked open, and pale light and the shadows of the men rushed into the storage area. Quietly, he shut the door and snuffed the light. He led John through the dark, shuffling across the room, stirring hymns of debris until they reached the other door.

Each flanked the door. Waiting. Wanting.

VI.

Rani stumbled on the landing, expecting another step but unable to see anything in this stygian well. It pressed upon her, an amorphous being of suffocating bulk that blocked all sight, sound, and breath. She strained her eyes and ears. Hoping for anything, anything but this morbid stifling.

Putting her hands before her, she tiptoed forward. Her heart was a machina of fear, valves slamming, chambers pumping panic and adrenaline-thick blood through her arteries. Her heart throbbed so hard she breathed her pulse. Crimson thoughts were all she had, and she feared a red-out.

She waded through the dark, through the hush, and imagined things moving aside her, things without eyes, without form, with only chasmal mouths hungering for marrow and milk.

At her breasts, she felt a wet chill. Her nipples tingled, and Rani understood that milk was leaking from her breasts. Milk that would've been for the angel's child. But like the child, her milk was wasted.

She hit an obstacle—wooden, hinged, key-holed.

Come to light, come to death.

And she opened the door and finally saw lights in the darkness as hands grappled her and fists knocked against her skull . . .

#

Consciousness came in fragments, much like the aborted fetus, all red and horrible.

. . . her wrists bound in cutting wires . . .

. . . her body hanging by hooks and chains, and her bottom resting excru-
ciatingly upon the point of a pyramid . . .

. . . the hooded man running the Cat's Paw deeply across the front of her
shoulders and draping her skin in the red silk of her blood . . .

"I am the Magian," he said, but she heard *I am the murderer.*

The Magian slammed the *Book of Enoch* onto the rack.

. . . howling voices of the Sufferers gnawing through the ancient pages and
choking the air with damnation's scoria, the esoteric slag amass in her lungs . . .

"The spirits have refused me for years. But they won't refuse you,
the whore of their fathers. You are the key. Call the Nephilim, call the
dead giants of the angels."

. . . unwilling shadows whirling and wailing around the skulls . . .

In his hand, he held a clawed device that glowed hot, and the man
with the voice of midnight and murder gored her breast with those
four iron-prongs. His eyes beastly bright and his beatific grin
flashing menace as his hand twisted the Breast Ripper.

. . . torque of skin and fatty flesh pulling away, torque of agony . . .

. . . teeth ripping into the pendulous sack, ripping deep as if to sink into
her marrow, bursting open distended glands and vascular gristle . . .

. . . her breast tearing away in blood-warm sprays and gross snaps . . .

Her blistered mouth obeyed the Magian's demands, screaming the
tribal names of the Rephaim, Emim, and Awwim.

Spirits of the Nephilim charged down, lightning-scorch of their
landing upon the concrete, acrid smoke in their steps, striking
serpents of flame in hand. Virulence of the Phantoms, Terrors, and
Devastators were aglow on their bronzed flesh. In molten waves of
orange and red, the colors of flames feasting on flesh, of fresh macer-
ated wounds, of the vibrant slain.

In an onslaught of the ogrish dead, crimson lashed the walls.

The Freemasons gathered for her torture hit the floor with hollow
splatters.

But the Magian escaped with the milky-blood dripping mass of
her left breast.

CHAPTER TWENTY-SIX

For clothing She is covered with a doubled cloak.
The mountain in morning She roams.
In grief, through the forest.
She cuts cheek and chin.
She lacerates Her forearms.
She plows like a garden Her chest,
Like a vale She lacerates the back.
"Baal is dead!
Woe to the people of Dagon's son!
Woe to the multitudes of Athar-Baal!
Let us go down into the earth."

The Baal Epic

I.

Hours after she had left him, Michael still huddled in the corner, hugging his knees, futilely warding off the cold and shock. His body ached for the scars. His mind ached for the end of these visions.

Of the rains of blood, of angels bowing in the scarlet waters of the sacrificed, of the dark god prowling the shores for children abandoned by their fathers.

Rani had ignored him, same as his father had ignored him sitting there with red-vivid trails upon his arms. She hadn't even noticed the cuts upon him that had spontaneously split his skin when the angels had come. Cuts at his temples sent bloody tears down his cheeks. Cuts in his throat salted his breath. And, along his arms, the old wounds had opened up and showed all his heart's seeping sorrows.

Everyone he'd ever loved had left him in one manner or another, and Michael realized Rani had been missing for a long time even though she had never gone away. He felt like the "hero" of the *Wasteland*, living in that land of winter and loneliness and death, hoping for that spring renewal. But the clouds which would bring the rains and the trees, which would bring the blossoms would only bring blood.

In the pane, the remaining pieces of glass tinkled like tiny bells in the wind. Broken chimes.

"Can you love me?" he asked the wind again but heard only the cold silence.

He knocked his head against the wall and sighed. Rani was but a reflection of himself, a walking wound, consumed by the despair that healing would never come because no one could love them enough. No one could love away the hurt. For them, even loving caused pain.

Exhausted, Michael closed his moist eyes and slept on edge, dreaming of a dark genesis.

#

The day looked no different than the night, the sky squalid with storm, sunlight smudged away by the gray-heavy clouds. Snow fell down in such volumes the city appeared to have been covered in a dense swirling fog.

With his iron knife in hand, gripped tight enough to crack the wood and horn of the handle, Michael pushed against the blistery gales down Bleecker Street. Snow and sprites raged in white wrath all around him. Thunder cracked and rumbled as if the sky was falling apart, as if heaven was being rendered by war. He wondered if the strange taste of the snow was the blood of angels.

Things had changed in the world. His dreams and his mediumistic bones proclaimed it, and things would become darkness, the way of the end, the way of the beginning. But he knew nothing was ever set in stone but always changing.

Thumbing the blade, Michael hoped to affect the fates.

He reached the West 4th Street subway station and descended the stairwell, thinking how all cycles in life were about this. This descent into the underworld.

Once on the train, with his hand and its knife resting on his lap, he laughed, and a few of the other riders regarded him with wary eyes. One woman led her toddler daughter away, farther in the compartment, putting other potential victims between her and him. He laughed even harder.

Jade dreams. He'd been caught in the jade dream of immortality, trapped in the deep echelons of alchemy and illusion, when the truth had been within him the whole time—even the gods must die, must descend into the underworld and defeat death before they can rise to life again.

Michael still chuckled, quieter, scarier, as he changed trains at Broadway, taking the 6 down to Canal Street. He knew why he had his jade dreams though, because he feared, like many, that a mere mortal could not defeat death. But dreams were still dreams, not part of reality.

Thrust once more into the icy wails, he trundled around the flow of people down Canal Street. The familiar smells of sour trash and musty sewers enveloped him as he worked his way deeper into Chinatown. The area was as flurried as the storm, traffic, vendors hawking and shouting, tourists and the Chinese immigrants crowding the colorfully stocked shops. With fat smiles, Buddha charms and statuettes promised good fortune, while watches and other trinkets, such as small animals crafted with real cat fur, begged for superfluous fortune to be spent. The food shops carried cheap vegetables and cheaper seafood, with dead chickens hanging like foul ad signs. Michael wondered how anyone could buy food from these shops that smelled of atrocious rot.

The crowds thinned on Mulberry, with only authentic Chinese restaurants and tea apothecaries for the locals. Few cars squeezed through the narrow lane, and he breathed in relief to be away from the mob. Down an alley, even further removed from the hustle of the normal world, he stopped before a plain brownstone. Michael tried the knob, which turned easily in his hand. The door flew open, thrown by the winds.

He stepped inside. Inside the slaughterhouse, the air reeking of heaped composts of carrion, the floor littered with strays bits of decomposing flesh, flesh black and furred with rot that looked as if the pieces could have crawled away from the whole. The very walls were bloated with gelatinous death and sweating chum.

How much carnage had he walked through in the last few days?

Too much and not enough, he chuckled.

Squelching step after squelching step, Michael made his way down the stairs into the basement, into the Mao Shan underworld. Only one corpse confronted him. Blue mist and flies covered the body, giving it the illusion of a mystic mountain upon which had grown those jade dreams. Jichun's body buzzed.

You like my breath of dragon?

You like my bite of dragon?

Michael stripped off his coat and shirt, then knelt beside the body, disturbing the flies, and the flies exploded in a pyroclastic swarm, pelting him as if with black ash and rock. Their buzzing struck him as well, like chainsaws in his mind. He fell back onto his haunches, arms thrown over his head for protection, and waited for it to end.

Because of the echoing din of the flies, he did not notice their absence for several minutes. He lowered his arms when the last tickle of insect leg, real and imagined, disappeared.

Beneath the flies, layers of maggots sheathed the body, mummifying Jichun in a moveable feast of white. Michael scraped the grubs and sacrophagic mange away from his face with the knife. He dug out those cyanic eyes.

"I like your bright eyes of dragon," Michael mocked the corpse. "Best tools for seeing in the dark."

Then Michael reached around his back and, by rote, carved a theurgy into his left flank, and called up the spirit of the Mao Shan master and imprisoned him in the gemstone of his flesh and blood.

Best tool for bringing back the dark beast.

And then he would have the spirit of the god who defeated death.

II.

Lilith had put wicks in the tallow of the slaughtered, and hundreds of visceral candles burned in the temple of her Gomorrah. The floor looked as if it were made of fire and burning flesh. Upon the altar, she sat with her knees up and spread wide, serpentine flows of blood running from between her legs, an offering for her brother.

The horned god approached her.

His resurrection premature, Ba'al carried the waste of the underworld upon his flesh, ulcers scarlet-black and spreading like a necrotic-contagion pox. Those shadow-sores threatened to chaw him away until nothing remained. But she would revive him, as she always had.

His pomegranate-saccharin breath steamed against her bleeding cunt. His claws gripped her ass, his thumbs poised at the edge of her livid genitalia. Lilith pushed forward on the altar slab, raising her ass off the stone, thrusting her cunt against his wine-dark mouth.

"Suck me," she said. "Drink my blood; eat my flesh."

Ba'al lapped and chewed greedily at her, famished for so long from the rites of spring.

"Rise, my Lord." Gasping, bucking her hips.

But this was winter, and other forces intruded upon them, stealing the horned god from his carnal feast. Ba'al vanished from the temple, and half the candles were extinguished with the cold winds of summoning.

Letting out a guttural yrowl, Lilith raked her cheek and chin with her nails. She slashed across her breasts, and she too, like the mother of gods, gave forth rust-sweet milk.

She was Anath all over again, enraged and eager to wash her hands in the blood of the slaughtered, in the dews and rains supplied by her brother Ba'al.

. . . *raiding the valley of men, battle-dressed in her serpent skirt, shorn penises hanging from her goatskin apron* . . .

. . . *violently killing and gloating, wading waist-deep through the blood, the heads of soldiers tied to her belt* . . .

. . . *cutting, grazing, exalting as she plunges her knees into the blood, her loins into the gore of the warriors* . . .

...as she descends into the underworld and dismembers Mot, god of death, scattering his sterile remains, and, with her revived brother, undertakes war against the gods of heaven ...

Eyes burning with blood-lust, Lilith walked through the fire and flesh and sought the offender son of Eve.

III.

Shaking, sweating off the pain, Michael remained on his knees and cut the theurgy in deeper. He summoned the dark beast as he had long ago, his voice laced with the necromantic spice of spirit and the blood of children.

The flies returned. Wings not buzzing, but whispering, whispering in the song of rain upon flesh.

The bestial dark breathed upon him again, steaming his flesh, wetting him with the black dew of Aliyan Ba'al, which was the dew of death.

" ... as an offering to Aliyan Ba'al ... "

Michael continued his summoning despite the trickle of lotic terror in his veins. He breathed in the flies and the lord of flies, and reeled in the virulent whirring of possession, slumping to the ground.

Shadow looming, the *hsien* came and straddled his body. Her eyes were magmatic as she lowered upon him. She gripped his hair in one hand, pulling his face against hers, crushing his mouth, and, in the other, his balls, pulling them as well, castrating him.

Fangs nipped his lips, over and over. Venomous agony sheered his mouth, caustically dissolving the tissue of his lips and gums, his soft palate, his sinuses. He felt the tissues acid-sizzling within his skull. But he couldn't scream. He had no mouth, no vocal cords, only an excruciating crackling and boiling of his flesh amplified within the confines of bone.

Then the venom reached his brain and turned his mind to froth.

CHAPTER TWENTY-SEVEN

In truth I found myself
upon the brink of an abyss,
the melancholy valley containing
thundering, unending wailings.

Dante, The Inferno

I.

Phantoms of the giants unhooked her and brought her down from the wires, stanching the bleeding of her iron-masticated breast with their tongues. They moved from ruined breast to swelling belly. Delirious from pain, Rani didn't know whether their terrible mouths upon her belly were kissing her or eating her. The Nephilim ended their homage to her impregnated flesh, retreating in bloody flames and smoke, disappearing into the skulls, and the gems within the eye sockets glowed.

Around her, the ghost-voices of his ancient wives, the mothers of those sons, cried of emptied wombs, of dead birthed sons, of taking bone against breast. Rani struggled to her feet, swayed in the sight of the fleshly residuum and lumbered toward the skulls.

The Magian had trapped the spirits within the skulls, evident in the ebb and flow of astral light within the gems as if the spirits breathed in the bone. On the gems, she spotted sigils of the pyramid and sun, and hammers with which temples were built. The skulls, icons of death and unnatural mystery, were destined for the walls.

And the Brothers of these signs would learn the ways of the angels and the heavens.

Secrets of smiting spirits wisped in her mind.

Her hands shook as she removed the lustrous gems, which dimmed in her sweaty palm. Her breath caught and tears rolled down her cheeks, and the mothers in her innards roiled in gaseous shrieks, as she hefted a bulbous skull.

Drawing her arm back, Rani gathered her strength then pitched the skull against the wall. Bone exploded against the stone. Skull plates shattered apart and fell to the floor, shattering into smaller fragments, crumbling into a hybrid debris of dust and cindering ore, of human and angel dead. Smoldering away into caterwauls; corroding into unfathomable silence. Into darkness beyond darkness, where invocations were never heard.

One by one, the skulls crashed apart.

Rani heard thunder beyond the old church between loud cracking skulls and knew something terrible was happening in the world, in the hells and the heavens, in all the spaces of time. And she wept.

Her womb wept too, in tears of blood.

But still, she felt the beating heart of the child within her, strong as the thunder. Which in turn made her strong.

Mother of the sons of the sons of God, who would nurse life with blood.

Smearing the dust of bone across her chest, she sealed the wound of her missing breast. Her phantom nipple tingled with the touch. Rani tried not to think about how lopsided she looked, how incomplete as a fertile idol she looked. Unlike Asherah with her twin breasts full as the Harvest moon. *Rabbit moon*, the enigmas within her whispered.

. . . *rabbits in the grove, moon in the night, semen and blood coloring the eggs of Asherah* . . .

Heavy heart, mind, and belly, she left the antiquated church and headed home. The other skulls were crying for her.

##

Rani stood on her steps, aghast at the change in the facade, the bricks literally crawling with glaucous vines and red-tipped thorns. On the second floor, the curtains billowed in and out of the broken window like lonely wraiths welcoming her home. Sheets of snow buffeted against her and surely into the house. She felt like she had gone through the wardrobe and stood in the land of ever-winter. Soon the ice witch would come.

When she opened the door, she retched. Michael on the ground, drifts of snow swept in a powdery circle around him, his arms and legs spread like Solomon's pentacle, his flayed skull, his skeletal mouth frozen open in unheard screams.

The ice witch had already come and left her warning.

II.

Shaken, Julian cuddled with the Enochian tome, all he had left of the provisions he'd taken to the church. Even the beautiful box had been left behind. But then he'd brought home something else, the whore's breast like some kind of mammiferous red rose with its fragrancy hint of immortal mystery of mysteries.

The snowstorm created a brumous picture beyond the window, and the longer he stared, the more he believed he stood on the other side of the window, upon the clouds, swallowed in a swirling quagmire. He didn't understand what happened in the church. He had the enruned skulls, the book, the whore.

"Sssssilly Julian . . . "

Turning his head, he caught the shade of Lilith, the antithesis of snow, slink into the bathroom. Waters thicker than water splashed in the tub as she no doubt stirred her hand in the glamour-bath. Lilith was like a cat stealing a drink from the toilet bowl, her fingers and tongue sticking in places where they didn't belong.

Julian followed her into the bathroom, the *Book of Enoch* clutched to his chest as if the knowledge would seep through the mite-ridden pages and osmotically into his heart and blood.

"I warned you about the angels," she said, dunking the pink floater of the dead child. Those milky eyes were even wider in fear.

"But these were not the angels. Only the spirits of their sons."

"Even worse then. Remember, even God could not keep control upon their destructions. The only measure was destroying them." Lilith bent down and blew grumous bubbles in the bath.

Her flesh shifted from scale to skin, skin to scale, and in a range of chameleon colors, and the ridges of her spine protruded through her back. She looked prehistoric, alien, monstrous.

Her Adamic children perhaps were human on the outside, but inside, Julian believed, they were positively reptilian, cold and brutal. And thriving well in the modern, seemingly godless world.

In these times, God had wiped his hands of the wicked and stepped aside, calling instead on faithful servants to do His reckoning.

Serve His will . . . take up the serpent . . .

"Then we will destroy," Julian said.

"The angels will not allow it. But I know of ways to fell angels, and they would not be able to do anything but defend themselves. I will help you, for a proper exchange of course." Lilith smiled, her mouth horribly wide.

Julian nodded, unable to speak because he couldn't swallow his fear.

Lilith fished the freshened corpse from the tub. Death no longer dappled the flesh, and the child looked as if he had come straight from the uterus, womb waters dripping off raw, healthy-plumped skin. As she held him up by the back of his neck, Stephan flailed in the air, his movements more animated and fluid than before. He was the perfect illusion of a living baby, despite those hallowed eyes.

Even his cries were louder, strong enough to reach into his mother's chest and rip out her heart with sound alone.

III.

Once upon a time, Rani loved the winds. She would stand in the swaying alfalfa fields of the country estate, her face toward the sun, her arms stretched out, and embrace the invigorating spirit of the earth. But now that spirit was devastating.

Stephan, his cry upon the winds, carried all the awful tones of darkness and agony.

Her knees hit the floor. She fell forward, caught herself on her palms, and landed at the skull-head of Michael, his eye sockets full of ichorous sight, his mouth full of empty screams. Which bothered her as much as the wind.

"Michael," she wept, holding her fingers inches above his mouth, his mouth which for many years had melded with her own. Her lips hummed with the vivid memory, with the harsh reality that she would never feel them against her again. Emptiness kissed her now.

She squeezed her eyes, squeezed out the tears. As the tears flowed down her face, anguish flowed from her mind into her heart, into her gut, into the aching core of her. Black emotion that flowed and felt like a cold lethal serum, which rued and vexed her delicate insides. Her bones could not protect her from the gravity and weight of sorrow.

The wind joined her weeping.

Surrounded by all this death, Rani didn't know if she could pull herself from the floor and discard all the things she feared, all the things she felt, all the things she should do out of those feelings and fears. She didn't think she could go on without any love left in this world.

Celestial secrets clicked in her mind like millions of snapping teeth.

Rani turned her head toward the coffin against the wall. Her intuition awakened and enhanced, she knew the Brotherhood had buried those skulls within her son's grave, knew they would eventually return for their treasure-stashed corpus. She knew her course as well. *Rent a car, pack it full of the death in her keep, and undertake that two hour drive north to the country estate, where all her disturbing secrets were buried.*

The nihilistic wind blew horrid laughter around the room and into Michael's fleshless mouth, and called her home.

#

She had repeatedly played Wolfsheim's CD during the monotonous drive, completely absorbed in those sad-romantic songs, but killed the radio once she entered the gravel drive toward the estate house—a fine example of Carpenter's Gothic, the steeped roof, the lacy bargeboards, the steep cross gables, the oriel windows, and all the vertical board and batten trim. Her mother had painted the ostentatious house in perfect candy-floss colors, which reminded Rani of the candied home of the witch from *Hansel and Gretel*: white frilly frosting on the yellow-tiered cake of the home, pastel sugared ornaments in the intricate woodwork, licorice of wrought-iron and leading, hard candy of the windows in sour apples and cherries. The trap for unhappy children.

On the second floor, the windows of her sister's and her bedroom were like the witch's hungry black eyes staring down at her. Rani floored the gas and turned the car off the driveway onto the grounds, heading toward the woods of lost children, anxious to escape the fattening on unhealthy memories and the oven heated for her pain. But then the skulls within the coffin cackled as they bumped together, and she knew there was no escape.

Fish-tailing on the snow-covered field, the Subaru groaned and swooshed along, the chains on the tires barely effective, and Rani worried the only thing she would bury tonight would be the four-wheel drive vehicle in the snow. Steering column clenched, her knuckles ached. Her neck ached too, as she leaned forward, her nose almost pressed against the frosting windshield. The defrost blasted on high, but still the windshield fogged crystalline, with only circles breaking here and there upon the glass as if they were the blank eyes of invisible Watchers.

Her nerves were cracking ice as the Subaru slid sideways, as the rear end torqued forward and put the car into a spin. And made symbols of the sun in the snow.

By the time she regained control of her car, she had lost control of her nerves. She sat there, panicking, her heart sledging against her chest, adrenaline wiring her and numbing her all at once. Deer in the headlights. Pending road-kill.

Her huffing breath steamed against the windows, whiting out the already white world beyond. Unsteady, she decided to forego the wheels and go by foot, and stumbled from the sporty wagon. Not far ahead lay the edge of the woods. Rani dragged the coffin of skulls from the car and along the powdery ground, making better time than she had hoped. The snow made it easier to sled the box along.

Once she reached the inner sanctuary of the woods, the place Satrina would take her when the sky went indigo-dark and the fireflies danced for the symphonic evening, where she spoke of the gnomes which fed upon the moonlight and grew into hulky beasts which fed upon the sleeping, she dropped the end of the coffin. The skulls clamored within. But that was the only sounds in the grove.

Rani retrieved the skulls from the coffin and arranged them around the grove, stationed like guards for the center grave intended for Michael. Michael, the theurgist turned theurgy. In his dead body lived the witness of the angels, as well as other supernatural spirits, things which the Brothers of the sun would enjoy getting into the light of. She had to rid his body of such spirits and secrets.

Her hands tingled with cold and with colder intentions.

Returning to the car, she had trouble pulling Michael from the trunk, his body stiffening and gaining gaseous pounds, an unwieldy and unwilling slab of flesh. But then she couldn't blame him, if he knew what she planned . . . even she shivered with all the things she must do by the end of this night. The last of the midnights and winters.

Rani trudged backwards, holding Michael under his arms and pulling him along. His heels bumped along the uneven packed-powder, and his lower jaw bounced up and down, his flesh-less mouth opening and closing in soundless protests, his ever-scary grinning teeth clicking and clicking. Clicking precious time away before the Brotherhood came to light, to bring death.

Sweat chilled her skin beneath her coat and sweater, and her muscles ached and quivered with the exertion of digging shallow graves. Early evening had crept upon her, in rich tones of grey and blue, in spits of snow and blinks of the rising moon between the clouds.

Sisters of the moon and blood.

Rani rubbed her numb hands together and blew warm breath on her fingers. Breath that puffed about her and hissed with her sister's eerie laughter. Her sister, the moon. Blood was the only missing element, but she didn't think it would be missing for long.

Back at the car, in the driver's seat, she flipped the vanity visor down. She braided her hair, applied antimony to her eyes and an iron-oxide pigment to her lips, the same reddish pigment used to mark burial bones, and somberly nodded at Jezebel in the mirror.

All the while, the wind tolled the ice in the trees. And her son tolled his voice of death, louder and louder, as the distance between them shortened.

CHAPTER TWENTY-EIGHT

Silver moon, silver snow
Darkness of midnight blue.
Silent storm, silent night
Cryptic murmur of ice.
Bitter chill, bitter end
Winter dead blue with cold.

T. Jacobs

Thou, unknown, terrible, and indistinct,
Yet awful thing of shadows, speak to me!
Why dost thou laugh that horrid laugh?

Byron, Heaven and Earth

I.

Ice cut through her flesh like glass. Hot pain singed around her wrist, despite the cold of winter's blade, and she winced as she drew the piece deeper into her vein.

Blood stained the crystal facets of the ice crimson and dropped wounded angels onto the snow. Red invocation woke the groaning deep.

"Rani," a spirit sighed, rising from the dark of fresh burial ground, lured by the perfume of her blood and the ointment of eggs, milk, honey, oil, and the ashes of the dead she had smeared on her throat.

Buried only hours before, Michael rose and walked upon the unhallowed earth with bright spirit, as if with the sheen of frost and moonlight upon him. His spirit had yet to assume the shroud of shadows that guarded the wandering dead.

His splendid spirit, she thought, wringing her hands, the hands that dug his grave, the hands that were required to annihilate *his splendid spirit* before the Brotherhood discovered his corpse. Before they discovered her secrets of the Watchers within his wet decay.

December-sad wind nipping at her face, she wiped the single frozen tear off her cheek.

"You shiver now but wait until the chill of death racks through your bones." Michael knelt beside her in silver flowing mists. "The sharpness of the knife is dull compared to the manifold pain of the coldest cold needling into you. In the grave, you rest as if inside the Iron Maiden, long nails of icicles driven beyond flesh and bone, driven deep into your soul. Raw electromagnetic nerves compose your soul, and you feel every point. Every tear as you struggle . . . "

He shuddered. "Shackles unfettered, I continue to feel the icy claws of death bore through me. Exquisite agony, this phantom pain of death that maliciously haunts me. Do not release me . . . "

Imploring her with moist eyes, Michael reached for her with a hand of blue-white wind, and, upon contact with his frigid touch, her head snapped back. It was as if an electrode stuck to her temple exploded. Her head burned with illicit visions.

Rani writhed as the images of the Grigori flickered like flames in her mind and soul. A blood orgy with the Fallen—*of the multitude of eyes blazing gold with lust, of feathers ripped from wings to provide the down of the unnatural bed, of lascivious mouths raping serpentine tongues into every soft orifice, of angelic swords piercing her flesh and of their strange genitals thrusting into her gory openings.*

Orgasms ripped through her body.

Muscles in spasmodic, convulsive, palsied, quavery, violent states, she seized in full-body climax. Every millimeter of flesh suffered the rigor torture of pleasure *extreme*, and her rictal lips wrangled with screams.

Her knees buckled, and Rani collapsed onto Michael's grave, gasping as the scarlet visions echoic of memory faded.

The wind creaked through the tree boughs. Oaks and elms swayed in a dead dance, stiff trunks lumbering to bend, flesh of ice falling in chunks to the ground, bare branches clacking like bones.

Rolling onto her back, she gazed at the skeletal canopy. Moon and star shine scintillated upon what ice sheath remained on the trees, reminding her of the Grigori and the way their swords had caught the candlelight.

"You cast me aside for them," Michael said, his tone rumbling upon the wind and disturbing ice.

"I had no choice." *No choice but to succumb to them. No choice but to evoke their celestial powers and call them forth for sacrifice.*

Rani shifted to her knees and placed her hands upon the river boulder marking his grave, tracing the rough-hewn word chiseled into the rock. *Poet*, his memorial read in etched shadows and blood.

Byron-incarnate, he was the night's poet, the mage of arcanum and the dark beauty of doom.

Snow that capped the gravestone stirred in the flurry and blew into her mouth. She grimaced at its crisp metallic taste, the bitter taste of failed alchemy.

The winds groaned in the hoary reliquary of woods, and her skin prickled as the relics beneath the hidden cairns released their specters in ominous noise. The hulking things of shadows crept around her. Angel-progeny, they waited and watched with eager brimstone eyes.

"And again you plan on casting me aside for them." Michael rushed upon her then and tangled his spirit-tendrils through her hair, brutal-pulling at the strands. "But you will not release me."

Holding her head back, he pressed his etheric mouth against her exposed throat and planted hyper dermic kisses in its hollow. Biting-cold flowed into her. Not air, but his essence seeping inward, infecting, infesting her blood, her marrow, her soul.

Rani stiffened with the ichor of the dead. There was a certain poetry in his possession, the way he crafted her pose, anguished and suppliant, into the living marble of a cemetery statue.

Michael's spirit whispered wicked through her veins and along her flesh, and the ashes upon her throat became like the salt of ancient psalms devils wrote, destructive. Her skin and bones felt afire. She knelt the pillar of Lot's wife, salts devouring her flesh and silencing her wailing voice.

But the snow was screaming down.

In white thundering as the Watchers hailed from the heavens and raged upon the earth.

Shemyaza leading the others.

Sariel . . . Kokabel . . . Ezeqeel . . . Araqiel . . . Armers . . . Kasdeja . . .

The din of their names resounded in her head, strident waves crashing on the crags of her skull, and the tiny vessels in her nose burst.

Shemyaza trundled to her side, bowed deeply, and licked the streaming blood. His tongue was black velvet against her. Mouth silent, he spoke soothing words, but, as Michael recoiled within her, the blood poured forth copious and faster.

Mewling in hunger, the aborted offspring of the El and human women edged from the shelter of the shadows.

The night if it had a voice would have rang with a terror-stark shrill. Giganteus and malformed were the children of the sons of God.

Voracity lit their grisly eyes.

Mother bubbled from their twisted lips, and Rani trembled despite Michael's binds on her flesh.

Cutting through the stale cold, their womb-stench drifted into her shallow breath. Her lungs filled with visceral memory—*of howling winds and wretched cries, of the seething split of her vagina, of the fetal waste spurting like bloody diarrheal water onto the bed.*

The half-formed half-breed had slid slick and slashed into red smithereens across the satin sheet, soundless without its mouth but screaming none-the-less. Screaming in the gush of blood and uterine waters.

Rani mourned its loss. Mourned more that lost feeling of fullness, completion, perfection, she had known with her womanhood swollen with its divine life.

Mother, an empty plea.

The angel stayed at her lips, exhaling his sweet myrrh breath into her, and the dark delirium of his incense murmured beyond her lungs and thrummed in her heart. His breath, wondrous as a shimmery nebula of indigo and mauve, radiated into her core and inflamed her with bright yearning.

The other son crawled inside her womb, moving in such a manner it was as if serpents were swirling within her, as if Shemyaza's cock were sliding in and out and all around.

Michael was shrieking within her.

Shrieking laughter as his spirit was lit with red-hot pleasure, as the Seraphical vim seared through him like a branding iron through springy brain furrows. Shrieking disappointment as the angel withdrew.

Oh, gods, how I envy you, being their priapic toy. Imagine the hard throbbing-gristle whip of cock against cock, Michael moaned in the voice of her thoughts.

Winter fondling rough, her flesh tingling on the verge of numb, she could only imagine death lashing into her bones and its ice-fire licking away her marrow. Then the Brotherhood would no longer need Michael's corpse, having hers rot-ripe for the taking . . . *their fingers itching to purl the muck within her entrails and pull the sticky residue of her memories from her purplish organs.*

Her bowels cramped at the threat.

Her heart tightened its rhythm with the lingering coil of pain . . .

. . . *body hung on wires and hooks, a fine red sheath of her fluids dripping onto the cement floor, wet ticking of brutal time . . .*

. . . *the ripping torture, the purloining of her flesh and crimson milk, the continual ruin of her fertile symbols . . .*

In the pit of her belly, echoes of the slaughter gurgled, mimic of the way the Nephilum had crouched in the squelch and fed sloppy upon the men's semi-liquid remains.

The Magian escaped into the gray zone, didn't he? Michael hissed through her mind. *He fled with the fibers and fat of your breast, didn't he? And he will track you down with his fleshly talisman, won't he?*

"Yes," she exhaled, her voice soft as snow swirling along the ground.

His smile will mock the curve of the blade he will bring to murder you — the shades stalking the woods and sulking beneath the river's ice speak of your fate.

Michael's cords of soul wound around her heart.

Fragments of your fear empower me. The Freemasons, the bastard sons of Enochian magick, will never necromance your soul, lover, because I have it in fatal bondage.

Wrists bound in metaphoric wire. Body hung on the hooks of his despair, of his refusal for black release. Soul-sweat glistening on bluish flesh, stinking of his death. Rani knelt, waiting, watching hungry-horrid children and disobedient fathers.

My turn to dangle your soul before gloom and its wasters. Michael chanted in graveyard tones and called upon the Grigori, challenging her to the ultimate power struggle.

Knots of dread upon her, she breathed their names...*Shemyaza*...*Sariel*...*Kokabel*...*Ezeqeel*...*Araqiel*...*Ar mers*...*Kasdeja*... succumbing to the needs of sacrifice again.

The Watchers exuded wrath with eyes of smelted ore and breath of Israel's desert winds, and Rani braced against the coming of their withered faces and their melancholic weapons of perdition. Against what she had no choice but to evoke.

Talons sheared through her clothes. Unearthly canines tore apart the day-old lacerations on her mutilated breast and bit into the nurturing meat. Glorious agony. Her screams echoed to the stars, and their light blinked into darkness.

Snarls and snaps of monstrous jaws, the Grigori beckoned their sons. Sons they had watched die.

The spirits of the aborted Nephilim crawled through the barriers of overgrown roots and seized her. Savage as they milked her blood and sucked down Michael's soul.

Rani felt him flow from her body, the riddling of his cries through her opened scars, the rankling seep of his cemetery cold, the releasing throes of his harrowed hooks. Seeming a pain without end. Condemned as the Grigori in cruel darkness.

But the Nephilim gave back even as they took from her, giving her sensuous warmth and somnolent freedom, and she drifted in dreams. Dreams of the Watchers as they returned to the fifth heaven and waited and watched for the advent of the Brotherhood . . .

CHAPTER TWENTY-NINE

Do not give what is holy to dogs,
neither throw your pearls to swine
that they may never tromple them
under their feet and turn around
and rip you open.

Matthew 7:6

I.

As if reading runes in her breast, Julian inserted his fingers into the subcutaneous concave, into the gristly fatty meat of the glomerate-lobular milk glands and lipid giblets, and along the networks of ducts of longitudinal and transverse elastic fibers and blood vessels. All of it, stringy, spongy clustered and slick against his prying fingers, like sticking his hand into the innards-full cavity of a quail.

The moist murmurs of her flesh were coy hints of the soft keys to come from her heart and bones.

He smiled as he popped one swollen milk gland between finger and thumb. Droplets of yellowish milk spurted into the silver cup, and, one after another, the glands burst between his fingers and emptied their liquid gold into the cup.

"Hand me the child," he told Lilith, who had been licking the clotted fluids from his refreshed body like a wolf cleaning the birthing scum from a newborn pup.

She laid him upon the ground and pushed him over with her foot as she sucked on her messy fingers. Lifting the child up by his arm, dislocating the shoulder with an audible snap, the bones inside still brittle with death, Julian placed him in his lap and offered the cup to the corpse.

His mother's milk touched his cherubic lips.

But Julian withdrew the cup, denying him his mother's milky comfort.

Taunted with the taste, Stephan wailed in sirens of pity and and aching need. Sirens that disturbed not only air but water, and, within the cup, the milk boiled up visions of the whore-mother in some northern grove. Wearing the face of the harlot and the shadows of the grave.

Julian poured the milk onto a map and called upon the guardians of the wind to show him the path, and the Wings of the Air did not fail to heed his call.

II.

Moonlight, its icy light cutting through the clouds, plunged upon her and only her it seemed, the peripheral wood cast in night-shades. Her womb grumbled. Grumbled like hungry gnomes. Rani stripped off her clothes, and her skin was luminous white-gold, the skin of the moon.

Nipped by sheer cold, she groaned as deep shivers ached through her neck and flanks and thighs. Her belly though was warm, almost hot with fever, and growing bigger and bigger by the breathful, inflated as if with breath, fed as if by moon.

As gnome within her womb became an ogre.

Secrets within her bones unnaturally widened her pelvis, her cervix, her mouth in screams as the birth of a giant began.

III.

By the interior light of the car, Julian read some of Enoch's prophecies to the dead child who continued to raise his grievous voice to his mother.

"From them I heard all things, and understood what I saw, that which will not take place in this generation, but in a generation which is to succeed at a distant period, on account of the Elect.

"Upon their account I spoke and conversed with Him, Who will go forth from this habitation, the Holy and Mighty One, the God of the world.

"Who will hereafter tread upon Mt. Sinai; appear with His hosts; and be manifested in the strength of His power from heaven.

"All shall be afraid, and the Watchers be terrified.

"Great fear and trembling shall seize them, even to the ends of the Earth. The holy mountains shall be troubled, and the exalted hills depressed, melting like a honeycomb in the flame. The Earth shall be immersed, and all things which are in it perish; while Judgement shall come upon all, even upon the righteous.

"But to them shall He give peace: He shall preserve the Elect, and towards them exercise clemency.

"Then shall all belong to God; be happy and blessed; and the splendor of the Godhead shall illuminate them."

Thunder rendered the sky like megalithic stones rolling and rumbling as the heavens turned to ruins. *The earth and heavens trembling and troubled.* Lilith giggled, amused at the strange sounds of winter storm, mumbling about the golden age of the first war and the light and dark of the second.

Stepping out of the car, she flopped onto the snow and wriggled. She stood and surveyed her angel of serpent.

"I can smell the salt upon the snow, the sweat of the Lady Ashera of the Sea. I can smell the roots and dirt of her tree, and hear the boughs cracking through the army of angels," Lilith said, awe and anticipation making her voice husky.

Blasts of cold and snow cannoned into the car. Odd snow, not melting against his warm skin, but sticking and spearing into him.

"We'll have trouble pulling him from the battle."

But Julian had hope. The Book of Enoch read: "Behold He comes with ten thousands of His holy warriors, to execute Judgement upon them, and destroy the wicked, and reprove all of flesh for every thing which the sinful and unGodly have done, and committed against Him."

In the woods, banshee-shrills echoed and thinned out the infant's strident cries. Loping shapes, drawn by the sounds of like those of an animal being killed, edged into the darkened grove, howling, leaving a trail of their own echoes behind.

"She's birthing," Lilith said, her eyes reptilian slits glowing with moonlight and hunger, and she stalked away, snuffling like those dogs for the piquant scent of the uterine dump.

Birthing, he mulled, never considering the whore carried another abomination. But there was *flesh for every thing which the sinful and unGodly have done, and committed against Him*, and the warriors would come.

Julian stepped from the car and laid the bundle of bait onto the white ground.

Holding the knife before him, he faced east.

"Before me Raphael."

"Behind me Gabriel."

"At my right shoulder Michael."

"At my left shoulder Ariel."

He unwrapped the dead child. With his knife, he cut the Qabalistic cross upon his stomach and a rose over his heart, and the blood which had soaked into his necrotic skin soaked into the cuts. Beautiful red rose, bright red cross. Bounteous scarlet screams.

"One while let he be known and another while a stranger: because she is the bed of the Harlot, and the dwelling place of Him that is Fallen. O you heavens arise: the lower heavens underneath you, let them serve you! Govern those that govern: cast down such a fall! Bring forth with those that increase, and destroy the rotten! No place let it remain in one number: add and diminish until the stars are numbered! Arise, move, and appear before the covenant of his mouth, which he has sworn unto us in his justice. Open the Mystery of your Creation: and make us partakers of Undefiled Knowledge."

Then Julian withdrew the periapt from around his neck, the thing Lilith had given him in return for much of his blood. Blood which she would wash between her sinuous thighs and fertilize her monstrous womb.

In his hand, he held the twined saffron hairs and shuddered.

Millions of mouths and tongues of damned souls were within the cords, all wailing for mercy. The din was horrible. Julian could only wonder how much more awful the owner of these hairs.

He turned his body south and presented the saffron halo to the direction heralded by the angel who is as God.

He lit the halo.

And the millions of mouths implored in burning tongues for Archangel Michael to come battle the angels of darkness.

IV.

Rani squatted and bore down and caterwauled in curses and vehement pain. She split like she had when Shemyaza dragged his sword from her anus to her clit, and the hybrid-son of an angel pulled himself from her womb, his claws reaching out of her and gripping her thighs. He birthed himself. A messy, mewling sac of muscle and sinew and giganteum bone, vibrant corpus-collage against the white canvas of snow.

Although premature, his flesh translucent and viscose-red, he had the build of a child, not an infant. And claws and teeth, with which tore himself away from the umbilical cord, and strong limbs with which he raised himself upon and stood between her legs and the waste between them.

She fell to her haunches, weakened and near black-collapse, staring at the thing that inspired terror. But she felt no wire-string of fear wrapped around her heart and held out her hand, beckoning him to her single aching breast. Mouth and teeth upon her, she slipped in and out of her mind, between reality and dream, delirious and drowsy from that somnolent bloody sucking.

Dogs howled in the woods.

... *thrown down, her blood splattered the walls and the horses trampled her* . . .

... *dogs howled in the city of Jezreel* . . .

... *as dogs ripped her apart* . . .

... *only her skull, feet and the palm of her hands remained in the dust, left to turn to dust* . . .

Winds groaning with more than dogs and the cries of her children, the Watchers returned, their wings stirring a whorl of hissing snow. Their eyes were bright, brighter than she'd ever seen any star in the sky. Thousands of thousands years of waiting had ended—they came for their son born, to be reared for slaughter.

The Nephilim child walked away from Rani, and again her arms were vacant and aching, all made worse the sight of one son disappearing into the darkness of the forest and another coming into the moonlight of the grove, in the arms of his murderer.

V.

Stealth of shadows converged upon the woodlet. Eyes lunar-reflective pierced through the white-dark gloom, and the air literally steamed in a circle around the exhausted mother, as ravenous things breathed in the scent of her hot womb-spilled blood and waited. Waited for the thunder to subside. Waited for the rumbling earth to settle.

Ears pricked, the dogs hunkered low upon the ground and watched for the coming of the walking thunder.

Silver-blue flashes struck the trees, felled the monumental pines in a cacophony of gunshot cracks and roars of other unnameable weapons, as well as the splintering shriek of bark and pith. A path cleared for the mammoth.

The smell of heaven was upon the earth, but like scorched flowers and blasted minerals and bitter myrrh.

Confusion riddled Shemyaza. Stay the ground and defend her. Sneak into the woods and squirrel away his only living son before the chariot wheels ran him over.

But he made no choice before the great angel Michael emerged from the wood afire in God's wrath, his saffron hairs like rutilant flames flaring upon his body, all the many faces and mouths and tongues howling like the burning damned.

"Deliverance" was all the Heavenly slayer said before his mercury-luminous swords swung toward the Fallen.

VI.

Chaos of the genesis and the end erupted in the grove, mirror of the devastation in the heavens as the Tree of Life forfeited her prisoner and the Queen fought for her throne of heaven and star and sky and sea and earth, and all her roaming children. The dark angels battled with the angel of light. All of creation and non-creation poised on the brink of rendering into an abyss. Skies threatened to fall in fire and clouded smoke, and the earth would shake apart and open up and swallow everything into bottomless black, and the seas would swirl and drain into the well of nothing.

Through destruction comes life.

New life, new earth, new heavens.

Poised on the brink of revelation, but without judgement.

Around her neck, the Seal of Solomon singed her skin, its powers awakened by the arcane words she breathed. Words she heard in the stars and in the winds through the trees, words of creation which she repeated. Rani stood on birth-strained legs and hobbled toward the Magian, the umbilical cord swinging like a wet corded tail between her legs.

She tilted her head downward, with her kohl-dusted eyes raised, seductively angered, and approached him. If she had horns upon her head, she would've charged and gored him. But he held Stephan before him.

Stephan. Her baby, looking as if he had never died with rose-blushed flesh as if blood flowed in his veins, moving as if he had never died, his arms reaching, reaching for her.

For a moment, the image of him muddled her mind, and she feared perhaps he had never died that winter. That bruises never ringed his tiny throat. That his flesh never failed to give warmth. That the stillness of his breath and heart was her madness, her delusion, and that she had buried her son alive. That she had murdered him.

The Magian laughed, as if he read her mind, her confusion, her fears. Crazy laughter. Mad moon laughter. Laughter which always preceded corruption and calamity.

Lifting Stephan by the nape, he presented him, and all the glaring cuts upon his body were shown. Marks of signs that kept him in darkness and agony. Marks of signs she would destroy.

But he had not finished with his marking of signs.

Against Stephan's throat, he pointed a double-twisted blade. He smirked as he dragged the blade across the tender flesh, making a blood-gem choker, and Stephan wailed, and Rani screamed. She watched her son curl into an afflicted ball, every muscle trembling in tension, his face scrunched as it had when birthed, before that first painful breath, his mouth open and terrifyingly silent. But she heard the screams regardless. Those screams of winter and midnight that haunted her, which never ended. Screams of his death that ended her life even though she breathed.

Rani hurt as her baby hurt, vicariously feeling that knife in her. Mother and son, bonded once in body, bonded forever in heart and soul.

"Little Boy Blue and his ring of rosies," the voice of murder and darkness sneered.

Her hands shook. Shook for knife, for bone, for destruction.

Once again, the Magian put the knife to his tender flesh.

Rani ripped the pentacle from her neck, the silver links sawing into her neck before the chain snapped off, and held it before her, as the Magian held her son before him. Like shields and wards.

No words passed between them but shades of indignation ranged across his face at finding the Seal of Solomon in her possession. He faltered with the knife against her son.

Her son, his snowy eyes upon her . . .

. . . *snuggled in her arms, warm and perfumed with powder, eyes blue as the spring sky, long eyelashes blooming open like fine petals, her son looking at her with unbound trust and love . . .*

. . . *butterfly kisses against his cheek . . .*

. . . *staring into those eyes, the endless garden of beauty and hope and joy, that was all hers to behold . . .*

Staring into those eyes, sheathed by the cold of death, beholding only despair. That black bond which she would break.

Though the Magian broke their spell, imbedding the knife within the cavity of his decayed heart. Stephan cried, a cry that resounded through the woods and deep within her, echoing of all the collective pain of the world, of all the souls waiting in darkness and agony.

Her heart was breaking over and over and over again.

And all she wanted was peace, silence to this long drawn-out shattering agony.

Lurching forward, Rani grabbed Stephan from his murderer's arms and fell onto the ground. She hugged him against her, holding on tightly to her child taken an eternity ago, years too long to bear, too long to fathom. His cold body settled in the cradle of her arms. His cries quieted, and all seemed silent even though the clash of titanic angels raged on.

Rani kissed him over and over, his lips salty from her tears.

But she found her son, her fairytale all hidden in a dark and lonely wood. She held her little prince, faces touching, his snowy eyes, all glittering and pure, warming her in this emotional coil.

"I will avenge on Jezebel the blood of my servants the prophets, and the blood of all the servants of the Lord," the Magian hissed.

From the corner of her eye, Rani saw his shadow coming.

She kissed Stephan once more, her lips and tears lingering as she placed the Seal of Solomon on him.

"Mommy loves you," she wept. "More than there are stars in the heaven."

And his snowy eyes melted, and his body burned in golden flames, his pink flesh scalding, simmering, smoldering, his mouth scored away by flames, gaping and releasing suspirous smoke and spirit.

No more haunting cries, no more darkness and agony for him, no more Stephan at all.

By her hands.

Sometimes we must destroy in order to create new life.

Rani stood the painted Harlot and faced her enemy, exposing the wounds of her womb and the dark power emanating from her. The Magian's eyes were like mad-stones as he lunged for her with the knife. Over and over, the knife stabbed into her secret red places. Darkness shrouded her. She heard the sloshing of her flesh, the grunts of her murderer, and the clacking shift of stars. She smelled the burning myrrh of the angels, the acrid smelt of heaven's weapons of war, and the salty, rust-scented death coming from her.

She smelled the end of misery.

And the dogs began to smell her.

VII.

In great hunger, the dogs stalked from the woods and converged upon her fallen body. They ripped into the Jezebel-flesh, quarreling and snarling and snapping as they fed, devouring her until only her bones remained. These the dogs gnawed upon, and the secrets within the bones came to light.

Her skull wailed.

www.ingramcontent.com/pod-product-compliance
Lightning Source LLC
Chambersburg PA
CBHW020829260626
47169CB00003B/896